Never Trust A
Scoundrel

By Gayle Callen

Never Trust a Scoundrel
The Viscount in Her Bedroom
The Duke in Disguise
The Lord Next Door
A Woman's Innocence
The Beauty and The Spy
No Ordinary Groom
His Bride
His Scandal
His Betrothed
My Lady's Guardian
A Knight's Vow
The Darkest Knight

If You've Enjoyed This Book,
Be Sure to Read These Other
AVON ROMANTIC TREASURES

How to Propose to a Prince *by Kathryn Caskie*
In My Wildest Fantasies *by Julianne MacLean*
The Perils of Pleasure *by Julie Anne Long*
Untouched *by Anna Campbell*
The Wicked Ways of a Duke *by Laura Lee Guhrke*

Coming Soon

A Notorious Proposition *by Adele Ashworth*

GAYLE CALLEN

Never Trust A Scoundrel

An Avon Romantic Treasure

AVON

An Imprint of HarperCollins*Publishers*

AVON BOOKS
An Imprint of HarperCollins*Publishers*
10 East 53rd Street
New York, New York 10022-5299

Copyright © 2008 by Gayle Kloecker Callen
ISBN-13: 978-0-7394-9478-3

First Avon Books paperback printing: April 2008

To my daughter, Laura:
Though it will be difficult
to let my last child go off into the world,
I watch the beginning of your journey
with anticipation and pride,
knowing that you'll find your way.

Chapter 1

London, 1845

Grace Banbury, out of breath, her heart pounding, slammed closed the front door of her brother's town house. She'd been knocking for many minutes in the darkness, hoping a servant would let her in. And when that hadn't happened, she'd tried the door, and as if God had answered her prayers, she found it unlocked. Now she locked it quickly behind her and put her back against it, dropping her portmanteau to the marble floor, struggling with the enormity of what she'd done.

She'd run from her village home without even the company of her maid, traveling by public coach for the first time in her life. In her reckless fury, she'd barely remembered to take the coins she'd been so frugally saving.

She told herself she was safe—for now. But what would Edward do when she told him that their mother had gambled away the ownership of both this town house and their little country manor?

In humiliation, her mother had fled just last night, leaving no clue to her whereabouts, except a note promising to earn back enough money to recover what she'd lost.

Earn back money with more gambling, Grace thought furiously. As if that ever worked.

Nausea threatened again, but she forced it back down. The future was a yawning, frightening blackness that would swallow her if she let it. Better to think of one thing at a time.

How could their mother betray them? She was supposed to be a lady, the widow of a gentleman, but for most of Grace's life, she'd conducted herself as a woman who could not long be separated from the risks and excitement of cards.

And now a stranger had dared her to risk everything.

Grace had a small dowry that her father had legally kept from her mother, with no access to it except through marriage. She had always wanted to marry for love, had hoped that she could succeed where her parents had not, but just last year she'd badly tarnished her own expectations. If necessary, she supposed she could seek security as a companion.

But what about her brother? He was a gentleman; these two small homes were his inheritance. How would he live now? Who would marry him?

The house was eerily silent, with an empty echo that felt wrong. No one had come to the door, and obviously Edward was out for the evening. She could only assume that not even a servant was at home. But how could that be?

There was a lamp burning on a solitary table in the entrance hall, and it cast flickering shadows on the bare walls. Now that Grace had gotten over her useless emotions, she realized something was wrong. Bare walls? She lifted the lamp and walked through the first door, only to find a dining table and chairs, an empty sideboard, and more bare walls. What had happened to all their possessions, the china, the paintings Papa had collected on his trips to Europe? She might think that the house had been ransacked, but it didn't have a feeling of violation. What it had was neglect, a light coating of dust on the large table, as if no one could be bothered to clean it.

Or as if no servants lived here anymore.

What had Edward done? Her feelings of worry, waiting with patience in the deep recesses of her mind, now surged back to tighten her throat.

No, panic would not help. In the morning, she would tell Edward everything their mother had done. He would explain why the town house was so bare. Together, they would come up with a plan. They'd only ever had each other, and now that bond was all they had.

But some part of her knew that Edward would have no good explanation for the condition of their home. For several years, she'd been seeing the signs of the gambling fever he'd caught from their mother, his restlessness, his need to be in London. She had tried to distract him, to lecture him, and finally to plead with him. He had always laughed off her concerns, swore that all gentlemen gambled, and that he was in command of himself. But the condition of the town house said otherwise.

She checked the kitchens and found no one, then moved to the small pantry that had been converted into a bedroom for the cook, whose gout prevented her from negotiating the stairs. But even that room was empty. She ran up the stairs to the third floor and found every servant's room just as deserted.

She'd never spent a single night of her life alone, though that wasn't nearly as frightening as the gaping uncertainty that was her future.

She walked back down a flight to the family bedrooms. To her relief, Edward had left hers alone. There was still her favorite painting of the sea at Brighton on the wall, and a little vase that her father had brought her from France.

When her stomach growled, she went down to the kitchen but only found biscuits and apples. After lighting a candle and leaving the lamp in the front hall for her brother, she carried the food back to her room and ate in silence, trying to ignore the tight heaviness in her stomach.

As she changed into her nightgown, she was glad that she'd worn clothing she could remove herself. She had wanted to bring her lady's maid, Ruby, but how would Grace be able to pay her wages? But oh, she missed her cheerful company. Ruby somehow managed to walk the line between servant and friend in a way that made Grace feel perfectly comfortable.

Of course, there was no water in the pitcher, and she was not about to pump from the well in the garden at this time of night. It was summer, so she could do without coal burning in the grate. But still, she wrapped her dressing gown about her and climbed into bed with her journal. A chill moved through her, making her shiver.

She always tried to write in her journal every night. It provided the thread of her days, gave her things to refer to when she wrote long letters to Edward. She gritted her teeth as she remembered how infrequent his letters had become. Maybe if she wrote about her mother's betrayal, the reality wouldn't hurt so much.

Several pages later, she sat back and looked at her cramped writing, splotches of ink, and to her horror, the smudge of a single tear.

How had she become such a weak creature? She'd known what her mother was capable of; she'd spent a lifetime learning to protect her feelings. Every time her mother swore things would be different, there was always a dark part of Grace's soul held in reserve, waiting for her mother's inevitable slide back into the gambling she couldn't control for long. Now Grace's whole life had been gambled away.

Suddenly, the slamming of the front door echoed through the house.

Edward, she thought, walking quickly from her room. She was relieved as well as sad, for she'd have to tell him what their mother had done. He was a year younger than her twenty-three years, close enough that they'd grown up together. He was her dearest friend. She could make him see that it wasn't too late for him, that he could stop gambling now.

As she hurried down the stairs toward the entrance hall, a solitary man looked up, and she stumbled to a halt, still halfway up the staircase.

It wasn't her brother, but a stranger, dressed in elegant black evening clothes.

She caught the banister, feeling off-balance. Some distant part of her knew she should be frightened, but she couldn't quite feel that, not when he looked like every girl's fantasy of a dashing nobleman.

She could tell he was tall by the way he dwarfed the bare hall. He slowly crossed his arms over his chest. He wore a cool, contemplative look as he studied her, as if he sized up everyone for their weaknesses. Well, she wasn't weak.

The lamp below him cast a yellow glow across his face, with its harsh lines and steep angles. His brown hair was dark and a touch too long, showing little concern for Society's fashions. His eyes were the deep brown of cocoa that burned if you sipped too fast. He showed his disregard of politeness by glancing down her body instead of only at her face. She suddenly remembered what she wore, and though she longed to clutch the dressing gown closed at her throat, she wouldn't let herself betray such vulnerability.

She coldly said, "How rude to force yourself into a home not your own. If you wish to see Mr. Banbury, he's not here. You may show yourself out."

His smile was slow and dangerous, and she began to worry about more than bodily harm, even as her skin heated. She had been foolish enough to come to London alone; what if others saw her arrival and knew that now a man visited as well?

"I didn't know that Banbury had a mistress," the man said, his voice of a deep timbre that rumbled within her.

She stiffened. "I am *Miss* Banbury, his sister. And again, I must ask you to leave."

To her surprise, he straightened as his smile faded. His arms fell to his sides stiffly, almost as if he faced her across dueling pistols. She didn't understand his wariness, and wanted to take a step back up the stairs, but feared he would take it as a sign of retreat, emboldening him.

"I don't have to leave," he said. "I'm Daniel Throckmorten, the new owner of this town house."

The coldness that had been hovering in the pit of Grace's stomach now spread across her skin, shivering out to her fingers and toes. This man had gambled against her mother, took everything a weak-willed woman could offer, took the only two homes that Grace had ever known.

"You are a bastard," she said in a low, furious voice.

He arched a dark brow. "No, not a bastard, but a man who plays cards."

"With a woman."

"Yes, a woman. I don't discriminate or think women of less intelligence. They're fully capable of being wily enough to gamble."

"It does not bother you that you are putting out an entire family?"

"I know nothing of your family or its situation," he admitted, tilting his head. "Should you not be directing your ire at your mother?"

"I cannot, because after telling me about the loss of the property, she left."

But not before she'd taken the antique violin that had belonged to Grace's father. Grace had been promised it since childhood, but it had disappeared the same night, another casualty to her mother's need for gambling stakes. If Grace had it, she would discard her sentimentality and sell it if it were enough to buy them out of this predicament.

"I have the deeds," Mr. Throckmorten said simply. "That makes me the owner."

She had too much pride to beg for them back, and knew just by looking at his ruthless demeanor that it would be pointless. In all honor, he had won. She should not fault him—but she couldn't help it. He had preyed upon the weakness of others. Someone had to make this man understand that gambling hurt far too many people. Her mother was no innocent, but any man should have been able to see that she could no longer control herself where betting was concerned. Or did only winning matter to him?

He smiled. "I have never cared for my own town house. It is cramped and in a declining part of London. I much prefer this place. The company is far superior."

Could he possibly think she would find him amusing?

"Come back in the morning to speak with my brother." And she would have more time to think up a way to stop all of this.

He ignored that and walked the same path she had, peering into the dining room. "I came tonight because I'd hoped to be here before everything I now owned was cleared out. Too late."

"It was not done because of you," she said begrudgingly.

"Ah." He narrowed his eyes. "Was it your mother or brother with the run of bad luck?"

"Does it matter?"

"Your brother, then. I don't think you'd be defending your mother after all that's happened."

Something in the tone of his voice alerted her, but she didn't understand to what. She watched him prowl the entrance hall, looking at all the blank spaces on the wall, conspicuously lighter than the wallpaper around them.

"Are you going to stay halfway up the stairs all night?" he asked.

She foolishly took the challenge, descending several steps to him. "You need to leave. A gentleman would—"

"But you already have proof that I am no gentleman." He came to the edge of the stairs and looked up at her.

They were so close that if they both reached out, they would touch fingers. She should be frightened, but she was not. She felt reckless with her anger and disappointment. After what her mother had done to her, nothing this stranger said would truly matter. She was at his mercy—if he expected her to beg for it, he would be unrewarded. And if he expected something else, he would discover quickly that she had learned the hard way how to take care of herself.

But he was still looking at her, and to her chagrin, she felt overly warm everywhere his regard touched her. What was wrong with her?

And then he glanced at her mouth. She had a sudden image of feverish kisses in the dark.

She mentally backed away from the thought, knowing from experience the heartache that would follow.

Gritting her teeth, she forced herself to be humble. "Even if you are no gentleman, you must have some compassion. Give me time to make plans. Perhaps we can come to some sort of agreement."

"Do you have the money to buy either home?"

"No." It was so difficult to pretend calm when she wanted to fly down the stairs at him, to pound his chest in punishment for what had happened to her.

"Then we won't come to an agreement."

"I need time to find a position for myself."

He cocked his head in curiosity. "A position?"

"I am unmarried, sir, as well as unbetrothed. I will need to earn my way."

"Are you educated enough to be a governess?"

"Yes." She fisted her hands, wishing she didn't have to stand here and take his interrogation.

But he was watching her far too closely, and she had the strange feeling that he was humoring her.

"You have another choice, thanks to your mother."

She stiffened.

"She was getting rather desperate to continue the game, and another player wanted her to sweeten the pot, beyond her property."

"What more did she have left?" Grace asked bitterly.

"You mean besides the violin?"

"You have it?" she whispered.

"I do."

"What else could she have possibly offered this other player? How greedy was he?"

"Too greedy." With a shrug of his shoulders, he added, "I had really only wanted the violin, but instead I won . . . everything."

"Just tell me," she said coldly.

"I won *you*."

Chapter 2

Daniel Throckmorten watched the blood drain from Grace Banbury's lovely face. Would she cry and plead? He hated when women used those tactics, all to make him feel like a bully.

"How could you have won *me*?" she demanded, her jaw clenched, her eyes dry.

He was reluctantly impressed. She had an abundance of composure for a woman who could not yet have twenty-five years.

"Do not think the worst of your mother," he said dryly. "She did not offer the right to bed you."

She flinched, and he saw fury dancing in eyes as green as summer grass. Her hair was light brown, the color of new wood cut in the depths of a mysterious forest. It was caught into a heavy braid that snaked over her shoulder. Perhaps she made him think of the outdoors because of the freckles scattered across her cheeks and nose, as if she spent time out in the sun without a parasol. She was small but generously curved, easy to see without the restriction of corset and heavy fabrics. He wanted to see more.

She lifted her chin. "You are making poor sport of me, Mr. Throckmorten."

"I'm not. This particular player had apparently been unable to court you. He wanted to marry you."

"Who is he?" she demanded.

He spread his hands. "I do not know. We all need privacy in our vices."

"But if he wanted to marry—"

"Your mother offered the exclusive right to court and marry you."

"And he *accepted* that?" she said in obvious outrage.

"He did. And that's when I began to wish that I had not entered the game. But I did want that violin." It had been of the same class as one his father used to own. He'd sold it to support them when Daniel's grandfather, the duke of Madingley, had not given enough spending money to his daughter.

Her mouth opened, but she said nothing at first, as if she didn't know where to begin. "But you won that dreadful game."

"I did."

She came down another step, temptingly close, leaning above him to point a finger in his face. "I refuse to marry you. Surely there is no way to enforce such a thing."

She smelled of lavender, of moonlit nights in a summer garden.

What kind of foolish romantic was he turning into? He'd known from the moment she'd appeared out of the darkness above him that he desired her, but he never allowed lust to cloud his judgment.

But it was difficult not to think such thoughts when, in a deserted house, a beautiful woman in her nightclothes was showing such spirit and passion.

He almost wanted to tease her, to insist they would marry immediately, just to see her reaction. But even he wasn't that much of a cad.

"Do not worry, Miss Banbury. I have no intention of marrying you."

"I will go to Scotland Yard and—" Her mouth shut and she blinked. "Oh. Thank goodness you see the ridiculousness of—"

"But I am in the market for a mistress."

A blush of warmth colored cheeks that had been too pale. Her lips curled, and she covered her mouth. At last he realized that merriment twinkled in her eyes.

And then she giggled. "Oh, dear," she said, sitting down on the stair behind her and wiping a tear from her eye. "As if I would ever be your mistress, no matter what you say you've won."

Daniel loomed over her, watching his shadow slide up and cover her. She leaned back on her elbows to look up at him, which left her lovely breasts on shadowy display through her thin nightclothes. She seemed innocent enough not to realize it.

"Miss Banbury, I think you underestimate my charms," he said softly. He rested one foot on the stair beside her legs, and then his forearm upon his knee, his hand dangling very near her.

Her smile faded, but she didn't move away.

"There have been only a few women before you who thought they could resist me," he continued, "but they were mistaken. If I wanted you as my mistress, it would not be difficult to persuade you."

And then she laughed, but with more bitterness than amusement.

He narrowed his eyes, letting his gaze wander down her garments, where he could see the press of her nipples beneath the linen. The fabric was caught between her thighs, and fell in folds that revealed her bare feet. Her small toes seemed so very intimate in the dark entrance hall.

Since no one had come to investigate upon hearing his entrance or their loud voices, he'd already guessed they were alone. She must know it, yet she so brazenly resisted him. He admired her bravery and determination, and the thought of her as his mistress was appealing.

It occurred to him that she was a gentleman's daughter, most likely a virgin. But, that had not stopped him with other women. . . . And the challenge was so much more exciting.

"You can step back now," she said coolly. "Your intimidation and boasts will not work."

He remained where he was, leaning over her. "Miss Banbury, I don't need intimidation or boasts. I am confident of my skills and my appeal."

"So you send the women swooning, do you?" she asked, tilting her head.

"And more," he said softly. "If I wanted you as my mistress, and set about to persuade you of the reasons you'd want to succumb, you would eventually do so."

To his surprise, she looked at his mouth. The arousal that had been toying with him now became an aching erection. What was it about this woman that so drew him? Surely it was only her scanty clothing and her pretty face and body.

"You think I would so easily forget my virtue—not to mention what your gambling has cost my family—and take you into my bed?"

"I didn't say it would be easy. I thrive on challenges."

She started to stand up, and when he didn't move, she gave his shoulder a push. He almost felt the warmth of her hand through his layers of clothing, so attuned to her was he. But he slowly straightened and allowed her to stand. She was several steps above him, but they faced each other straight on.

"So this is a challenge?" she said.

He raised an eyebrow. "Do you want it to be?" He hadn't thought she would be the kind to join the game so willingly. The warmth of her breath caressed his face. He could feel his blood thrumming through his body, his every sense aware of this woman, from her creamy skin to her delicious pink lips to her hair, in which he longed to press his face and inhale.

"And what do I get as you prove your inability to sway my morals?" she continued speculatively. "The house?"

"Of course not." He played a hunch. "The violin."

She took a deep breath.

Yes, he had guessed correctly. "And of course, if I win, I get you in my bed, willingly."

"You won't win."

She seemed far too sure of herself.

"You cannot cheat by avoiding me," he said. "You must allow me to try to seduce you."

She colored. "Very well. And you cannot cheat by claiming possession of the house right now. I have to live somewhere. And you cannot allow it to be known that you own the house."

He gave a faint smile. "Or you really will look like my mistress?"

"No one can know about this."

"Whatever you think of me, I do not go around ruining women's reputations—unless they want me to. There is no need to unveil to Society what I wish to enjoy in private."

She nodded. "Will you shake on it?"

He looked at her slender hand, then slowly took it, letting her know who held the power as he swallowed her fragileness within his big hand.

"Why are you doing this?" he asked.

She inhaled, not lowering her eyes, standing up to him in a way that was maddening. It suddenly seemed like a long time to wait to claim her.

"Because someone has to bring you down, Mr. Throckmorten."

"And because you enjoy the challenge, just like the rest of us gamblers?"

When she gasped, he thought he'd gone too far, equating her with her mother, with him. He sensed she did not see herself as the weak creature she thought they were.

She pulled her hand away. "I've stated my reasons. We've shaken on it. You can attempt to seduce me, and I will resist. But if I surrender and become your mistress, you win. If you break your word on any rule we've agreed to, I win the violin by default."

"Very well."

"And we cannot wait forever for you to prove that you cannot seduce me."

"Forever is a long time."

"Exactly. And you'd be waiting that long."

"Cocky, aren't you?" he said, reaching to capture her hand again before she knew what he was about. She wasn't even trembling. He knew she had probably never held a suitor's hand without gloves between them. He took advantage by pressing a kiss to the back of her hand, then turning it over and pressing another to her palm. Lavender seemed all around him now, burned into his brain. Whenever he smelled it again, he would remember this night, the challenge of this woman. He touched her with his tongue, and although she stiffened, she did not gasp or frantically pull away.

"A time limit, Mr. Throckmorten. You have one week to prove my supposed inability to resist you," she said with subtle sarcasm. She removed her hand from his.

"Three weeks."

"Two," she shot back.

"Very well."

"And all I have to do is resist you." She sounded as if she would be getting off lightly.

"And soon you won't even want to do that, Miss Banbury."

"I'll be doing other things as well, have no fear."

"Against me?"

"Against you."

"Ah, I look forward to it."

Then neither of them spoke, and they just looked at each other. Daniel wondered if she were taking his measure, as he was hers. He was suddenly glad that he'd won that card game.

"You may leave now, Mr. Throckmorten," she said softly.

"I look forward to our next visit, Miss Banbury."

Strangely, it took effort for him to turn away from her. He wanted to sweep her into his arms, carry her up the stairs, and prove to her that she would be no match against his seduction.

But that wasn't part of the game.

When he reached the door, she said, "Mr. Throckmorten?"

He glanced over his shoulder, and she held out her hand.

"The key, please."

"I own this town house."

"And you agreed not to reveal that fact. While I am living here, you will not find it so easy to enter again. The key, please."

He walked back to her, noticing with amusement that she still had not come all the way down the stairs. She liked meeting him eye to eye. And he didn't mind giving her the key—he still had one to the kitchen door. He placed the key in her palm, and before she could pull away, he folded her fingers around it.

"Clutch it tightly, Miss Banbury," he said in a soft voice. "I won't willingly give up anything else."

She pressed her lips together, but all she did was nod.

He bowed. "Good evening."

As he closed the door behind him, he heard her turn the lock. He didn't look back as he descended the stairs to the street, where his horse waited. He felt lighter than he had in a long time.

He'd been restless lately, on edge—bored. He was almost thirty, and the life he'd been leading since he'd been sent down in disgrace from Cambridge years before no longer seemed enough. He had accumulated a fortune, and the making of it now seemed too easy. Even gambling, taking wild risks and winning, had lost its appeal, for he was talented enough to win at anything that required skill—including seduction.

But now he had a new challenge to focus on. He sensed that Grace Banbury wasn't used to someone with his control. Her mother surely had none. By the sight of the bare town house, her brother was not much better.

Grace most likely took care of them all, as she was trying to do now. The violin couldn't be all she wanted, although he knew it would bring a pretty penny. She'd just been betrayed by her mother, had just lost the security of a home.

But she was playing her own game with him, and he wouldn't deprive her of it.

Or deprive himself of the chance to have her willingly naked in his bed. Daniel didn't need the lengthy commitment of marriage. He had no need to please his family, for he wasn't the real heir. He and Grace would tire of each other and move on, the inevitable result, but until then, he would show her pleasures that she had never imagined.

Grace didn't trust him. She stood near the window beside the front door, watching between the draperies as he mounted his horse and rode away. The gaslights illuminated his figure down the length of the street, and she watched his straight back, the easy way he rode his horse.

He thought he had command of everything.

With a groan, she sat down on the bottom step and put her face in her hands. What had she allowed to happen?

There was a sick feeling, a twisting of her gut inside, as if she were somehow surprised at what her mother had done. So many times over the years, Grace had thought her mother could not possibly do anything worse. And usually, Grace was unpleasantly surprised.

But this—

She swallowed heavily. Her mother always believed she would win, always assumed the risk smaller than it was. Because a man wanted to marry Grace, her mother had used that against him, "sweetening" the winnings.

I am not a prize to be won, Grace thought bleakly.

But thank God, Mr. Throckmorten had not wanted her to wife. He was not foolish enough to try to enforce such a prize. And she wasn't even offended that he didn't want to marry her. He didn't know anything about her.

Except that he desired her.

She shivered, and she admitted to herself that it wasn't unpleasant. She had always reacted this way to men who looked at her with appreciation. To her dismay, she had always enjoyed every moment of it, basking in the attention, flirting as only a too-confident woman could.

Until it had almost cost her her reputation and her self-respect.

If she dwelled on that, she'd make herself sick. She had learned long ago to get on with the repairs of her family, to make things right. The newest plan had come to her in the middle of Mr. Throckmorten's boasts about his prowess in seducing women, and Grace had seized on it with a foolhardiness that couldn't be helped. She needed that violin. Sadly, it was not for the childhood memories, but for its monetary worth. She'd been told it was so rare that collectors would pay thousands of pounds for it. Would that be enough to offer as the initial payment toward one of the family's properties? And then she'd own it, and her mother would have no control.

But to get the violin back, she'd had to make a bet with a gambler, something she'd sworn she would never do. The sick, hollow feeling came back, almost eating her up inside. Was she truly more like her mother than she'd ever thought?

But no, she was only doing this to fix her mother's mistake, to give Edward the home that had been taken away from him. She had no access to her own dowry money; it was locked up too tightly in the bank so that even her mother couldn't get at it. And if she married some man out of desperation, there was no guarantee he'd even allow her to have any part of the dowry.

Grace was confident in her ability to win. There was no risk at all. Though Mr. Throckmorten could try all he wanted, she would never allow herself to be seduced when so much was at stake. She had learned her lesson.

Chapter 3

Grace sat still, afraid to think about what she'd done. A key rattled in the front door, and with a gasp, she came to her feet. But this time it was the familiar, beloved face of her brother, his brown hair mussed, his chin shadowed with a day's growth of whiskers, his expression shocked and concerned.

"Grace, when did you arrive?" he demanded with confusion.

Before she could answer, his gaze took in her nightclothes, his eyes widened, and he glanced back outside.

"But I saw Throckmorten leaving here. I thought I must have accidentally left the door unlocked. I'm still so used to having the butler—" He broke off with a wince, then his stormy gray eyes settled on her once again. "Did you speak with him?"

"I did," she said gravely. "When he arrived, he didn't know I was here."

"I don't owe him anything—"

"No, but Mother does. Or did."

He only looked bewildered. It was obvious he'd

had a bit too much to drink, but he wasn't drunk, and for that she was grateful.

"Come up to the drawing room, Edward. I have so much to tell you."

When they were seated across from each other on two sofas, Edward listened to her story while wearing a weary expression. She hated seeing the hurt in his eyes when she had to tell him that their mother had lost his only inheritance. He looked confused and crushed, not the same young man brimming with vitality that she remembered. She kept waiting with dread for him to say he'd win it all back, but he didn't.

And she found that almost worse.

When the time came for her to explain how their mother's bet related to her, the words stuck in her throat. It was too embarrassing, and Edward didn't need to know. For then he'd ask what Mr. Throckmorten had said about a marriage between them, and she'd be forced to lie somehow. And she didn't want to lie to her brother. It was bad enough keeping things from him. But how could she tell him that his sister, still reeling from her foolish conduct with Baxter Wells, had just challenged another man to try to seduce her?

Edward would forbid it. He would try to protect her, might challenge Mr. Throckmorten to a duel, for heaven's sake.

But he did deserve to know that she had some kind of plan. She trusted her brother; she just didn't trust his judgment anymore, she thought sadly.

"He has the violin, Edward," she said, wringing her hands and looking away.

"The violin that was to be yours? Mother gave that away, too?" he added in disgust.

"Yes, but I think I can persuade him to give it back. And if we sell it, surely we can afford to rent a place to live, maybe even one of our own homes."

"But how can you get it back?"

She didn't know what lie to tell him. "He did agree to allow us to live here for a while. He was not so cruel as to put us onto the streets."

"How nice of him," he said sarcastically, "when he has so many family homes to choose from."

She sighed, grasping at ideas. "I . . . challenged him for ownership of the violin."

Edward frowned as his gaze searched her face. She went on quickly.

"He doesn't believe that I could convince him to give it back of his own accord, but I can."

"How? He will want too much from you, Grace."

Now he was hitting too close to the truth, and she couldn't quite meet his eyes. "I don't know, Edward. I had thought first of revenge, of course, but in the end, it is not his fault that our mother is . . . what she is." Her mind was working frantically—only a different sort of man would give back the violin. She stiffened. Would Edward believe that she could change Mr. Throckmorten? She had no better idea. Before she could change her mind, she said, "I decided to try to turn him from a gambler into the kind of man who, for honor, would give us back at least the violin."

Edward sat back, looking at her through bleary, puffy eyes. "I don't understand. How can you make him give up gambling? If you were capable of that miracle, our mother would be here with us."

There was a tense silence, as they both wondered where their mother had fled to, how she would survive. But knowing their mother, Grace thought, she'd taken something of value with her. And for now, it was a relief not to have to deal with her.

"You need to stay away from him, Grace." Edward leaned forward on the sofa, staring at her with sincerity. "He is not a safe man to be around."

"I don't plan on being alone with him," she said quickly.

But how could she know what Mr. Throckmorten had planned for her? she thought with a too-pleasant shiver.

"Grace," he said with exasperation, "don't you know who he is?"

"Well . . . his name was familiar, but I had no time to search my brain for the reason why."

"His father, Baldwin Throckmorten, was a famous composer before his death."

"Oh yes, that is why I know him! I own sheet music to his father's symphonies." She tried to imagine young Mr. Throckmorten growing up in a household surrounded by music, but she couldn't even picture him as a child. He surely had made any household miserable with cunning pranks and ruthless demands.

"His mother is Lady Flora, daughter of the late duke of Madingley."

"He's related to a duke?" she asked in surprise. This might even help her plans. Surely he would care what his family thought of him.

"Just listen. Lady Flora also loved to compose music, but was never successful."

Grace frowned. "But I own music by her as well."

"You're getting ahead of my story," Edward said in a low voice. "When they first married, her husband was very poor, and her father supported them. That was a scandal in and of itself, that she married so far beneath her. She tried for many years to have her work published, but was unsuccessful. Baldwin Throckmorten became more and more famous. And then he fell off the balcony at Madingley Court and died."

With a gasp, Grace said, "How old was their son?"

"Young, but I do not know the exact age."

She didn't want to feel sympathy for him. He was a gambler and an overconfident seducer of women.

"Worse was yet to come. Servants heard Lady Flora say that it was all her fault that her husband was dead."

"Oh, surely she was just grief-stricken."

"But then not six months later, she emerged

from mourning with an incredible symphony, and she never again composed another. Though there was no proof, everyone believed that she'd killed her husband. She lives reclusively in the country and never comes to London. Throckmorten has become just as scandalous as his parents. The duke's other children are no better, but that gossip can be saved for a different time."

"Surely Mr. Throckmorten's scandals cannot top his parents' rumor of murder."

"Of course not. But he gambles with anyone, even over foolish things like how many callers the newest Original receives in a day, or how many times Queen Victoria makes a public appearance in a week."

Or if he can seduce a desperate woman into his bed, she thought, gritting her teeth.

"He dabbles in business too much for a gentleman. He is notorious for his ability to . . . persuade even the most reluctant of women to become his mistress."

Her face was hot with a blush, and her resolve to resist the man strengthened.

"He shows no interest in marrying," Edward continued, "so the young ladies stay away from him."

"He sounds like a foolish man," Grace said. But he also sounded like a man who would do anything to win, which would play right into her plan. Could that be his weakness?

Edward shrugged. "I've been told he's beyond wealthy." There was a tired envy in his voice.

"Was his father that successful?"

"I think not. Throckmorten is a genius with his own finances."

"And he'll ruin it all with his wild ways." Grace turned away, and spoke without thinking. "Does he not understand that once the gambling fever takes hold, it might never let him go?"

Then she realized what she'd said and looked back at Edward.

His eyes watched her with sadness, the wariness gone. "It doesn't have him like it has me, Grace."

"Don't say that! I was thinking of Mother."

"I can't even be angry with her. I might have done the same."

"You're wrong! You don't have to be like her. You can stop the gambling now."

"It's in my blood, don't you know that?" he said, his voice sounding as weary as if he'd given up. "But not you, Grace, thank God."

She felt sick. If he knew how recklessly she was gambling with her own reputation, he would be so disappointed in her. "I have my own flaws, Edward, as you well know."

He sighed and put his arm around her. "Wells played you for a fool, Grace. I had thought he was my closest friend—I had even encouraged you to attach yourself to him."

"You didn't know, Edward," she whispered. "And it was my fault that I—" She broke off, unable to even say the words.

"You were an innocent, Grace. He took advantage of you, said he was going to marry you. Even I believed him. Why wouldn't you, a girl in love, believe him, too?" He ground his fist into his open palm. "He's steered clear of me in London. Knows I'd pop him in the face for how he treated you."

She hugged herself, and then leaned her head against his arm. Poor Edward, so close to her, yet she'd been too humiliated to tell him everything that had happened between her and Baxter Wells, including the several days where she'd snuck away to lie in his arms.

"Promise me that you won't discuss this with Mr. Throckmorten, Edward," she insisted. "I think he'll respond to me better than you. I'll get that violin back."

"I hate using you this way, Grace."

"I promise I'll be careful."

At last, he nodded. "For what it's worth, I won tonight."

"Oh, Edward," she whispered forlornly. She wanted to beg him not to bet any of it, but she could not show him her distrust.

"We'll be able to pay the bills for a few weeks, maybe even buy you a new gown. If you're going to redeem Throckmorten, you'll need to see him wearing your best."

"Redeem?" she echoed.

"Isn't that what you're doing?"

Redeeming a gambler, she thought morosely. She'd spent her life trying to do that, first with her mother, then her brother, and now Daniel Throckmorten. And it never worked, not down deep

inside. But if she couldn't redeem Mr. Throckmorten's soul, maybe she could redeem him in
Society's eyes?

With this plan, she could convince Edward
she'd won the violin legitimately.

And she could thwart Mr. Throckmorten's attempted seduction.

When Edward left the room, he did not kiss her
cheek, or put his hand on her shoulder, as he once
would have done. Tears pricked her eyes, but she
willed them to dry. She wasn't finished fighting—
not just for her own freedom, but for her brother's
recovery. For what sort of life would he have without the social standing of land?

She took a deep breath and tried to calm herself. She was tired and distraught. She told herself
that for now, they had a place to live and food to
eat. She had confidence in her ability to resist Mr.
Throckmorten. And by resisting, she could win
the violin. To save Edward, she'd try anything.

Grace woke up at dawn, because she always
kept country hours. With Edward usually in
London, and her mother sleeping late, Grace had
been the one to consult with the steward every
day, to do the household accounts. She'd begun
to read books on agriculture that the bailiff had
suggested to her, so she'd understand what he
was discussing. She'd always considered it time
well spent, for she wanted to make a useful wife
someday.

Not a mistress.

When she thought of a mistress, she pictured a selfish creature, given to pleasures of the flesh rather than the hard work that came with preparing for marriage. She couldn't imagine why a woman would rather devote herself to a man for money only. Of course, now she knew how easily a woman could be tricked into losing her virginity. And there was always the fear that on her wedding night, her new husband would realize she had not come to him pure.

Her confrontation with Daniel Throckmorten had made her rethink some of her ideas, had even confirmed things she knew about herself. She was far too easily attracted to a man with handsome looks and a dangerous air. She wasn't worried that she'd succumb to any pressure on his part, not anymore, but she was disappointed that once again, she was proving to herself that men seemed to be her weakness. For her mother and brother, it was the risk of games of chance. For her, it was the age-old game between men and women.

And the new game she'd begun with Mr. Throckmorten.

How did he plan to proceed? she wondered as she ironed a gown to wear. Would he show up at unexpected times, imposing on her with his presence? Would he "court" her, visiting every day, having conversations as if they were getting to know each other for marriage instead of a more illicit purpose?

Grace washed and dressed, vowing to have Edward help her carry buckets of hot water to her room that night so that she could have a proper bath. While she was in the ground-floor library, writing a letter to send for her maid, she heard noises from the back of the house. Thinking it was Edward, she went to the kitchen, only to find a young boy eating pieces of dried apple, looking at her with big, wary eyes. After some questioning, Grace learned that Edward still retained a horse and the services of this young groom, Will, to take care of the stables and apprentice as Edward's valet. It was surely cheaper than his last perfectly trained manservant.

She sent the boy on a new errand, parting with another of her coins. He was to find Daniel Throckmorten and follow him for the day. She had to know what kind of man he was, his favorite haunts, and his friends in Society. Her plans for him needed witnesses, and she already had one in mind.

Later that afternoon, Grace rode a hackney to the fashionable town house of Baron Standish to make her morning call upon his wife, whom she'd known so many years ago as Beverly. They had gone to school together, before Grace's mother's financial situation had changed. Grace and Beverly still occasionally wrote, but when Beverly married and began having children, the letters became more infrequent.

But Grace still trusted Beverly's friendship, and if anyone could introduce Grace to the correct matrons and hostesses, it was she.

While Grace waited for the butler to take her card upstairs, she thought about what she might be involving Beverly in. She was keeping so many secrets, although she thought she could trust Mr. Throckmorten's love of a challenge to keep their . . . relationship quiet. But what about those other two men who knew that he had won the right to marry her? One of them had obviously wanted her, she thought worriedly. She could only pray that he would not want to risk a scandal by bringing his part in the affair to light.

At last the butler showed Grace upstairs to a lovely drawing room, where the sun shone through sheer curtains.

"Grace!" Beverly came toward her, looking more mature, but still with that lively sparkle in her eyes that meant mischief. Blond and pert and happy, she was obviously a very contented woman.

Grace gladly hugged her. "Beverly, it is so good to see you."

"You should have written when you were arriving! I would have invited you to a dinner party last night."

Grace found herself blushing, remembering whom she had spent last evening with. "I didn't know myself until quite recently. I'm staying with my brother."

"Do sit down and tell me everything. I admit my last letter to you was surely sometime ago."

Grace didn't want to say that it had been over a

year because she understood how busy the woman was. They chatted about Beverly's children and Grace's occasional suitors. When at last polite conversation was exhausted, and an expectant silence replaced it, Grace didn't quite know where to start.

Beverly gave her a kind smile. "Do tell me why you're really in London. You never wanted to leave your mother before."

I couldn't trust her alone, Grace thought with a sigh. But inwardly, she began to recite the story she'd conceived because she could not possibly tell Beverly the truth.

"I am twenty-three years old," Grace said in a soft voice. "I have not been meeting men who suit my fancy in Hertingfordbury."

Beverly smiled. "And here in London we have a veritable feast of men. You'll meet someone to please you."

"My brother can introduce me to his friends, but he's a bachelor, of course, and—"

"Say no more, my dear! Allow me to be your sponsor in Society. You come from an old family name. I am certain you will be well received."

Grace felt a surprising sting of tears, when she would never have considered herself an easy crier. But Beverly was proving herself a true friend—and Grace was lying to her. She consoled herself by remembering that she really did want to marry, so at least that part wasn't a lie.

"I must be honest, Beverly." *Partly honest.* "My

mother always had something of a reputation as a woman who enjoyed games of chance." *What an understatement.*

Beverly leaned forward and touched Grace's arm. "I remember, dear, but I'm sure others won't. It is how you present yourself that matters. As long as you are well-bred, and possessed of a dowry as well as your beautiful face, you will have no problems."

Grace gave her a relieved smile. Thank God for Papa, who'd thought to protect her dowry. At least she didn't have to lie to Beverly about that.

The butler stepped into the open doorway. "Lady Standish, Mr. Throckmorten is here to see Lord Standish."

Grace took a deep, quivering breath and tried to appear disinterested as she studied the small statue of a bird resting on the nearby table. Oh heavens, how had he come to be here at the same time? Was he following her? she thought, affronted. But of course, she was having him followed right this moment. She bit her lip, quelling a bubble of hysterical giggling as she imagined looking out the window and seeing Will watching from across the street.

Beverly clapped her hands together. "What perfect timing!"

Grace winced.

"Do show Mr. Throckmorten up," Beverly continued. "I think we can certainly rid him of any disappointment that my husband is not at home." When the butler had gone, she turned to Grace, and whispered, "Here is a most eligible man. His grandfather was the delightfully scandalous duke of Madingley, and his sensible cousin now has the title. Mr. Throckmorten himself has had to put up with much scandal, but it seems contagious in that family. And he has shown no preference to any young lady."

Of course not, Grace thought. *He preferred a mistress.*

Beverly leaned toward her. "You might be just the woman to make him interested in Society again. The mamas would thank you!"

Grace held back a snort.

And then Mr. Throckmorten entered the room. If she thought the sheer effect of him would be less imposing in comfortable daylight, she was wrong. If anything, the shining sun made him seem so much more a creature of the night, dark in coloring, sedate in his choice of clothing, as if he had no need to preen with vibrant colors. He bowed to the two women, and they returned the formality with curtsies.

"Lady Standish, do forgive my interruption."

Mr. Throckmorten spoke in that smooth, deep voice that made Grace shiver inside. Why did even the man's voice attract her?

"I wanted you to come up, Mr. Throckmorten," Beverly said. "Miss Banbury, may I present Mr. Throckmorten."

His eyes focused on her, betraying not even a hint of the amusement he must surely be feeling. He thought he'd gotten the best of her.

"Miss Banbury," he said, with another bow.

Grace inclined her head, using all of her skills at hiding her emotions as she responded, "Good afternoon, Mr. Throckmorten."

They all seated themselves, with him sitting directly across from her. But at least he concentrated that devilish smile on Beverly for the moment.

"I am sorry my husband is not at home to receive you, Mr. Throckmorten," Beverly said. "Did you have an appointment that he forgot?"

"No, my lady, I merely had a question about a railway investment we're both a part of. It can certainly wait."

Beverly glanced at Grace. "My husband always says that Mr. Throckmorten has an uncanny sense for which investments will bring the best rewards."

Grace smiled politely. This confirmed her brother's assessment of him. "So you know the best risks to take, Mr. Throckmorten?"

"Always, Miss Banbury. And I only choose to participate in something at which I know I will win."

"Is that a gambling reference?" she said, tilting her head. "Gambling is a terrible habit to have. I always feel sorry for someone caught within its spell."

"Luckily, there are those of us who can safely navigate its treacherous shoals."

"I can say that I, too, enjoy winning."

Their hostess looked curiously between them.

"Mr. Throckmorten," Beverly said, "Miss Banbury only recently arrived in London. I will be sponsoring her at all the best events of the Season."

"She is very lucky to have your help," he said.

Grace smiled at her old friend. "I agree."

Beverly nodded as if she were embarrassed at the praise. "Mr. Throckmorten, I hope you will make her feel welcomed by making sure all the young men ask her to dance."

"I'm certain I will be at the head of the line," he said.

Grace barely resisted rolling her eyes. "If there is a young lady you are paying calls to, please don't let me interfere."

"There is no one I am interested in, but thank you."

"Mama!" The wail drifted down the staircase from the second floor.

Beverly sighed.

A servant hurried in. "Lady Standish, please don't concern yourself. The nurse assures me that—"

"Mama!" This time it was a shriek.

Beverly rose to her feet and gave Grace an apologetic look. "Please excuse me for a moment. It is almost dinnertime, and her nerves are often frayed when her little belly is empty."

She strode from the room like a maternal whirlwind, leaving the door to the corridor wide open.

Grace gave Mr. Throckmorten a wary look, but he didn't notice because he was gazing down her body with an intense stare. She inhaled, feeling a little fluttery, a little unsure of herself. He had obviously masked his intentions for Beverly's benefit, but now he was making it very obvious what he was thinking.

Winning the challenge.

Chapter 4

Daniel allowed the silence to continue for a few moments, until he thought Grace wanted to squirm. She looked so moral, so prudish, as if she couldn't believe what he might try.

It made him hard. By the devil, everything about her made him hard.

"You followed me here," she said in a low, cool voice.

"Of course. You'll be seeing a lot of me. Who knows where I'll turn up?"

She narrowed her eyes at him.

"Who is the little boy you've enlisted to follow me?" he asked.

Her lovely cheeks blushed, though he imagined she willed them not to.

She lifted her chin. "My brother's groom."

"He's not bad for a lad. I might try harder to lose him tomorrow."

"Do you have something to hide?" She batted her lashes sweetly.

"No, but I enjoy upsetting your plans for me."

"Oh, believe me, sir, I have not even begun my plans."

"Well, that's good to hear. I would have been disappointed otherwise."

Clenching her jaw, she glanced at the open door. He knew she would not want anyone to overhear their scandalous conversation. So he slowly rose, avoiding even a glance at her, although he was aware that she stiffened as if he were going to pounce. And it was a tempting thought. But instead he strolled casually about the drawing room, looking at knickknacks and paintings until he came to the sunny window behind the sofa Grace was seated upon. They were now only several feet apart, and she did not turn to look at him.

"You look lovely in that green gown, Grace," he said in a low voice.

He thought she'd be offended at his use of her Christian name.

"Thank you, Daniel."

He wasn't surprised that it would take more than that to ruffle her. She had spirit along with her tempting innocence.

"Christian names," he murmured. "That speaks of a new intimacy."

"Or rudeness."

"Then allow me to be even more rude when I say that the color brings out your eyes—"

"Why, thank you," she interrupted.

He smiled to himself at her disappointed tone. Did she think he was so unoriginal?

"You didn't let me finish. The color also manages to make the skin above your breasts even more creamy."

He heard her inhale but not release her breath.

"You cannot see such a thing!" she whispered fiercely. "My neckline rises to my throat!"

He could not stop himself from glancing over his shoulder to watch her. "I can imagine. I want to lick you there, and trace a wet path down between your breasts."

She finally remembered to breathe, but it was a faint little gasp that made his stomach tighten. Now simple breathing was enough to make passion rise in him?

She tilted her pretty little head, her light brown curls bouncing, and he wished he could see her expression. But he preferred being just behind her, making her wonder at what he would do next. He found it . . . exciting to think that he might be the only one who'd ever spoken to her this way, had ever tried to seduce her with words alone.

But of course he planned to do so much more. It already obsessed his thoughts, and he'd only just begun . . .

"What will you taste like?" he mused softly.

He could see her hand clutch the pillow beside her.

"Hmm, strawberries and cream, I imagine." He dropped his voice to a guttural whisper. "Creamy flesh, strawberry pink nip—"

"I'm back!" Beverly called from the corridor.

He turned his head and looked back out the window, but not before he saw how Grace's hand trembled when she straightened it upon that dainty lace pillow. The first round surely went to him, he thought with satisfaction.

But he was uncomfortably aroused and hoped he could get away with standing behind the sofa for a while yet.

Grace woke up just after dawn. The first thing on her mind was the last thing she'd thought of before sleeping: Daniel Throckmorten's outrageous behavior at the Standish home. She shuddered and closed her eyes, biting back a moan. She could still hear his deep, rough voice saying words she hadn't imagined a man would say in broad daylight.

She would certainly not allow his scandalous words to affect her. After dressing, she went searching for Edward's groom/valet. After finding him in the stables, she brought him inside and made him some toast and eggs.

"So how did your assignment go yesterday, Will?"

He looked guilty, a bit of egg still in the corner of his mouth. "I didn't do too good a job. He spotted me quick, he did. Flipped me a coin, and said to keep up the good work."

She sighed. "So what did the gentleman do?"

"Went ridin' first thing, and I found out from his groom he does that near every mornin'."

Will told her about a bank Daniel had visited, and a lawyer's office, and even several businesses and a factory. It seemed the man was far busier than her brother usually was.

"He even visited a fancy mansion near Mayfair in the afternoon," Will said.

"I know, I was there," Grace said ruefully.

"After eatin' at his club, he sent me out a pastry like I never had afore," Will added blissfully.

If she weren't careful, Daniel would win the boy over to his side.

"Then he went to a blazin' palace on Park Lane," Will said with obvious awe. "I asked a coachman, and it were Madingley House, miss. But he doesn't live there. Got his own town house, he does. I forgot to tell ye—when I was comin' home late yesterday, I saw a man watchin' the house."

She frowned thoughtfully. "What did he look like?"

"Don't know—he left afore I got close. Since Mr. Throckmorten knows I'm watchin' him, could he have someone watchin' you?"

She shrugged. "I don't know, Will. I'll have to find out."

"I already saddled the 'orse," Will said. "Mr. Edward don't need it until afternoon. And you bein' up so early, thought ye might have a reason."

Grace ruffled his hair. "You're a smart one, Will."

"Ye want me to follow him again today?"

"Not right now," she said, not wanting the boy to see what she'd planned for Daniel. "I'll let you know."

* * *

Daniel never missed a morning ride. It was not an hour past dawn, and fog was hovering low over the Serpentine in the middle of Hyde Park. There were only a few riders at this time of the morning, and he felt alone and peaceful.

He thought of Grace, the woman he wanted in his bed. She could not be more different than his last mistress, a woman of the world, used to expecting the finer things in life in exchange for the pleasures of her body. Last month, she'd asked to be released from their arrangement. She had begun to want more intimacy than he could give her, even though he'd warned her from the beginning—as he did all his women—that their companionship would not turn into more.

But Grace would be a different mistress. He fully expected to make her as eager for his touch as he felt for hers. He had almost debated attending the musicale that Lady Standish had undoubtedly dragged Grace to last night. Now that would have caused a sensation, and it would have been far too obvious that he'd come only for her, since he never attended such affairs.

Instead, he'd gone to Madingley House and had his weekly fill of the loud voices and merriment of his uncle and aunt and cousins.

But not his mother, he thought, feeling the old twinge of unease that he had buried for so many years. She had not been to London since his father's death. He didn't think she cared about rumors that might still be lingering twenty years later. She socialized with the neighbors back in Cambridgeshire. But they all knew not to have music playing. Here in London, he thought she would fear such entertainment.

He couldn't avoid music, of course. He'd even heard the occasional melody of one of his father's symphonies, but he didn't go out of his way for an evening of music.

But then he was guessing at his mother's motives, for they never talked about the past. After his father died, she had retreated into her music— ignoring him. He still remembered those bleak days, when one servant after another took turns trying to keep him distracted from the closed door of the music room. He had known his mother was in there. She would eventually emerge at the end of the day to talk to him. But he was so young that over time he began to resent the piano, to resent even the melody in her mind that called to her more than he could. She kept telling him that she had no choice except to write everything down. When it was finally done, and she declared herself through with music forever, he'd been secretly glad. He'd never brought up music again, but had always wondered when it would pull her away from him, her only child. Now that he was an adult, he wished it would come back to her.

Here in Hyde Park, with only his horse for company, Daniel told himself not to think. He rode contentedly in the saddle as the animal cantered.

Until he heard a scream.

He stiffened, pulling on the reins until the horse came to a stop. He looked between the trees, up and down Rotten Row, but he saw nothing.

Then came another scream, closer this time.

Suddenly, a horse burst from between two trees, heading straight at Daniel. His mount danced to the side, its ears back. The scream was coming from the other rider, a woman, who seemed to be hanging on for dear life, sliding perilously to one side. Her hat was gone, her brown hair flying from its pins. Daniel urged his horse into a gallop, so that by the time the woman's horse flew past, he was keeping the same pace with a burst of speed.

He reached out, leaning sideways as the rough dirt path seemed to fly beneath him. He meant to grab her reins, but at the last second, he saw that it was Grace Banbury. Her beautiful face was stark white with terror. Letting go of his own reins, he caught her beneath the arms and dragged her across his lap.

Grace cried out as she found herself pulled across the gap between the pounding hooves of both horses. The ground raced below, the air rushed through her hair and past her ears, and she'd thought herself perfectly safe—until Daniel Throckmorten had decided to risk life and limb saving her rather than just take hold of the reins.

His thighs were hard beneath her, one arm encircled her back, and the other reached to slow her horse, making him lean perilously low over her. She gaped up at him, so shocked she almost forgot to pretend gratitude, as had been her plan. His face was hard with determination, brown eyes narrowed with concentration. It was thrilling and exciting—and difficult to remember to look terrified. When he finally pulled to a stop, she only had a moment to look around to see if anyone was watching. She saw three people on horseback, and thankfully, two were ladies, who were more likely to spread the tale.

Daniel lifted her even closer to him. Cradled in his arms felt as safe as being on the ground. He examined her face as if he expected to find blood.

"Are you all right?" he demanded.

"Oh, you saved me, Mr. Throckmorten!" she cried, a bit too loudly.

He frowned. "However did you get yourself in such a predicament? You live in the country. I would have thought you a better judge of a horse's temperament. This beast is your brother's, isn't it?"

"Yes, yes, it was foolish of me, I know—"

"Hallo, are you all right?" cried a man's voice.

Grace tried to sit up higher, but the pommel cut into her hip, and Daniel was still holding on so firmly. "Could you please help me down, Mr. Throckmorten? I do believe my limbs aren't shaking so badly now."

His frown grew even more suspicious, but there was also a hint of amused curiosity in those dark eyes. But their witnesses were riding toward them, and she could not afford more time to appease him.

She tried to turn to greet the spectators, but he hugged her close and whispered, "You've given me such a ripe opportunity, Grace. I wonder what they'd say if I just continue to hold you so indecently, as if we are far too familiar with each other."

"You wouldn't," she hissed, waving her hand before her face as if she would faint. She put the back of her palm to her forehead, trying for weak and distraught.

"But your acting is so marvelous. It would be a shame not to allow you a last grand performance."

She simply looked at him, their faces close together, their eyes daring each other.

"Only two weeks left," Daniel murmured. "I might have to do something desperate to ensure that I win."

"You're far from desperate," she whispered back, then smiled. "It's two weeks minus a day. And you wouldn't do anything that might lead to a forced marriage."

"And who could possibly force me into that?"

Before she could respond, others were upon them.

"Throckmorten, superb horsemanship," said a man who reined in his gelding as he reached them.

Daniel finally released her from his gaze. "Thank you, Colby," he said smoothly. "Always good to aid a lady in distress."

"Oh, my dear," cried a well-dressed woman

riding at the man's side. "Will you faint? Please don't fall off the horse."

"I would never allow it," Daniel said, holding her even more tightly.

The more Grace tried to appear weak, the more he pressed her against him, breasts to his chest, making it difficult to remember her purpose. "I can't quite get my breath," she said weakly.

The woman slid from her horse. "Do let her down, Mr. Throckmorten. I can help the poor girl."

Grace sensed Daniel's reluctant surrender, and she gave a deep sigh, using weariness to mask her relief.

"Let me dismount first, Miss Banbury," he said, "and then I'll help you down."

She gave a trembling nod, allowing him to do all the work of sliding out from under her. When he was on the ground and reaching up to her, she let herself slide weakly into his arms. It was difficult to forget that his hands were on her waist. She had a fleeting thought about what it would feel like if she weren't wearing a corset.

"Miss Banbury, is it?" said the woman behind her.

Grace gratefully turned to her and gave a shaky smile. "Yes, ma'am. I am newly arrived in London, and I hadn't ridden my brother's horse before, and didn't know the paths—"

"Of course, of course, it is very different here than in the country," the woman said soothingly.

She was perhaps twenty years older than Grace, a mature woman who had a vigorous air about her.

"I am Miss Parker. Do you need to sit down, dear?"

"Oh, no, I am certain I will be fine. Thank goodness for Mr. Throckmorten. I could have died!"

"Rescuing innocent maidens, Throckmorten?" said Mr. Colby with dry amusement in his voice. "Not quite like you."

Good, Grace thought with satisfaction. Just the reaction she'd been looking for. She glanced over her shoulder at Daniel but didn't allow any triumph to show. It was far too early in their challenge.

During several minutes of conversation, Miss Parker invited Grace to call upon her, Mr. Colby gave Daniel a rewarding look of approval, and Daniel appeared reluctantly amused. All in all, her plan to improve his reputation was succeeding.

"Thank you all for your help," Daniel said. "If you don't mind, I think Miss Banbury has had quite enough excitement for one day. I'll escort her back to her brother."

"Good of you, Throckmorten," said Miss Parker, speaking to an equal in her no-nonsense way. "Please do visit me, Miss Banbury."

"I will, Miss Parker. Thank you so much for your concern."

Without a mounting block, Grace was forced to allow Daniel to help her mount. She found the stirrup as quickly as possible, so that his hands wouldn't linger. But as the others rode off, he guided her knee around the pommel very familiarly.

"That's not necessary," Grace said softly, still attempting a smile, while inside she felt a tightening deep in her belly.

"I deserve some sort of reward for acting in your little play."

She looked down upon him, his hand still on her knee, and found herself feeling generous. "Very well, if it will make you feel better."

He arched a brow, but at last he moved back and mounted his own horse. "Should I lead you by the reins? We wouldn't want another accident to happen."

"I'm certain your masterful horse will keep mine well cowed," she said.

He rolled his eyes. They walked their horses sedately.

At last he said, "You made quite the conquest today."

"You mean besides you?" She batted her lashes at him.

He smiled. "Besides me. Miss Parker is quite the influential bluestocking, a spinster with strong ideals. She leads several charity organizations, and even holds the meetings in her own home."

"How fascinating," she said, thinking how well this might fit into her plans.

"So you're interested in charity work?"

"I never met a man who wanted to discuss it," she said slyly.

"It takes a special man to know how to seduce a virgin," he answered.

She felt her face grow hot and looked about. Although there were more riders as the fog burned off and the sun rose, no one was close enough to hear his outrageous conversation. "So you think only virgins want to talk about helping others?"

"So you admit you're a virgin?"

Even more heat washed through her, and she forced herself not to lower her gaze. "That is none of your business, Mr. Throckmorten."

"It was Daniel yesterday. Or was that too intimate for you?"

"Daniel."

"And believe me, Grace, your innocent status will only help me. You'll never know what to expect from me."

"I am not naive."

She broke into a canter, but not before she saw his speculative gaze.

"You seem to be intruding on all parts of my life," she said with deliberate lightness. "I'm surprised you thought it necessary to post a man to keep an eye on me. Surely my servant Will would tell you what I was doing if you asked."

He shot her a sharp glance. "Post a man?"

"My groom saw a man watching the house." Uneasily, she added, "You didn't hire him?"

"No."

She sighed. "It must be someone for Edward then. I do hope he isn't in any more trouble."

"If I hear anything, I'll let you know."

He sounded almost distracted. Edward's problems obviously didn't concern him, and she didn't want to involve him. It was a private, painful matter—bad enough that he knew firsthand what her mother was capable of.

Daniel glanced at Grace's profile and saw faint traces of sadness. She was a woman who understood a mother's distant preoccupation. She had had a brother to band together against their mother, and he had not, but at least his mother's neglect had only lasted a few months.

He found himself amused by how her mind worked. She had deliberately tried to make him look like a hero today. How was that supposed to counter his seduction? Or was it just a method to acquaint her with people he knew?

As they reached the end of the park and neared the heavier London traffic, she looked at him and said, "I assume I'll see you at Lady Irwin's ball this evening."

He eyed her, taking his last chance to look down her trim body. "And why would you assume that? I might have a very important game of hazard at a club tonight."

"But you're playing a new game now, Daniel, aren't you?"

He met her knowing gaze. Damn, but he liked the way she thought. "Yes, I am. I'll be there."

"Shall I save you a dance? Oh wait, you don't dance with young ladies."

"I'll make an exception for you."

She put a hand to her throat in shock. "I am so flattered."

"Don't be. When my hands are on you, you'll know why I did it."

Her smile faded, and they stared at each other. She might regret the necessity of their challenge, but he knew that something inside her thrilled to it. And that part of her called to him.

She said nothing more, just nodded before guiding her horse away from him.

He watched her go, admiring everything he saw.

Chapter 5

At the ball that night, Grace felt like a princess on her brother's arm. Edward introduced her to the hostess and several other couples, brought her a glass of champagne, stood with her, and commented upon the various bachelors, as if he were helping her find a husband. She would have been thankful if she weren't so suspicious of his motives. At least this was keeping him from one of those dreadful gaming hells she'd heard about. At last he excused himself to go off and laugh with several other young men. And he didn't bother to introduce her, she thought with a huff. How like a brother.

As for Daniel, she kept watching the receiving line for him, but never saw him enter. Had he been teasing her about attending the ball? He was known for avoiding these sorts of affairs.

Then at last she caught sight of a man taller than many others, his hair brown, his broad back to her. It had to be Daniel, she thought. She was the reason he'd come tonight, and somehow she would have to make that clear to the *ton*. If Daniel were seen to be back on the marriage hunt, he would be distracted, giving her an edge. She felt a thrill she attributed to the resumption of their challenge.

Was this how her brother felt whenever he was about to sit down to a card game?

Grace's excitement dimmed. She bolstered herself by remembering the good that could come of her association with Daniel. Even now, she still had a home and food on the table, through her own wiles.

Like a mistress.

Those words froze her, but only for a moment. She wasn't Daniel's mistress, and she never would be.

She knew the moment he saw her, felt the shock of his direct gaze from across the ballroom. This morning he'd been pleasant and concerned for her, but the night seemed to bring on the dangerous Daniel, the man who meant to hunt her as a private trophy.

And she saw another side of him, too, the one he showed the public. The crowd parted for him as he came toward her. People whispered with speculation as he passed. Young girls looked at him longingly while their mamas steered them away.

Just before he reached her, she saw several women give her a faintly pitying stare. Was it so obvious that she was his next target? Something deep inside her stiffened, and she turned to Daniel, sweeping into a curtsy.

"Good evening, Mr. Throckmorten," she said in her silkiest voice.

His eyebrows rose a bit, but he bowed and took her gloved hand for the correct brief moment. "Miss Banbury, you look lovely, as always."

"But you haven't known me long enough to form such an opinion, sir."

"I have a good imagination."

He was openly staring at her neckline, and feeling a perverse need to tease him, she deliberately took a deep, bosom-lifting breath.

His gaze shot back to hers, and she only smiled and blinked at him with feigned puzzlement.

"Not so innocent at all," he might have murmured.

"Pardon me?"

"You saved me a waltz, I presume," he continued blandly.

"You are in luck, sir. I have been introduced to no other gentlemen."

"I can see them all wishing it weren't so, Miss Banbury, but most will stick boringly to the rules."

She tilted her head. "But not you?"

"For once I've come down on the correct side of etiquette, especially since it benefits me. We've already been introduced. Which means you can dance with me."

He took her hand as the first notes of the waltz rang in the air.

"You didn't even bother to ask," she teased, trying to hang back.

"I was so very certain of your response. And it is your first London waltz, is it not?" he added softly.

She looked wistfully at the dance floor, where at least three dozen couples were gathering. At most, she'd danced in a cramped Assembly room floor above a tavern, with four other couples. It seemed like a fairy tale to dance beneath a thousand candles in chandeliers, to have so many people watching her, and to know that she was with the most handsome man in the room.

His hand felt so very different than hers, cool and large, rough and strong. This would not persuade her to grant him any sort of intimacy. It was only a waltz.

But what a wonderful waltz. The sound of the orchestra echoed through the ballroom, swelling and rising until her heart seemed to beat to its tempo.

But then Daniel swept her into his arms, and everything else faded away. She knew the dance well, had practiced through her girlhood in happy anticipation, but she could have been ignorant, so masterfully did he lead her through the steps. He spun her between slower couples, swirling and dipping, holding her closer by slow degrees. His hand seemed so big on her back, making her feel feminine and fragile. Then his thighs brushed hers, jolting her with an even more intense awareness of him. Her smile faded, her body concentrated on his, as if waiting for another casual, intimate touch.

As he guided her past another couple, his thigh slid smoothly between hers, a brief, erotic press, leaving her with the lingering shock of desire.

It took every bit of concentration not to stumble against him.

Oh heavens, even a dance with him was a seduction, rather than making him appear like every other normal man, as she'd intended.

At last the dance was over, and he led her near the open French doors, where a cool breeze attempted to penetrate the overwrought heat of the ballroom. She stared vaguely about her, then found a glass of champagne in her hand.

"Drink," Daniel said.

She took several sips.

"Better?"

She eyed him. "Better how? Am I now refreshed? Yes."

"Are you cooled down?" he asked in a soft voice. "I believe you were . . . overheated."

Her face was now hot with a blush. Oh, he knew what he did to her, womanizer that he was. He must believe that the seduction of an "innocent" would be easy for him. She admitted that he could tempt her, but she would never allow herself to give in. It was a dance, and he knew how to use his body as a weapon in their challenge. She would learn to deal with it.

He regarded her with a serious look that she didn't believe.

"No, I think you are in danger of becoming faint from the heat, Miss Banbury." He suddenly gripped her elbow. "Perhaps a breath of fresh air will clear your head."

With barely any effort, he steered her right out of

the ballroom. Short of creating a scene by dragging her feet or holding on to the door, she could not stop him. She was in the hands of a practiced rake.

It had been a long time since she'd walked in torchlit darkness with anyone other than Edward's business steward at their country estate. She hadn't allowed herself the temptation. Daniel's presence was like a powerful wall to one side, keeping her in line with just his warm fingers above her elbow. Her skin was bare there, and she realized with shock that he had removed his gloves since their dance. She pulled away, and he let her go.

As they approached the stone balustrade, a breeze with the scent of roses swept up over them from the garden below. Torches lined several paths, and she could see daring people disappearing within. At least Daniel made no move to herd her toward the wide stairs.

He leaned his elbow on the balustrade and watched her. A torch was behind him, leaving his face mostly in shadow but for the glitter of his eyes. The moon darted behind clouds, and the darkness seemed to settle around them.

He towered above her, dark as sin, with only the white of his shirt and cravat glistening in the moonlight. Her heart was beating much too fast, and she was disappointed that she could not control such an elemental response. But that was part of the game, wasn't it? Resisting herself as well as him. For she had her own weaknesses, and like any man, he must sense them.

Retreating seemed another weakness, yet she stepped away, in case others saw them. "Ah, a warm, moonlit night," she said. "Perfect for a man to practice his wiles on a woman."

"Trust me, I don't need moonlight," he said, putting his hand over hers on the balustrade. "Darkness works even better."

Smiling, she slid her hand away. "Think you I don't know what to expect from a man such as you?"

"There are so many men like me in Hertingfordbury?"

"So you've done your research."

"I read the property deed."

She stiffened but did not respond to the provocation. Was he deliberately trying to distract her from his true intentions?

He stepped toward her, she stepped back. Too late, did she realize it only got darker where he was herding her.

"And what do you expect from someone like me?" Daniel asked.

"That scandalous waltz, of course, and the way you took advantage of touching me before all of the *ton*."

"Most don't know who you are. They are just as intrigued by your mysterious beauty as I first was. So I displayed you to them."

"You don't dance much, do you?"

"No. Why?"

"To me, you displayed your open pursuit of me. They'll think you've finally decided to marry.

And now you'll be the next inviting target for all the young girls."

He grinned, teeth flashing. "I think you've overestimated your powers. They know any woman I choose to pursue only has one place in my life—as my mistress."

She shook her head, undaunted. "You've always thought your dreadful reputation and family scandal have kept you out-of-bounds. The mamas have thought that you don't want to marry, so they've ignored you. Trust me; soon I'll have them believing that you're back on the marriage block, just waiting to be bought. The chance to marry a wealthy gentleman related to a duke will dissolve many a woman's reservations."

He gave a low, hypnotic chuckle. "I think you underestimate the effect of one dance with you. A lifetime of scandal cannot be erased so easily. And what makes you think that each of my mistresses didn't start out believing she could ensnare me in marriage?"

He leaned over her, and she glanced around with deliberate casualness, realizing they were almost alone, that his body blocked from anyone's view what he might do. Her breathing seemed too suddenly out of her control, just like this whole situation.

But what could he do? she told herself in a panic. He was after seduction, not ruination.

But accidents happened, as she well knew.

She backed away again and came up hard against the corner of the balustrade. She was trapped. His hands settled on the stone on either side of her. No torch illuminated his face, only the silhouette of him from behind.

"But what if you truly are becoming another candidate for marriage?" she whispered in desperation.

He leaned even lower, and she felt the heat of him, the brush of his breath on her face.

"I have been doing this long enough," he murmured. "I know how to avoid people."

"Or force them to avoid you," she shot back.

Another voice said quietly, "Then you don't know how to avoid me."

Daniel stepped back, and Grace stiffened as she saw her brother standing there, hands on his hips as if he were barely holding himself back from throttling Daniel.

"Good evening, Banbury," Daniel said mildly. "And why would I wish to avoid you?"

"Not so difficult to figure out, when you steal my sister out of her first London ball." Edward took her hand and pulled her away from the balustrade and out of Daniel's reach. "Haven't you taken enough from my family?"

Grace groaned, looking about in worry. But when no one seemed to be paying them any attention, she made herself stay calm.

"Edward," she said, "we've learned over the years to place blame where it belongs. No one forced Mother to do anything she didn't want to do."

"And he's not forcing you?" Edward demanded, scowling down at her. "That's not how it looked to me."

"I was not holding her against her will," Daniel said. "If she had asked, I'd have let her go."

She winced. Her brother would want to know why she hadn't asked. And permitting Daniel liberties didn't seem to go along with redeeming him, especially not with her history.

Edward stared at her a moment longer, as if trying to read the truth in her eyes. He turned back to Daniel, and in a calmer voice, said, "Why don't you go fill up a few more dance cards, Throckmorten—if you can." He gestured with his head back toward the mansion.

Grace bit her lip, but remained silent, knowing that neither man would appreciate her interference.

Daniel gave her a brief bow and walked back to the open door.

She looked up at her brother. "Edward, I told you I wanted to make him into a better man, and by dancing with him, I showed all the eligible young ladies—"

"But he didn't just *dance* with you, now did he?"

She put her hand on his arm. "I can handle Mr. Throckmorten."

"You thought that the last time you were involved with a man," he said gruffly. "I let you have your way, and you ended up crushed."

"And now you can no longer trust me."

"I never said that! But if you suffer such hurt a second time . . ."

"I won't, Edward. I'm wise to the ways of men now."

He looked toward the mansion, a bitter tilt to his mouth. "Throckmorten is not like any of our country gentlemen, Grace."

"I know. And I am being careful."

She longed for her brother back, his quirky counsel, the humorous way he saw life. This Edward seemed . . . sad and defeated. And some of that was her fault because he'd thought he should have been able to save her from his best friend. She didn't know how to help him except to return his inheritance to him. Without property, he was just another poverty-stricken gentleman whom no one would marry. And it would destroy him if she had to marry someone she didn't love just to support the two of them.

"You're not just beautiful, you're smart," he continued. "Too smart. And you still have a dowry. You need to go back inside and charm a few men. I know many who would want to marry you."

She and her brother always did think the same thing at the same time, she thought fondly. "But for my money or my face, Edward dear? Marriage should not be based only on that. I think our parents' was, and look how unhappy they were." She leaned her head against his arm and looked up at him. "And I won't abandon you so easily."

He closed his eyes. "It's so difficult, Grace. I wish I hadn't come."

"What do you mean?" she whispered. "Watching me and—"

"No, I can't even say that's the worst part. It's . . . I know what the men are doing just down the hall." His voice was soft and strained. "I don't want to gamble. I keep asking myself why I need it, why it's so important. It's all I can think about."

"Oh, Edward," she said, tears filling her eyes.

"My mind is playing tricks. It keeps telling me that I can stop whenever I want to, that I'll just win enough to—whatever. And sometimes that happens. And that's worse, because then my mind has even more ammunition with which to persuade me."

"Then stay with me," she said. "We'll dance. You can introduce me to your friends."

He winced. "I should have done that when I came in, but all I could think about . . ." He took a deep breath. "You're right. I can control myself, if just for an hour. Then I'll leave."

As Daniel had surmised, his reputation remained unaffected by one dance with an eligible young lady. Perhaps she had yet to realize that he might have damaged hers. Though he talked with most of the men easily, when he was alone he remembered that the only reason he attended these affairs was to discover his next mistress.

Or to begin his seduction of her.

He spotted a tall, swarthy man moving through

the crowd toward him, nodding or speaking to several people, but never stopping his slow advance on Daniel. Behind him, people whispered in his wake, sent looks of awe at one another as if they'd just seen the prince consort.

Thank God for his cousin Christopher Cabot, the duke of Madingley. Chris wore a bright smile as he approached.

"Madingley," said Daniel dryly.

"Throckmorten," Chris said, not even bothering to repress a grin. "Was that you I saw—dancing?"

"I have been known to do so."

"And that is the reason I am here. I heard this afternoon at the club that you'd accepted Irwin's invitation. He was frankly worried about it, wondering what you intended."

"Always good to worry the host. So far I haven't done anything to offend him—simply danced with a lady."

"And dragged her off to the dark terrace. Surely you are not looking for a mistress here."

Daniel grimaced. "Watching me? So what family member put you up to that?"

"None. Took it upon myself. I am the head of the family, after all." He smiled. "Shall I tell them that you've found a woman worth being publicly alone with?"

"You know I'm not pursuing her for marriage."

Chris's grin faded. "No? Then what was that for?"

"You've never stolen a kiss?"

"I have," he said too gravely. "But usually with

a woman sophisticated enough to realize the game."

"Believe me, she's playing her own game as well."

"Is she trying to trap you?" Chris asked in a soft, wary voice.

Daniel shook his head, wearing a wry smile. "Not that. I promise I'll tell you more about it another time."

"But I've been dispatched as your rescuer. What am I supposed to tell them?"

"You mean our aunt and uncle?"

Chris nodded, his smile returning.

"It's too late to worry about their reputations, so they need to stop worrying about mine. You, too."

Chris shook his head. "Card game?"

"Lead the way."

After Edward escorted Grace back inside, he introduced her to the friends he'd greeted when they arrived, and she spent several dances well occupied by admiring men. At last she was able to catch her breath by hiding behind a potted fern. A champagne glass suddenly appeared through the leaves.

Grace laughed when Beverly poked her head through. "You read my mind," she said, taking a refreshing sip.

"I saw who you were dancing with."

"Then you saw me with several men."

Beverly waved a hand. "Only the first mattered,

of course. And to think, I introduced you to Mr. Throckmorten! What a catch."

Grace rolled her eyes. "It was a dance, Beverly."

"And a daring rescue earlier in the day, I hear."

Without thinking, Grace said with delight, "So the story worked its way about town? Wonderful!"

"Wonderful?" Beverly asked with suspicion. "You want people to know you're such a dreadful horsewoman?"

"Well . . . no, of course not."

"Then why would you care what people heard?"

Grace said nothing, tapping her toe and looking past the fern, as if watching the dancers.

"Grace Banbury, you do realize that our friendship has returned full force. And friends tell friends their deepest secrets."

Inside, Grace winced. There were so many things she wasn't telling Beverly. "I—I really can't speak of it here." She was only buying time, of course, because now she was going to have to tell the woman something eventually.

"Hmm, what a mystery," Beverly said. "For that, I can wait. But you have worked miracles already, you know."

"I have?"

"Throckmorten *danced*. Mamas were swooning in horror, young ladies were in awe—until he took himself off with his cousin."

"He's gone?" Grace asked.

Beverly laughed. "I cannot wait to hear this story. But no, he's not gone. He's playing cards with the gentlemen in the library."

"Oh." A feeling of disappointment stole over her, and she silently chastised herself for forgetting what he was. He was a man who enjoyed the amusements of a wealthy gentleman. She could hardly expect him to stop gambling just because he was sharing a private challenge with her. She had to remember that not everyone was as overcome by the lure as her mother and brother. But how could he not realize how easy it was to slip into obsession? "Did you say his cousin was here? Which one?"

"The duke himself. Madingley."

"Isn't he the one whose mother is from Spain?"

"Yes, she is." Beverly leaned toward her and whispered, "A commoner, and once Catholic, or so I hear. The *ton* still has not accepted her."

"But they must love her son," Grace said wryly.

"A duke? Him, they adore, of course. Now if we can't talk about the interesting Mr. Throckmorten and his family, you need to meet other people. And I know exactly the right ones."

Just like the first night when she'd arrived in London, Grace found a lamp lit in the entrance hall, as well as a newly stocked candelabrum. She was surprised at Edward's thoughtfulness. She gratefully lit the candles, leaving the lamp for him. He'd left the ball not long after their discussion, and she hoped he'd been able to resist the card game.

With a lot of tugging and squirming, Grace managed to remove her gown. She washed, donned her nightgown, braided her hair, and then crawled into bed with her journal. She wrote about her successful rescue that morning, and was halfway through the evening's excitement, when she heard a muffled noise.

She closed her journal and rested it on her knee, placing the quill in its inkpot. Could it be Edward already? But he was not usually quiet about his arrival.

For a moment, she thought about the man Will had seen looking at the house.

Oh, she was being foolish. This was a wealthy neighborhood—and she'd locked all the doors.

But all the same, she went to the door and leaned her ear against it, listening. Again, she heard something.

She just couldn't keep asking herself questions. She pulled open the door, went out into the hall and stood still, listening. Edward's door, across from hers, showed no light from beneath. She sighed, turning to go back into her room—and saw a faint light beneath the door of the master suite.

Had Edward moved into the larger room, and she just hadn't realized? She'd only been here one night. She tiptoed to the door and leaned her ear against it.

It suddenly opened and she reeled forward, off-balance, right into the arms of Daniel Throckmorten.

Chapter 6

Daniel hadn't expected Grace to fall so easily into his arms, so warm and soft and wearing only a nightgown. The scent of lavender surrounded him. She gasped and struggled in a panic.

"Grace," he murmured against the hair at her temple.

She stilled and gaped up at him, still caught so wonderfully to his chest.

"Daniel?" she cried.

"Hush." He pulled her inside and shut the door. "Are you allowing me to win so easily, fair Grace? This is like granting me a perfectly wrapped present."

With a flustered groan, she pushed against his chest, and he released her.

"What are you doing here?" she demanded. "You gave me back the key to the house!"

"I was not so foolish as to give you the only key that I had."

She put her hands on her hips in anger, probably not realizing how delightfully her uncorseted

breasts bounced. She likely wasn't wearing drawers, and with just a flick of his wrist, it would be
easy enough to see—

"You promised that we could live here, at least
for the month," she said angrily.

It actually took time to formulate a simple response, as his brain only seemed able to dwell on
how little she was wearing. "And you can. I just
thought I'd bring over a few things I might need—
a change of clothing, for instance."

Her eyebrows dropped in a ferocious frown
that looked quite fetching on her.

"And why would you need that?" she asked icily.

"Well, when my seduction succeeds—"

"*If.*"

"—then I need to be prepared. A gentleman
cannot begin his day in wrinkled clothing. My
valet would be appalled and worry that he would
be blamed."

And Daniel hadn't been able to forget about the
man watching her house, but he wouldn't say that
aloud. He hadn't thought about her alone with
no servants for protection until just this evening,
when he'd seen her brother gambling again. He'd
remembered the bare state of the house that first
night, no servants about to make it look lived in
when no one was at home. It felt strange to be
worried about a woman.

He needed to distract her, so he reached around
and caught her braid. "I like your hairstyle. I've
never seen it on a fashionable lady before. You could
make quite an entrance anywhere you went."

She tugged her hair, and he slowly let it go, a little bit at a time.

"This is the best way to keep my hair from tangling. You obviously do not have a sister. But you've had many mistresses, of course."

"And they kept their hair long and free, the way I like it."

He moved closer until she backed up against the door. He murmured, "I like the way a woman's hair tangles about our bodies when we make love."

She ducked beneath his arm and retreated to the center of the room, her face flushed. "It sounds painful for the woman."

"None have ever said so."

"They needed your goodwill—and your money."

He moved toward her again, and she darted around the far side of the bed.

"How many mistresses have you had?" she said quickly, obviously trying to distract him.

"A few." He leaned against the bedpost, casually stroking the velvet bed curtains with long, smooth strokes.

She watched his hands, her lips parted, her eyes wide. Then she swallowed and marshaled her determination.

"And how long does a mistress linger in your good graces?"

"Are you doing research?" he asked, lifting a brow.

She blushed. "Just curious."

"I had my first mistress when I was nineteen."

"So young!" she said in surprise.

"It lasted just six months—long enough to have me sent down from Cambridge in disgrace."

"But . . . do not other men have mistresses?"

"She was living with me in my room."

"Oh."

"It's a shame I didn't realize in time that we didn't suit. But it really didn't matter in the end. I was bored at Cambridge and had learned all I needed to. The rest of my education was through *experience*." He emphasized the last word, letting her think what she would.

Her gaze darted away but only briefly. Her curiosity was one of the things he enjoyed about her. It would prove so helpful to him.

"The classics would not aid me in this new industrial world, so I took my small allowance and began to invest."

"Successfully, I hear," she said dryly.

"I like your interest in me. It proves we suit. I always succeed at whatever I try. I'm good with numbers."

"Successful with mistresses, too?"

"Not always. But enough to keep all of us satisfied."

"And how long was the longest relationship?"

He put a knee on the bed, and although she stiffened on the far side, she did not scurry away. He climbed up and on all fours began to crawl toward her. He could see the green of her eyes darken like the depths of the forest, and he imagined the moistness of a summer heat. To his surprise, he began to perspire. He had a wild urge to fling off all his clothing and see what she would do.

Grace was frozen, caught in a subtle trap she had no answer to. Daniel was above her, crawling toward her like a cat, all smooth muscle beneath his clothing. She imagined him naked, doing the same thing, and she almost couldn't remember how to breathe.

She licked her lips and watched his gaze settle on her mouth, as if he would begin to nibble her there first.

"Are you trying to distract me from my question?" she asked in a quivering voice.

He stopped with his hands on the edge of the bed, his fingers splayed, his head swaying outward like a dark, shaggy lion. "I forgot it."

"What was the longest a mistress lasted?"

"Three years."

"That is a long time," she said, feeling intrigued in spite of the desire uncurling inside her. "And you broke it off at last?"

"She did."

Hearing such intimate words was making her even more vulnerable to him. The more she heard, the more he became a person to her rather than just an opponent.

When he reached for her, she took a step back, and he made no move to leave the bed. His fingers almost reached her breast, and she watched them with a gasp, until finally he pulled back.

"She left you for a man who offered her more?" she asked.

"She had no one else at the time," he said.

With a stab of disappointment, she watched him stretch out on his back, his arms out over his head. She stared spellbound at the rise of his chest and the width of his shoulders. With a pleasurable sigh, he folded his hands behind his head and crossed his ankles. She realized he wasn't wearing shoes, that his big feet in black stockings looked strangely intimate.

"Then why did your mistress leave you?" she asked.

"She said I did not talk to her enough."

"Not talk enough? You have barely closed your mouth since I met you!"

He laughed, long and low, a contagious sound that felt too good rumbling near her rib cage.

"Believe me, we talked in bed."

Her ears practically burned at the way he spoke of intimacies so casually.

"But she wanted more of my time and attention, and I could not give her . . . what I didn't have to give."

Grace risked stepping closer to the bed, so that she could see his face in the shadows. "She made the mistake of falling in love with you."

He shrugged. "She didn't say so, but I suspected that might be the case."

"So she was protecting herself by ending your affair."

"Perhaps."

"And you hurt her."

"I didn't want to."

So perhaps she had meant more to him than he'd realized. But he hadn't loved her.

She changed the subject. "It seems you are better at scandal, like the rest of your family, than you are at a serious relationship."

"My family is actually capable of serious relationships," he said, smiling. "The scandal part just keeps . . . happening."

Like the jungle animal she'd imagined, he suddenly pounced, pulling her onto the bed, his upper body looming above to hold her down. Chest to chest, breath to breath, they stared at one another. He'd left her legs free, and she could have kicked him, but instead she watched his taunting smile fade, replaced by a look of hunger that called to her at a very deep, primitive level.

"I've waited to kiss you all night," he whispered, his face just above hers.

His chest against hers was a pressure and a promise. She wanted to squirm, but not to get away—to pull him closer, to have him truly on top of her. He moved his chest against hers in a slow, circular motion, and without a corset, she felt each of his buttons like an intimate caress. One tugged at her nipple, and she shuddered. Resisting her own longings was even more difficult than resisting him. Why was this happening to her all over again, when she thought she'd learned her lesson?

"I watched you dance with those other men—"

"You did not. You were playing cards."

He leaned closer, and at the last moment, he pressed a soft kiss against her cheek. His lips, moist and warm, lingered, and she struggled not to turn her head to him.

"I saw enough," he said.

She didn't know whose heart was thundering so loudly, hers or his. For the first time she wondered if she would be truly strong enough to resist him. As it was, her hands were fisted in the coverlet. She struggled neither to touch him, nor to push back the lock of hair that fell over his eyes.

"When I had you alone on the terrace," he said, touching his nose to hers, "I thought I'd found my chance for a stolen kiss, but then your gallant brother interrupted."

"He could be home any minute. You should leave."

"Then I had better not waste this chance."

He lowered his head and kissed her, and though she'd braced herself to reject such an intimate invasion, his lips gently explored hers in a slow, sweet seduction, kiss upon kiss, warm, moist heat of desire that simmered quietly, deceptively.

With a moan she gave in, forgetting the mistakes of her past, thinking of nothing but mind-altering pleasure. She slid her hands over his shoulders and up into his hair, holding him to her, feeling the warm, silky thickness of it. It was as if the touch of her hands unleashed something inside him, because he turned his head and deepened the kiss, parting her lips with a thrust of his tongue. She'd been kissed before, but it had never set her afire with such masterful skill. His tongue explored the inside of her mouth, rasping against hers, taking possession. She pushed up against him, trying to get closer, and he pushed back.

She closed her eyes as he continued to nuzzle behind her ear, licking and nipping, and finally her brain seemed to function again.

"You must stop," she whispered.

He spoke against her skin. "This is a seduction. I don't want to stop."

"But it's not a seduction if I don't want it to go further."

He lifted his head and studied her. His wet mouth made her shudder.

"So I'm not seducing you tonight?" he asked.

"You think I'd let you win so easily, so quickly?"

He smiled wryly. "No. I knew you would be a challenge."

She stared at him. "Sadly, it seems I like challenges."

"Why is that sad?"

But she'd said too much. She liked being with him, wanted the pleasure of his attention. Surely she could have that and still defeat him in the end. She moved, and he slid to the side, allowing her to roll off the bed.

"You have to leave," she said firmly.

He lay on his side, head propped on his hand, and watched as she tugged down her nightgown. She felt like she was the evening's entertainment.

"I'll leave when your brother arrives home."

"But he would see you!" she cried, aghast. "He would think that I—that we—"

"He won't see me. This seduction is between you and me."

"But why stay? I am perfectly safe here."

He hesitated as his expression became serious. He sat up and swung his legs over the edge of the bed. "I don't like it that someone is watching your house. I didn't see him tonight, but I might have just missed him."

"Perhaps Will made a mistake," she said, wanting to believe that. "He's only a boy."

"I'm not taking that chance."

"Do you think there are people after Edward?"

"Or after their share of money."

"Then Edward could be in danger!"

"I doubt it. They want the money, and if they harm him, they won't get it."

She went to the door. "So you're just going to . . . stay here?"

"I can see the front of the house from the windows."

"And Edward can see the light."

"No, because I'm done luring you."

He gave a wicked grin, and then leaned over and blew out the candle. She could see nothing in the sudden blackness, but she thought she heard him leave the bed and come toward her. Fumbling behind her for the door, she fled out into the hall.

When she was in her own room with the door locked, she thought she would have a difficult time falling asleep. But Daniel followed her into her dreams, and this time when they kissed, he was pulling her nightgown up her body, and she was letting him.

When Grace entered the stables in the morning, she found Edward's horse already saddled and Will giving her a curious, wide-eyed stare.

"Will, thank you for anticipating what I'd want," she said.

"I'm not the only one, miss," he said, gesturing over his shoulder with his thumb.

Daniel stood there in his riding clothes, tall black boots up to his knees, brown trousers, and coat. On another man they might look plain, but on him the garments only emphasized his dark good looks. He was wearing a devilish smile, and when Will wasn't watching, Daniel let his gaze roam over her.

She was caught in the awareness of him, in the memory of his chest on hers and his lips giving her such pleasure.

"Have a good ride, miss," Will called, darting outside toward the house.

Daniel's mouth quirked.

Grace lifted her chin, trying to look composed, but she couldn't think of a thing to say.

"Will is your only servant?"

She frowned at him. "Yes."

And then he came toward her, stalking her just like last night. There was still a post between them, and she stayed on her side of it.

"You're not very talkative this morning," she said quickly.

"Talking isn't part of our challenge."

"Women like talking," she said. "I don't think you're very good at seduction. I think you're used to women falling into your lap."

His laughter was low and intimate, and it was difficult not to join him.

He reached for her, keeping to his side of the post, and she eluded him.

"Or money," she said. "You throw money at them."

"Money makes things easier sometimes. Is that what you want from me, Grace?"

She had no money of her own that she could touch. If there wasn't a deadline to their challenge, and it played out long enough, she'd have been desperate for her own money to survive.

But she wasn't there yet. She still planned to win the violin.

She turned, saw the mounting block perfectly positioned, and used it to vault into the sidesaddle. She went racing out the back into the alley behind the courtyard, passing Daniel's tethered horse. By the time he caught her, there would be witnesses that he was pursuing her. Again.

He caught up to her in the park, and to her satisfaction, she saw several riders make note of their entrance. This made two mornings in a row they had been seen together. It was true, at first people might assume he pursued her as a possible mistress, since it was his pattern. But she would make certain that everyone soon knew differently.

"You are quite the skilled rider, unlike yesterday," Daniel said dryly, tipping his hat as they rode past another couple.

She gave him a smug grin.

"How old are you?" he asked.

She frowned, wondering where he was leading her with such a question. "I am twenty-three."

"So certainly not in the first blush of youth."

She rolled her eyes.

"Why have you not married?"

"I have not had a proper Season, unlike most young ladies. The village had a limited selection of young men."

"But I'm certain you must have had some of them courting you."

"Sometimes." This was cutting too close to her foolish mistakes. "None of them were appealing. So how old are you?"

"That's a change of subject," he said.

"Not really. Just reciprocating."

"Very well, I am twenty-nine."

"Ah, ancient for a bachelor. Shouldn't you be married by now? Or have your mistresses taken up too much of your time?"

He frowned, as if he were giving her question serious consideration. She didn't think he would answer something so personal, and sure enough, he said, "Do you want to race?"

She stared at him, the challenge filling her. He was an unusual man. Even the thought of besting him made her pulse race and gave an added spark to her day. She knew it was making her forget about other things, and right now, she was glad for that.

She was still so very aware of him, wondering what he was thinking, what he planned next— and the thought gave her a secret thrill—but she was also contemplating her own strategy.

Having Daniel seen gallantly rescuing her and dancing with her at a ball, might eventually make him seem like he had become a marriage-able man in Society, but it would not make him a better man. And that's what she'd told Edward she meant to do. She had to succeed, or Edward would ask too many questions about how she'd really won the violin.

So it was time to think about trying a differ-ent tactic. She would have to call upon Miss Parker, the famed spinster and head of charitable organizations.

"Daniel, you're not changing the rules of the challenge, are you?"

"No, why would you think a race would do that?"

"Maybe you're becoming desperate. You have not convinced me to be your mistress. You'll have to do better than what you've tried."

"Oh believe me, I have several more ideas to pursue."

She shivered with anticipation.

Chapter 7

Returning from a call on Beverly, Grace let herself in the front door. She heard the unmistakable sound of several voices from down the corridor, none of which sounded like Edward.

How many strangers could invade a town house in just a few days? she wondered with exasperation.

"Hello?" she called.

At once, a man dressed formally in black livery came into the entrance hall.

"You must be Miss Banbury," the man said. "I am Woodley, the new butler."

Had Edward won so very much last night? she thought in surprise. "I didn't know you'd been hired, Woodley," she answered honestly.

"Our registry office was contacted just this morning, miss, by your brother's assistant."

An assistant?

"We have already been paid for the first month, Miss Banbury, and we certainly appreciate such thoughtfulness."

"We?" She swallowed heavily. How could Edward have afforded to hire more than one servant?

"There's myself and my wife, who is a fine cook and housekeeper, miss. This is a cozy home— we're all you need. And there's a fine bedroom for us right behind the kitchen." He bobbed his bald head. "We appreciate not having to climb the stairs."

She couldn't help but smile at his friendliness. "I'm glad you approve."

"Tell me you're hungry, miss, because my wife can have a roast turkey ready soon. Will Mr. Banbury be dining this evening?"

Already her mouth was watering. "No, I'm afraid my brother and I both have plans. But I look forward to tasting your wife's cooking soon."

She felt a momentary pang, wondering what Edward was doing, but she had long ago told herself she could not constantly worry about him.

The day became even better when her lady's maid arrived soon after from the country, along with several small trunks of Grace's wardrobe. Woodley and Will left the trunks in Grace's room, and the two women were finally alone.

Grace hugged her maid and stepped back to look at her with delight. A redhead, Ruby Grover was short and plump and mischievous.

"Miss Grace, ye took off so fast from home I feared someone was sick," Ruby said, playing up her disappointment. "And ye didn't even let me enjoy the fun."

"It wasn't fun at first, believe me," Grace said, as the two of them began to open the trunks and remove gowns to be ironed. "So tell me, did Mr. Throckmorten send his own steward to our manor? I hope he didn't try to change too much."

"Mr. Who?" Ruby said, puzzled. "No one came to visit us, Miss Grace. And who would have the nerve to change somethin'?"

Grace straightened in surprise, a pair of linen drawers dangling from her hands. "Nothing has happened at home?"

"Well, your mother be gone on a trip, but ye knew that before ye left."

"Then . . . you don't know why my mother left?"

"No, miss." Ruby wrinkled her upturned nose. "Is somethin' wrong?"

Grace took her hand. "My mother lost the deeds to both our homes in a card game, Ruby. I came here to see if my brother and I could somehow . . . fix things."

The maid blew out a sigh. "'Tis sad news, Miss Grace, and I'm so sorry to hear it for yer sake."

"And I'm sorry for *your* sake, and for all the good people who work—worked—for us. I don't know what's going to happen, but at least the new owner hasn't tried to change things immediately."

"So this Mr. Throckmorten is the new owner."

"Yes." Grace smiled without humor. "He was really only after the violin. His family is musical."

"Your papa's violin is gone, too? Oh, miss!"

Grace squeezed the maid's outstretched hand. "Don't worry about me, Ruby. I have a plan."

"Of course ye do," Ruby said. "So what is it?"

No one was going to know the true challenge but herself and Daniel. "I'm going to win back the violin by making Mr. Throckmorten into a better man."

Ruby frowned. "And ye say he really *wanted* the violin? That doesn't make sense, Miss Grace, if ye don't mind my sayin'."

"Did I mention he is quite the rake, Ruby?"

"No, ye didn't, but that explains why ye feel you can change him. Then ye're goin' to turn him over to some other young lady, and he'll be so grateful, he'll give ye back the violin?"

"And then I'll sell it and rent a town house."

"Sell yer papa's—" She broke off. "Ye have another plan, Miss Grace, ye got to, because I can't see this one workin'."

"We'll see." Grace went back to unfolding garments. She might as well start her own private wager for how long she could keep Ruby in the dark.

She was just beginning to plan what she'd wear to Beverly's house for dinner when she heard the pounding of boots up the stairs. She flung open her door, and then fell back as her brother strode in and closed it behind him.

"I thought you couldn't access your dowry," Edward said, hands on his hips.

She blinked at him. "I can't. What made you think otherwise?"

"Then how did you hire two new servants?"

After gaping at him, she managed, "I thought you hired them."

They stared at each other for a moment, and then he ran a hand through his hair. "Damn, it must be a mistake."

"I don't believe so. They said they were hired by your assistant."

"I don't have an assistant!"

"But—then who?"

"Mother? Out of guilt?" he said hesitantly.

She shook her head.

He sank down on the edge of the bed. "Could your plan for Throckmorten have worked already?"

"I don't understand."

"You're trying to redeem him, aren't you?"

She hesitated, knowing that that was only for the public's eye—and to quiet Edward's suspicions. "You think Daniel—"

"Calling him by his first name already?"

She saw his jaw clench, knew he was grinding his teeth together, his longtime method for trying to hold on to his temper.

"I misspoke. But you can't believe that Mr. Throckmorten is behind this." But was he? Did he think that by giving her an easier life, she would be more inclined to favor him? To lose control when he touched her?

"First he allows us to live here, and then he hires servants. He's taking care of us as well as pitying us."

She winced. "It isn't like that, Edward. I . . . assume he doesn't wish the place to be in poor condition if he takes it over."

"You mean *when*."

"No, I don't. I'm going to beat him at this game. You have to have faith in me."

"Then I'll have to," he said bitterly, "because I have no more faith in myself."

"Oh, Edward—"

"I want to refuse this pitying gesture of his, but I can't consign you to cleaning this entire house yourself. And it's *his* house."

She didn't know what to say that wouldn't make things worse. How many more blows could Edward take before he was overwhelmed?

Part of her wanted to refuse Daniel's "gift," because it made her feel even more like a kept woman. But perhaps he wasn't doing it for that reason. Deep down inside, could he have a conscience? Did he feel guilty for his part in their family's demise?

And could she use this unexpected side of him to her advantage?

Daniel approached Edward Banbury while he was eating dinner at their club, and the younger man noticeably stiffened and put down his spoon.

Daniel sat down across from him. "I have some things I want to discuss with you."

"I don't see what we have to discuss," Banbury said coldly. "You saw that I couldn't afford servants to make life easier for my sister, so you decided to provide them."

Daniel hadn't thought his part in it would stay hidden long, but a couple of hours wasn't much. "I'm not doing this to help you." He hadn't thought that his actions might be another blow to Banbury's already wounded pride. But what else could Daniel have done? He hadn't wanted to become so involved, but Grace was alone too much in a house that was being watched. Did Banbury even know?

"Helping Grace is even worse," Banbury said. "Unless you plan to marry her."

Daniel couldn't help but smile. "I'm not marrying her, and she certainly wouldn't want to marry me."

Banbury slammed a hand down on the table.

This had gone far enough, Daniel realized. "Someone is watching your house."

Banbury's defensiveness fled. "What? Why?"

"I don't know. Your groom spotted him first, and I saw him once, but not again. I assumed it was because of a debt."

Banbury shook his head. "My vowels are minor. Why would someone need to watch our house?"

Daniel rubbed his jaw. "I don't know. But something seems wrong to me."

"Until I know what's going on, I won't leave Grace alone at night."

Daniel nodded.

"I don't like this control you have over her."

Daniel waited, wondering if he was about to be

challenged over something he hadn't even done yet.

"I want to buy the violin back. I know Grace has these plans to get it back from you."

Daniel couldn't believe Banbury would be this calm if he really knew all the details. "Grace might want a say in this," he said dryly.

"But for family honor, let me try to earn enough to buy it back. Don't let her do whatever she's got planned. I've never been able to stop her once she's set her mind to something. She wants me to trust her, and I do. But I can't trust you, not with my sister. She's been hurt before."

Daniel nodded. "I understand." He rose to his feet. "By the way, if you're looking for a good investment, try the railways."

Banbury gave him one last penetrating stare and went back to his soup.

Daniel felt like an idiot. What had he said that for?

When Grace arrived at Beverly's house before the rest of the dinner guests, Beverly came down from the nursery to join her in the drawing room.

"I am so glad you were able to arrive early," Beverly said, sitting down beside Grace on the green-striped sofa. "My husband only just arrived home, and I had to tell you what he saw just this evening at his club. Mr. Throckmorten and your brother sitting down together at dinner."

Grace frowned. She had asked Edward not to

interfere. What could they be telling each other about her? Or were they discussing a gambling event they would both attend? Either possibility was terrible.

"I cannot believe that Mr. Throckmorten is already discussing his intentions toward you with your brother," Beverly continued, a look of anticipation gleaming in her eyes.

"He's not," Grace said.

Beverly's shoulders sagged. "Oh. I had so hoped that he was smitten with you already, especially after his behavior here two days ago. But then, he did refuse my invitation for tonight."

Now it was Grace's turn to sag. "Oh."

"Now, now, men will be difficult and try to withdraw as they realize they're falling under our spell."

Grace laughed humorlessly. "He's not falling under my spell, although he is trying to make sure I fall under his. But apparently, he doesn't care enough to be here."

Guests began to arrive, halting their discussion. Grace was introduced to several married couples, a few with eligible daughters, and then several bachelors, one extra to partner with her.

To take Daniel's place.

Grace was annoyed. She had promised not to avoid him and his seduction, and here he was avoiding her. She grudgingly realized that she had looked forward to seeing him. What did that say about her?

Although he was not in attendance, the ghost of

him was, because it was all anyone wanted to talk about with her.

And perhaps that could be used to her advantage.

"Oh, no, I'm not disappointed that Mr. Throck-morten isn't here," Grace said to the elderly Mrs. Radburn, who leaned on her cane and watched her with interest. "I have only just met him, you know."

"But you somehow persuaded him to dance," Mrs. Radburn said.

Grace could only shrug and smile.

Lady Putnam, tall and stately, said, "I think he did not come because of the scandal of the new earl of Martindale."

Several people who'd gathered around them nodded solemnly.

"What scandal?" Grace asked, telling herself that she was more curious than worried.

The older ladies gave her that faintly pitying stare again, but their daughters did not. Grace imagined that if Daniel showed interest in them, they wouldn't care about his scandals. These girls didn't want to be seduced as a man's mistress, and if they knew the truth—

They'd find a man's single-minded attention far too exciting, as she once had.

She of all people knew what could happen when a man got what he wanted. Right now, she might have Daniel's attention, and his secrets, but what would happen when he was done with her? How could she ever trust that in some card game, or when he was drunk, he wouldn't reveal the terrible secret that bound them together? She might live her life always wondering.

"The new earl just inherited the title," Lady Putnam continued, looking around importantly at the expectant faces. "He's young, only twenty-one, and it is his duty to renew the entailment on his land, so that the next two generations cannot sell the family property."

"But his family wealth has been decreasing for decades," Mrs. Radburn said in a hushed voice.

Lady Putnam nodded importantly. "So rather than do his duty by keeping the land in the family, he sold the country estate to Mr. Throckmorten."

There were aggrieved nods all around.

Into the silence, Grace asked, "And how does this make Mr. Throckmorten to blame?"

Every eye turned to her.

"The estate was in the family for hundreds of years," said Lady Putnam, looking down her nose. "Mr. Throckmorten is taking advantage of a young man's misfortune. How else do you think the man became so wealthy?"

Grace backed down, knowing that a dinner party was not the place to cause a scene. She needed the help of these people. But Daniel was only making it harder for her to improve his standing in the eyes of the *ton*. Why did he keep doing such things?

"Miss Banbury, you seem very interested in Mr. Throckmorten," Mrs. Radburn said.

Again, Grace felt herself the focus of the ladies.

"I do not know him well," she said. "We have only danced together once."

"You should be very careful," Lady Putnam said with condescension. "He is a man who takes what he wants."

"And you assume that because of his association with the earl?" Grace asked.

The younger ladies looked with fascination between Grace and their elders.

"You do know he has"—Lady Putnam glanced at the younger women around them—"female friends."

Grace inclined her head. "But has he ever harmed a *lady's* reputation?"

"Only when she was foolish enough to agree," Mrs. Radburn said to Lady Putnam.

Grace said, "I have spent several hours in Mr. Throckmorten's company. I believe that he is not the man people assume, and I know he will prove it to you."

Mrs. Radburn leaned toward her, her head slightly wavering with her age. "Miss Banbury, I do believe that in your innocence, you've decided to champion Mr. Throckmorten."

There were titters of laughter all around, and Grace met Beverly's worried gaze.

"Every young lady needs a project," Lady Putnam said.

Their open laughter was amused rather than cruel, and Grace just smiled. But she'd planted the seed that she meant to plant, and she would be curious to watch it take root over the next few days.

* * *

When Grace returned to the town house later that evening in Beverly's carriage, she searched the street for any lingering men before she got out, but saw no one. Perhaps Daniel was worried for no reason. The lights were ablaze in the town house, so Edward must be home.

And she found herself . . . disappointed.

She told herself she should feel relieved that Daniel couldn't use the dark of the night to press home his seduction. She'd been beneath him on a bed just last night, she reminded herself. She didn't really know him well; if he'd wanted to force her to do whatever he wished, he could have. She'd once trusted Baxter Wells, after all.

She found Edward in the library, reading a book on railways, of all things. When he claimed to be thinking of investing, she did not want to discourage him. To her surprise—and relief—he didn't even have much to say about his dinner with Daniel. Surely they could not have talked about her.

After wishing her brother a good night and getting an absent grunt in return, she went up to bed and found that Ruby had already prepared a bath. Soon Grace was alone, steeping in a warm bath. But she couldn't relax.

Was Daniel in the house even though her brother was home?

She felt exposed in her own bedroom, as if Daniel would have the nerve to invade without her permission.

Of course he'd do that if it got him what he wanted.

He'd find her naked, and she'd be trapped. Would he be able to see under the water? Would he lift her to him regardless of how wet she was? Her mind betrayed her as she thought of two naked bodies, entwined and writhing.

She remembered that feeling, had thought she'd convinced herself that it had been so wrong, that only when married would she be tempted again—until Daniel, and now he was all she could think about, even in her bath. She finished quickly, dried and dressed in her nightgown, but still he didn't come.

She told herself that she was only disappointed to be denied another opportunity to prove that he could not seduce her.

But she was only deluding herself.

Chapter 8

Daniel overslept. He washed and dressed quickly with the help of his valet, then rode to the park, because it was too late to surprise Grace at her stables.

As he watched her ride toward him and saw the look of relief that she quickly masked, he couldn't keep the satisfied smile from his face.

Part of his strategy was in the element of surprise, and he wanted her to think about him when he wasn't there. But the strategy had turned around on him, for he found he'd missed seeing her last night. He wondered what she'd been feeling lying alone in bed.

And then he'd wondered about her bedroom—and the bed itself. Although this was a challenge between them, he'd found himself more and more distracted by thoughts of her, by concern about what to do to make sure he won the challenge. For now that he'd set himself on this course, he didn't intend to lose.

For a man in command, he felt a bit adrift,

pulled along by currents he'd set in motion but could no longer so easily control.

Maybe he would have to look at that as part of the challenge.

She rode up beside him, and he let himself admire her flawless seat upon a horse used to taking a man's command. She wore a jaunty cap perched to dip toward one eye, as if she were a gentile pirate. And he wanted to ravish her.

He noticed that once again, the few riders on the lane were watching them. Grace either didn't notice, or didn't mind.

"Good morning, Grace," he said in a low voice.

She dipped her head, and the feather in her cap bounced. "Good morning, Daniel. Did you have a late night? I hope you didn't lose too much."

He chuckled. "So you think gambling could keep me away from you?"

"It is a passion of yours."

"But it holds no candle to the passion I feel for you."

She didn't break their shared gaze, but there was a light blush across her skin, and he wondered how far down it went.

She cocked her head. "Or the passion you feel for a bold challenge."

"You look like a bold wench this morning." He swung his horse about, and they rode side by side.

"A wench? I am so flattered by your high praise."

"You don't need high praise. You know that you're lovely."

"But now I know that you consider me a wench."

"Someday soon," he promised. "But no, I was not gambling last night."

"Then perhaps you were hiring servants for my other home in Hertfordshire."

He smiled at her. "Would you like me to?"

She didn't smile back, and her voice turned cool. "I didn't ask for your help. Edward is very upset."

"So he told me."

She studied him. "Did he tell you to cancel their services?"

"No. He didn't like the thought of you being alone in the house."

"Because someone was watching it."

He said nothing.

"Is that why you hired the Woodleys, Daniel? Are you worried about me?"

"I'm worried about my property."

Her smile formed slowly. "I don't believe you. And I don't believe you're particularly worried about some man on a street corner. This is all part of your seduction. If you think that feeling taken care of will make me more partial to you, you're mistaken."

"Then are you refusing their services?"

Her smile turned wry. "No. I am not that foolish. I tell myself that the Woodleys will keep the house in good condition until—and if—we hand it over to you." She leaned toward him from her saddle. "But really, I like their company and their service. And as long as no one knows you're paying for it, then I'll be practical and accept."

"Your brother believes I'm pitying him."

"Oh, I think not. Such emotion wouldn't be worth your time."

He smiled.

"Did you enjoy dinner at Lady Standish's?" he asked. "I had another dinner to attend that forced me to send my regrets."

"I hope it was worth it," she said lightly.

He saw the curiosity in her eyes, knew she would not directly ask him his business. And it was none of hers.

But he was beginning to realize that seducing Grace Banbury was not going to be simply physical. She was bound by proprieties, by an upbringing that didn't encourage a woman to share intimacies with a stranger. She probably felt confident in winning the challenge because she couldn't imagine submitting to a man she barely knew.

So he would have to allow her to know him. It was an . . . unsettling feeling.

She was watching him now with those eyes that shone with intelligence, with purpose. She thought she would only have to delay him, to outwait him, to win. He wanted to be the winner, even if it meant sharing more with a woman than he ever had before.

He was far too competitive, he knew, but he

wasn't about to stop now. Not when winning her was becoming all he could think about. Even the innocent movement of her body as she rode the horse was distracting.

He said, "The dinner party I attended was hosted by Mr. and Mrs. Lionel Hutton. He is a director in the Southern Railway company."

She gave him a surprised, searching glance. "Oh?"

"I'm an investor in the company, and I'm considering being a director myself." He paused, and then added, "It is my latest scandal."

"One of many, I am sure," she said dryly.

"How could I top almost working for a living, something a true gentleman would never lower himself to do? I could take Mr. Hutton's hint and marry his daughter."

"It would certainly be a step up for a railway director's daughter to marry the grandson of a duke."

"I believe that's what they were thinking," he said dryly. "And her dowry is quite impressive."

That was a mistake. Surely Grace had little or no dowry. But she only smiled, as if she weren't offended.

"According to the ladies at the dinner party last night," she said, "you have another new scandal."

He tapped his chin. "Let me think. There are so many."

"The new earl of Martindale?"

"Ah, the land recently released from entailment. He needed money more than land."

Her smile faded. Had she thought it wasn't true?

Martindale had come to him out of trust, because although he needed the money, he'd asked Daniel to hold on to his land for him, rather than sell to an unscrupulous buyer who wouldn't eventually sell it back. And Daniel would honor the request.

She believed his motives the worst. People usually thought so of him—he'd noticed it from the time he first went to school. And he'd always played upon their beliefs, enjoying the scandalous reaction to whatever he did.

But he was pursuing Grace for the basest of motives. She should learn not to think well of him, or she'd be disappointed.

"Are you busy this afternoon, Daniel?" she suddenly asked.

He glanced over at her in surprise. "Nothing pressing."

"Would you like to attend a picnic with me?"

Now that was an interesting idea. He immediately began to think of ways he could lure her away from whatever party she was asking him to join. Romance hidden behind trees could be exciting.

"I would be happy to attend," Daniel said.

He saw her relief and wondered why she would think he wouldn't want to be with her—considering that he was attempting to seduce her. Up to this point, he was proceeding slowly, allowing her imagination to engage her as well. But perhaps it was time to pick up the pace.

"You may call for me at noon," she said, and then glanced at him with amusement. "You do have a carriage, do you not?"

"I do. And you will be pleased with its privacy."

She arched a brow and looked away. "This event is in the middle of the day, sir."

"You'll be surprised what we can do in the middle of the day," he said, thinking about secret gardens even as he wondered where the picnic would be held. He would let her surprise him.

When Daniel called for her that afternoon, Grace stared at the closed carriage in surprise, wondering if he thought he'd have clandestine privacy with her in there. Then she watched his face when her lady's maid followed her down the stairs. She thought she glimpsed a brief tightness in his eyes, but he only nodded to Ruby, who eyed him with open curiosity. Grace used his distraction to quietly give the address to the coachman, who bobbed his head in acknowledgment.

Grace gave Daniel a bright smile, and he bowed to her. It was a bow of surrender, she knew, for she'd already taken the first victory of the afternoon. As if she'd go off in a carriage alone with him!

Even though a secret part of her would like to. Heavens, but she was enjoying herself.

"Mr. Throckmorten, this is my maid, Ruby," Grace said. "She arrived from Hertingfordbury just yesterday."

"Your house is getting more crowded by the minute," he observed.

And he had been a part of that. Did he regret hiring the servants now?

"There are people on every floor at all times of the day and night," Grace said brightly.

A corner of his mouth lifted in a smile.

She knew she was practically challenging him to try to gain access to her home so easily, as he had the other night. Knowing his sense of competition, he'd try.

Daniel helped Ruby into the carriage, to the maid's surprise, and she settled into a corner and looked out the window, obviously trying to pretend she wasn't there. Then he took Grace's hand, and their eyes met for a moment.

He leaned a little too close. "She won't stop me for long," he whispered.

She smiled at him, trying not to show him how, with just a touch and a word, he made her breathe too quickly, with too much excitement. "I don't know what you're talking about, Mr. Throckmorten."

In the carriage, he took the seat opposite her, and as they got under way with a jerk, she felt his gaze roam over her. She glanced at Ruby, who was looking pointedly out the window, and almost wanted to elbow the maid so that she'd watch Daniel. But that would be too obvious, so Grace forced herself to return his stare with one of her own. It was warm in the carriage, and she felt flushed even before she could feel his focus moving down her body, lingering on her breasts as his mouth lifted at one corner.

She tried to be bold and stare at him the same way. His body narrowed from his wide shoulders down to his waist. Then, to her shock, he subtly spread his legs a bit, as if he thought she wanted to see—

Her wide eyes flew back to his, and he looked far too amused and knowing. Her cheeks felt hot, and it took all she had not to look away in defeat.

Instead, she lifted her chin and said, "Mr. Throckmorten, will you be attending Lady Barlow's musicale this evening? I hear her daughters are quite accomplished with both voice and instruments."

"As to their talent, you heard incorrectly, or so I've been told. But no, I shall not be attending."

"Surely the son of a famous composer would be invited to every musical event of the Season," she said.

Was she mistaken, or did the mention of his father make his gaze a bit more . . . shuttered?

"I was invited."

When he didn't elaborate, she said, "But you turned the poor lady down?"

"I do not attend musicales, Miss Banbury."

"Why not?"

She thought he would cover himself with a flip remark, and was surprised when he regarded her seriously.

"Questions from the curious about my mother

still haven't gone away. Music is a painful subject for her. After my father's death, and her one
musical composition, she never wanted to hear
it again." He smiled wryly. "I imagine you've already heard all the rumors."

She nodded. "I have. And I'm sorry for what
you suffered."

"You mean what she suffered."

But not him? she wondered, and then continued, "It is a shame that such talent is associated
with sad memories."

He shrugged.

"Did she forbid you from listening to music?"

He frowned. "No."

This was becoming far too personal, but she
couldn't help her curiosity. "What questions do
people ask?"

He tilted his head as he watched her, and a faint
smile hovered at his lips—but he wasn't trying to
seduce her with his gaze anymore, which should
make her feel relieved.

"She has not been to London in many years—"

"Since your father's death?"

A flash of surprise showed briefly in his eyes.
"A good deduction. Yes, the questions and curiosity proved too much for her."

"And all the memories they induced."

He nodded.

She couldn't believe that he was talking like
this to her. She wanted to shy away in politeness,
feeling too intrusive on private emotions—

And she wanted to know everything about

this man, who would shun events because of his mother's painful memories.

Or his own? Was there truly a different man buried beneath the rake he showed the world? She should stop prying, but something she didn't understand drove her.

"And now the questions about your mother are too much for you?" she asked. "Surely they only admire her talent and want to know how she is doing."

"Miss Banbury, these are the people who believed her a murderer," he said with no emotion.

She stiffened.

"The sort of people who believe that a symphony is worth killing over."

"People kill over less."

She was assuming his mother innocent, but maybe she wasn't—did even he know the truth?

"Society loves to whisper, even when it is unwarranted." She hesitated. "Yet, at the time you wouldn't have known that. You were only a little boy, who'd just lost his father tragically."

To her surprise, she felt her skirts stir, and realized that he had slowly slid his toes under her hem.

Distracting her, she knew. Of course he didn't want to talk about his family tragedy. Or had he changed so much that those emotions were locked away, and he thought they no longer affected him?

But he didn't attend musicales.

Still smiling sweetly, she pushed her heel hard into his toe, but all he did was grin.

Ruby glanced between the two of them, and Grace realized that they'd stopped speaking rather abruptly.

"So where are you taking me on our picnic?" Daniel asked, glancing out the window.

Grace saw the frown that slowly came over his face as he saw that they were no longer in Mayfair.

"It's a surprise," she said.

"Quite."

Miss Parker was a woman who obviously understood that for society ladies to help—and donate—they had to feel comfortable. The "picnic" was really a long row of tables set up in a littered park in Bethnal Green. As their carriage came to a stop, and Daniel opened the door, Grace could see a dozen ladies supervising servants as they unloaded wagons and carts filled with crates and covered cauldrons. Other servants wandered the edges of the park, trying to look unobtrusive, but they were obviously for security. Scores of people in threadbare clothing had already begun to gather around the edges of the park, holding the hands of excited children. Grace smiled. This was really a good cause and not just a way to make Daniel more accepted in Society.

But he *was* the only gentleman in attendance. As more and more ladies saw him walking toward them at Grace's side, heads began to turn, and whispers were exchanged.

Miss Parker, after directing a group of men in the building of small cook fires, came to them when others hung back.

"Miss Banbury, I am so glad you were able to join us for such a worthwhile endeavor." She glanced at Daniel. "But you did understand the purpose, did you not?"

"That it was to help London's deserving folk?" Grace asked brightly. "Of course! And when I mentioned to Mr. Throckmorten what we were doing today, he insisted on coming to help."

Daniel bowed briefly to Miss Parker, who eyed him with surprise and amusement.

"Helping is not the only thing he's doing," Miss Parker said, glancing meaningfully at Grace.

Grace pretended not to understand. "Pardon me?"

Miss Parker obviously thought that Daniel was only trying to impress Grace. Maybe she'd tell the other ladies the same thing. All of which would help them believe that Daniel finally had softer emotions.

To her surprise, Daniel left them and went to assist the men unloading the wagons. As Grace helped set out plates and cups, she couldn't help watch with the rest of the shocked ladies as Daniel hoisted a keg of beer onto his shoulders, heedless of his expensive frock coat, and carried it across the field.

"My, my," said one woman, who fanned herself so briskly that everyone around her laughed.

"He is really trying to impress you, Miss Banbury," Miss Parker said.

Young ladies and old all looked between Grace and Daniel, and Grace hoped they saw the marrying potential in him rather than a man who collected a string of mistresses. What man of their acquaintance would help the poor with the sweat of his brow rather than just a check?

Grace felt pleased with her accomplishment as an hour wore on and the food was served. Needy Londoners moved down the line holding their tin plates, and thanking each woman with appreciation for a ladle of stew or another piece of bread. Grace saw several ladies looking rather faint at the disreputableness of some of their guests, but everyone continued to do her part. Daniel stood with several male servants, pouring tankards of beer to set on the table near them. He had removed his coat, and his shirt seemed so white and . . . bare. She couldn't hear what he said, but there was much laughter. He fit in so easily, as if he'd been raised on the streets rather than in a duke's palatial home.

Had he become good at fitting in because he'd had to do so much of it when he was young? She thought again of him at eight, his father dead so suddenly, his mother accused. Had he even realized what was going on? Or had that come later, with age and the cruelty of other children?

Since he easily took charge of any situation, she imagined that he'd tried to help his mother, who was shocked and grieving. He still cared about her feelings, when it had all happened over twenty years ago. She found herself curious to meet his mother.

As the luncheon attendance began to dwindle, and people were scattered at tables and seated on blankets eating, Grace saw a pair of young ladies stroll casually by the beer stand. They made it a point to talk to one of the servants, while trying not to eye Daniel too obviously. He looked amused, and then glanced up to find Grace watching him.

Oh, dear. Before she could even look away, he'd raised a beer tankard to her.

"He is such a disreputable man," a woman said in a low, angry voice.

Grace turned around to find a woman of middle age, her white gloves still pristine, where Grace had long since removed hers. She wore the black of mourning. She was speaking to another of similar age, but both stared obviously at Grace. They must have meant to be overheard.

And Grace couldn't help herself. "But he is here today, giving of his time, is he not?"

"Young lady, you don't know who I am, do you?" said the first woman.

Grace opened her mouth, but the woman went on quickly.

"I am Lady Swarthbeck, cousin to the earl of Martindale." She lifted one eyebrow imperiously.

Grace realized that she referred to the earl who had just sold his ancestral land to Daniel.

"Good afternoon, Lady Swarthbeck," she said politely. "I am Miss Banbury."

"I know who you are, girl. Mrs. Radburn told me about your sympathy for Throckmorten. I assure you, it is misplaced."

"I believe that—"

"If I had known that *someone* would have temerity to bring *him* to this honest gathering, I never would have come."

"But we are all so needed here," Grace said softly.

The woman drew herself up even higher, bosom thrust forward on her broad chest. "Do not instruct your betters, girl. You are ignorant of all that has gone on."

Grace wanted to debate that, but knew that Lady Swarthbeck wasn't the sort of woman who could hold a rational conversation right now, after being hurt by her cousin's actions. Grace felt sorry for her. But her cousin was the one she should scold.

Lady Swarthbeck turned away in a huff and marched toward the beer stand. She took hold of the arms of the young ladies still flirting with Daniel and pulled them away.

Grace couldn't hear all that was said, except for something about "few morals," and "a blight on good society."

Gritting her teeth, Grace took a step toward them, and then found herself restrained by Miss Parker.

"Miss Banbury, do not make this worse," Miss Parker said softly. "The day has been a success. Let others confront their problems elsewhere."

Grace nodded absently, all of her focus on Lady Swarthbeck and Daniel. Daniel said something in a low voice, and the noblewoman simply turned her back and walked away. So much for all the members of Society accepting Daniel.

Grace had begun this plan to "redeem" Daniel merely to quell her brother's suspicions of the real terms of the challenge between Daniel and her. But she'd found Daniel's childhood sympathetic, and thought that some of his reputation stemmed from family scandal over which he'd had no control. Of course, that did not excuse his treatment of women.

Originally, she'd been so confident in her ability to resist him that rejecting his attempts had been a game to her—exciting and dangerous and thrilling.

She still knew she could win, but each time she was alone with him, her tenuous grasp on control slipped a little more.

And now she felt sympathetic toward him. Perhaps she could end this challenge feeling better about what she'd accomplished—besides rejecting him.

He suddenly looked right at her, and she didn't look away.

She was a fool; she should run, salvage her pride while she still had some. But she didn't want to.

What if she really could redeem the duke's scandalous cousin?

Chapter 9

As the sun beat down on Daniel's shoulders, and he heard the coarse voices of the men around him, he found himself caught in the spell of Grace's serious, intent regard.

What was she thinking in that devious mind of hers?

She'd seen Lady Swarthbeck's cut, and she couldn't be surprised that Daniel was rejected by Society after the things he'd done.

Then Grace turned away and set about helping a young mother with three children. Grace took the babe from her arms so that the woman could help the others with their plates. Soon Grace had a smudge on her bodice, and a lock of light brown hair had tumbled out of its restraint.

She had certainly outwitted him this afternoon. He'd thought to have an intimate picnic—or at least the kind where they could find themselves alone quite easily.

But not here in the middle of Bethnal Green, a neighborhood of dubious character.

What had been her purpose bringing him here?

It couldn't be just a distraction from his pursuit of her. She could have accomplished that quite easily by doing this without him.

But she'd invited him. Had it been a challenge, to see how he'd handle himself? Did she assume he'd scandalize himself further by rejecting such an unusual outing?

But no, that didn't make sense with what he knew about her. He watched her smile at the poor woman she was helping, the way she looked tenderly down at the babe wrapped in no better than rags. She found a clean blanket for him at the table filled with used clothing and goods.

She seemed a pure, good woman. How had she turned out that way, raised by an unscrupulous gambler of a mother?

She was volunteering her time helping people, when her own home was bare, and she probably couldn't have fed herself without Daniel's intervention.

He finally turned away to lift the next keg into place and begin pouring. He wanted her in his bed. She was a different sort of woman than his usual mistresses, and the challenge had given him new purpose.

At the end of the afternoon, after everything had been cleaned and reloaded on wagons—and Grace had insisted they remain until the end— Daniel donned his coat and escorted her and her maid back to his waiting carriage.

When they were settled on the plush benches, the two women facing forward, and Daniel across from them, he watched the satisfied expression on Grace's face. But he made her wait a half hour into their journey before he spoke.

"Did you accomplish everything you'd hoped, Miss Banbury?" he asked.

"All of our guests seemed well pleased with the feast," she said, smiling. "My thanks for all of your help."

"Even though I was not asked or informed."

He saw the maid glance suspiciously between them.

"I knew you'd want to be a part of such a charitable cause," Grace said.

"I do many things that are charitable. I keep dealers and servers employed."

She rolled her eyes, and he thought the maid's lips twitched with amusement, but she was stoically doing her duty by trying to pretend she wasn't there.

"And although I admire the efforts of Miss Parker and all of the ladies," he continued, "such charities only relieve suffering temporarily and do not help with the root cause."

She frowned at him. "But it is something we women can do, because we cannot affect the political course of our nation."

"Not yet anyway," he said dryly. "But a different age is dawning, where men are more equal and are judged by what they accomplish for society's good, not how they were socially born."

"Are you including women?" she asked with disbelief.

"Of course. Women like Miss Parker want to be heard—and someday they probably will be."

"It may be a new age, Mr. Throckmorten, but the suffering is only increasing for those with no choice but to work in your new factories."

"*My* factories?"

"I'm including you with all the members of your sex."

"If you want to know of which you speak, you should tour one of my factories. I do not tolerate children working, nor do I allow adults to work in unsafe conditions or for long hours."

"My, aren't you enlightened," she said, giving a rueful smile.

"I try."

"So that is why you are far too busy with your investments than to do your duty to your family and marry."

"I have no duty in regards to marriage, Miss Banbury. That is for my cousin Madingley to worry about."

"Are you not his heir, Mr. Throckmorten?"

"So you know the family tree so well?"

He saw the blush rosying her cheeks.

"People talk, sir," she said. "And no, I don't know much about all your relatives."

"Then let me tell you something that you can admire about me," he said, leaning toward her, forearms on his knees. "Naturally, I give monetary contributions to worthy charities."

She leaned forward as well and gave him a polite smile. "How easy for you."

The maid was openly fascinated now and watched as if they were a performing a play for her amusement.

"And I do something on a much more personal level as well."

Something in her expression changed, grew more focused, and much to his pleasure, she licked her lips. "Do tell."

"I read to the blind."

She blinked her eyes, and then sat back with a flounce, crossing her arms beneath her lovely breasts. "You don't need to tease me."

"I'm not teasing. Someday I will prove it to you."

Her maid glanced out the window, then cleared her throat. "We've come to the town house, miss."

"Thank you for noticing, Ruby," Grace said. "I might have sat here far too long listening to Mr. Throckmorten recount fanciful stories."

He grinned. "You'll regret your disbelief, Miss Banbury. I promise to demonstrate my charitable activities quite soon."

The door was opened from the outside and the stairs lowered by his coachman. Grace pointedly looked at Daniel, waiting for him to get out first.

"Tell me one more thing, Miss Banbury," he said. "Today you must have been showing me off to your new Society friends. And the other night, you wanted me to dance before them all as well. Why?"

"Why?" she echoed, trying to seem surprised.

He didn't believe it. "Are you trying to marry me off to some unsuspecting young lady? Your attempts will not stop my . . . courtship of you."

Wide-eyed, she made a little snort in her nose, an aborted laugh. "I would never do that to an unsuspecting young lady, Mr. Throckmorten."

He sat back on his bench and frowned, studying her so deliberately, hoping to discomfort her. She didn't break, but after several moments, her maid sighed loudly.

At last Daniel descended from the carriage and helped both of them down to the pavement. He took Grace's gloved hand and bent over it.

"Thank you for the pleasant day, Miss Banbury," he said softly.

She pulled away and gave him a perfunctory smile. "You're welcome, Mr. Throckmorten. I hope the lesson was not lost on you."

"Only time will tell."

He watched her walk up the stairs and disappear inside the town house. Right now he was in the mood to follow her inside and use a man's intimate persuasion to find out what she was up to. But damn, he'd hired those bothersome servants.

When Ruby and Grace were safely inside the town house, Ruby turned to stare at Grace, hands on her hips.

"And what was that about, miss?" the maid demanded in an exasperated voice. "Are ye playin' a dangerous game with that man?"

"I already told you, Ruby," Grace answered softly. "It's all part of the plan to redeem him."

"It seems all part of a plan to stay near him, if ye ask me."

Grace threw up her hands, even as a hidden part of her knew that Ruby was right. "How can I redeem him if we're never together? Just think how the *ton* will talk now that he has gone with the ladies on a charitable mission."

"They'll just think he's after somethin', like any man."

Before she could say more, Mrs. Woodley, plump and efficient, came down the hallway from the rear of the house.

"Good afternoon, Miss Banbury," the house-keeper said. "Will you be having dinner at home this evening?"

"Yes, Mrs. Woodley, thank you, although I will be going out again to a musicale this evening."

"But not with that Mr. Throckmorten," Ruby said to Mrs. Woodley. "He doesn't go to 'em."

"What a shame, but not surprising," said the woman, nodding with sympathy, then heading back toward the kitchen.

Grace followed her down the corridor, knowing Ruby trailed behind. "What do you know, Mrs. Woodley?"

The woman leaned against the worktable in the kitchen, where she was rolling out dough. "Surely you know about his parents, Miss Banbury. Besides the rumors of murder, they're the sedate branch of the family—they don't like music anymore. The rest of the Cabots always have something wild going on. Their house parties in the country are legendary."

If the woman wanted to gossip, Grace was glad to talk. "Mr. Throckmorten doesn't seem the type to have such a family."

"Oh, not him, miss. Mr. Throckmorten is an only child, you see. But his mother's sister married this professor, and there was a scandal about dead bodies and his research and—" She broke off, looking worried. "Am I saying too much, miss?"

"Of course not," Grace said quickly, propping her chin on her laced fingers. "I'm so new to London that I know nothing about the *ton*."

"Well, the professor and Lady Rosa, Mr. Throckmorten's uncle and aunt, have a son and two daughters. The duke's father had his own scandal, of course. On his Grand Tour, he married a Spanish girl, common and everything."

"That's not so scandalous, compared to murder and research on dead bodies," Grace said, smiling.

"Well, no, but she's the duchess, and that has never set well with some of the finer folk. She has a son, the current duke, and a daughter, too, so that Mr. Throckmorten has a lot of cousins. Someone is always hosting a party at Madingley House."

"Does Mr. Throckmorten go?" Ruby asked.

Grace should have shushed her, but she wanted to hear the answer, too.

"Sometimes," Mrs. Woodley said, using her rolling pin in smooth strokes over the dough. "Or so I hear."

Slowly, Grace began, "Are they all . . . happy as a family?"

She couldn't help but think of Daniel as an eight-year-old, his father dead, with no siblings to share his grief.

"They're close, miss, and care for each other. But that Mr. Throckmorten has always done things on his own."

Grace nodded. She didn't need anyone to tell her that. He was a man who did what he wanted, whether gambling against women, skirting the line between being a gentleman and a new man of industry—or targeting the next woman he planned to conquer. And now his focus was on her, and though she fought her feelings, she relished his attentions.

She remained in the kitchen for a few more minutes, watching Mrs. Woodley work. Ruby gathered up several irons to begin pressing Grace's gown for the evening. Instead of a bare, echoing tomb, the town house felt more like a home again since the servants had come. She couldn't help but be relieved they were here, and not just for their invaluable help. They were also protection against Daniel's thinking he could visit whenever he wanted, hoping to catch her alone. She told herself to be satisfied they were interfering with his plans, but she gritted her teeth in disgust, knowing that part of her was a bit disappointed.

* * *

When the musicale was over, Grace felt relieved.
It wasn't that Lady Barlow's daughters weren't talented, but her mind was distracted by thoughts
of Daniel. He had not gambled last night—surely
tonight that was where he'd be.

And she was bothered by it.

He should be here, appreciating the music. She
wondered, with two gifted musicians for parents,
if he played an instrument himself? Or had he
once, but given that up?

She was so preoccupied, that as she waited for
the hackney coach she'd hired to pull up, it took
her a moment to hear someone calling her name.

Finally, the word penetrated her fuzzy brain,
and she looked around. Although several guests
were climbing into their carriages, or talking as
they waited, no one seemed to be looking at her.
So who—

"Grace!"

She whirled around at the whisper, but there
was only shrubbery behind her. Then someone
caught her arm and pulled her through. Before
she could even be frightened, she found herself
face-to-face with Daniel.

She gaped at him. "Lurking in the shrubbery
seems beneath you!"

"Shh! I paid off your hackney driver, and no
one else was paying attention."

"But—"

"You should be more careful," he said, frowning,
still holding her hand. He began to walk down the

length of the house and into the courtyard behind, talking over his shoulder. "You were lingering too far away from the safety of the other guests."

"Well, that certainly worked in your favor."

There were streaks of light through the darkness from the lit windows of the house, and she could see the gleam of his white teeth as he grinned back at her.

"It did," he said.

"So what do you intend to do with me?"

They were in the courtyard now, moving down gravel paths, skirting foliage and flowers.

"I intend to escort you safely home," he said, unlatching a gate in the rear wall.

"What if my maid is back there waiting for me?"

"You didn't bring her."

"Have you been spying on me?" she demanded, not really angry. This was a contest, after all.

"I only watched you waiting for your hackney. She would have been with you. Tonight I was lucky."

"You'd been hoping I wouldn't bring a maid to the picnic this afternoon."

"Daylight in a carriage can reveal so much. But I'm good in the dark, too."

Her mouth went dry, and she stumbled.

A carriage loomed above them in the shadows of the alley. Even the coachman was dressed all in black. Grace felt a thrill of excitement, knowing that she would be alone with Daniel in a close, private—dark—space.

He helped her up inside, and she was relieved to see a lantern swinging gently over her head. He stepped up, the carriage rocked with his weight, but instead of sitting beside her, he sat across. She told herself to feel relieved.

But he spread his legs so that her wide skirt would fall between.

She wouldn't have to counter his advances for long. But she had a good sense of direction, and the coachman turned the wrong way out of the alley.

"Surely you're taking me home," she said into the tense silence.

"Of course."

His voice was smooth and low. He was again the dangerous Daniel of the night. During the day, she often thought she was beginning to know him, but not at night.

"But the traffic will be less congested on a different route," he added.

She didn't believe him.

But what did it matter? She had his word that he would not damage her reputation. She would be home soon enough. And until then, she would prove to him how easily she could resist him.

He said nothing more. With the lantern above, his eyes were in shadow. He was obviously watching her, but she couldn't tell where, and it made her feel shivery all over.

Again, he slipped one boot beneath her skirts. Short of climbing onto the bench, she had nowhere else to go, so she let him toy with her. In the weak light, she could see the bump in her gown from his boot, and followed it as it moved to the center of her skirt. And then the bump came higher, toward her, as if he would lift her skirt high enough to peer beneath. She quickly held it down at her knees and glared at him.

His smile was devilish and disarming, but he lifted his boot no higher. She felt a draft of air on her knees, the bare skin between her drawers and stockings. When the lump of his boot started to recede, she felt a wave of relief, which came to an abrupt halt when she realized that on the way back down, his boot brushed her calf. She waited, uncertain if it was a mistake, but then he casually slid it down the length of her leg.

She squirmed, unable to help herself. It was as if her skin were coming alive, and if she didn't move, she might burst right out of it.

She kicked him, and he laughed softly.

"You have me at your mercy, Daniel," she said. "It seems unfair because I cannot retreat."

"Knock on the ceiling whenever you'd like. My coachman will stop to see what we want. He'll save you."

Knowing that she had a way to protect herself suddenly made everything seem different. It was a new challenge, to see who would break first here in the darkness and privacy. What would she let him do before she'd admit defeat by summoning the coachman? Kiss her? Touch her?

Her trembling returned.

Or would she even be able to stop herself?

Daniel must have seen the panic cross her face, but he said nothing, did nothing, only watched her, his look full of challenge—and eventual victory.

She straightened as her courage returned. He would be waiting a long time.

Then he sat forward, opened the lantern, and blew out the wick.

The plunge into blackness made her gasp. She could hear and feel her own frantic breathing—and at last she realized that the blinds were open, and every minute or so they passed a gaslight, which shone dim illumination between them.

But not on Daniel, who was a vague, lighter shadow in the darkness.

He reached both hands out, arms spread wide, and closed the blinds. She could see nothing.

She thought he would pounce on her then, but the silence remained unbroken. Instead of feeling relieved, her tension and excitement only increased. What was he doing?

She heard the creak of his leather-covered bench, and she flinched.

He was at the bottom of her skirt again, and though she was prepared to hold it down, she didn't feel it lifting. His hands were skimming her legs on the outside of her garments, moving steadily upward as if he were looking for something. His fingers pushed down on the fabric to brush between her thighs, and without thinking, she moved her legs apart to escape his touch, which teased and burned.

And then she heard his weight shift and realized too late that he'd come off his bench and dropped to his knees on the carriage floor.

Between her spread legs.

She tried to close them, and felt his thighs, his body, blocking her. He wasn't pressing himself up against her, but just the thought of him looming over her, positioned to do anything he wanted, should have made her panic and fight him and knock on the ceiling.

But she did none of those things. She had never imagined a challenge would make her risk as much as she'd risked once before.

She would not let him defeat her.

And a dark part of her wanted to feel the pleasure he could give her. Just a touch, a kiss, that's all she wanted. She would stop there.

She waited there in the darkness. He was so close, she could hear his breathing now, too, and to her delight, it was as fast and shallow as hers. Would he kiss her? Would she feel his lips tugging at hers, opening her to him, pushing inside—

His hands suddenly clasped her waist. She jerked in his arms and he waited. Did he think she would push him away? Then he didn't know her.

She leaned back on the bench, looking up to where she thought his face was. She was growing so desperate for his kiss that she almost reached for him.

But that would be a form of surrender, and she couldn't do that.

His hands slowly began to move up her sides. She stopped breathing. She felt his fingers trace the lower curves of her breasts, meet in the center, and move up over her bodice, so gentle, barely touching. When they brushed over her nipples, even through the corset she felt like she was seared by him. She drew in a breath on a gasp, her body tense, her head thrown back.

And then she felt the warm brush of his hair against her cheek, and the wetness of his mouth on her bare shoulder. She groaned, fisting her hands in her skirts so that she wouldn't touch him. He still wasn't touching her with anything but his mouth and hands, and it took everything in her not to arch up, to meet his body with hers, to use her legs to pull him against her.

His tongue licked a path along the bare skin above her neckline. At her cleavage, he dipped down inside, leaving her shuddering. His hands slid behind her back, molding her flesh, pushing her up as if bringing her breasts to a feast.

To her surprise, she felt her dress loosen, a tugging on her corset from behind, and then with sudden impatience he pulled down on her corset at her waist, and her breasts slid free. Only a chemise covered them now, soft linen that brushed against her erotically.

And then through her chemise, Daniel took her nipple into his mouth, wetting the fabric, sucking on her. She cried out and lost the battle to withhold herself from him. Her hands slid up his back, through his tousled hair to hold him against her, where his lips and tongue brought her such exquisite pleasure. With his tongue he circled and teased, and at last he used his teeth to pull the chemise away from her bare skin. His hands cupped and kneaded her, lifting her breasts to his mouth to continue his sensual exploration.

Chapter 10

She tasted like the sweetest fruit, strawberries and honey and the warmth of summer. Daniel feasted on the moistness of her, reveled in the way her nipples hardened just for him. Her little cries of passion maddened him, and he finally pressed his hips into hers, though his garments and layers of her skirts separated them. He turned her until she was leaning back across the bench, letting him push harder. He rolled his erection against the depths of her, lingering, circling in a way he knew she would like. He groaned when he felt one of her legs circle him, clutching him. As he moved his attentions between her breasts, kissing and licking, he slid his hands higher beneath her skirts, reaching for the drawstring of her drawers.

And then suddenly she was sitting up, knocking him sideways and almost off her. He heard her frantic knocking on the ceiling and felt the carriage slow to a halt.

He muttered a curse and drew back onto his own bench, feeling as stiff and awkward as an old man. He could hear her fumbling with her clothing and the occasional muttered word.

"Can I be of assistance?" he asked, glad that his voice only sounded a little husky. He was amazed he could even get the words out, so lost was he in what he wanted to do to her—with her.

"I think you've assisted enough," she responded tartly.

But not angrily. She was a fair woman, and had been enjoying him just as much as he'd been enjoying her.

"Oh—hook my dress, please," she said primly, as the carriage slowed to a stop.

He reached forward and found her back already presented to him. He laced the corset, and fastened the last two hooks.

"So you *are* good for something in the dark," she said.

He laughed.

In silence, they felt the carriage sway as the coachman descended. When he opened the door, faint light from the street washed in. To Daniel's surprise, Grace looked almost normal. She was watching him expectantly, and he realized he was supposed to come up with a reason why they'd summoned the coachman.

"Tyler, our lantern went out," Daniel said. "Can you light it from yours?"

He handed out the lantern, and when she remained silent, he said, "I'm surprised I could think so quickly on my feet."

"Why?"

He stared at her curious expression, her intelligent green eyes. "Because all I can think about is you, and what we have yet to finish."

She ducked her pretty chin, slanting her glance away from him. "We are not finishing."

"No? That was a close call."

She gave him a pointed look. "A close call would have been nudity."

"Are you offering?"

She rolled her eyes and let her breath out on a sigh, just as the coachman handed back in their lantern. When they were on their way again, Daniel didn't talk; he found himself brooding as he watched her, more disappointed than he'd anticipated. It wasn't as if he thought she'd freely give in to him so soon in their challenge. But she'd granted him enough that he was frustrated.

And he couldn't help but remember the way her leg had circled him. It had seemed . . . unusual, for a woman as innocent as she.

Or perhaps she was just a natural.

The thought alone made him close his eyes and take a deep breath.

"You are in pain?" she murmured.

He opened his eyes and smiled. "No, just . . . thwarted."

"I'm told it hurts for a man to stop."

He stared at her. "And where would you hear something like that?"

"One of my female friends," she said.

He was surprised to discover that women talked of such things.

He leaned forward and tried to take her hand, but she pulled away. Even by lanternlight, he could see how red her face was. "If we were naked together, and I was almost inside you—"

She turned away.

"—it would be terribly difficult to stop."

"But would you, if I told you to?"

She was staring at him now, her green eyes serious and wary. This was about trust, and to his surprise, he wanted that from her. Since when did he ever care about that with a woman?

"I would," he said.

She looked at him a few moments more, and then nodded.

"You know I want you in my bed," he said after a pause.

She glanced at him. "After all of this, I would assume so."

"You have friends who've told you about men. Have they also told you what happens between a man and a woman in bed?"

She nodded quickly, biting her lip as she looked away.

Daniel was glad. One less impediment between him and fulfillment.

A while later, when the carriage slowed again, he opened the blinds and peered outside.

"Are we at my town house?" she asked.

He didn't correct her as to the house's owner. "We are."

"Then stay in here, please."

He frowned.

"If my brother is looking for me, I don't want him to see you."

"I understand."

She slid forward in the seat, waiting expectantly for the door to be opened. Without thinking about it, Daniel cupped her head and leaned forward to give her a quick kiss. When he pulled back, she stared at him, eyes unfocused, lips moist and parted with surprise.

Then the door opened, and she descended quickly.

He slid back in his seat with a sigh, opened the other blinds and looked out into the night, away from the town house. Just seeing those lit windows would make him think of joining her there.

So he stared out at the park in the center of the houses—and saw a man standing just beyond the light from a gas lamp. Daniel couldn't see his features, for he wore a hat and dark clothing. He was looking at Grace's house, and at the carriage. He stilled, as if he somehow realized that he was being watched.

And then he started to run.

Tyler chose that moment to urge the horses forward, but Daniel slammed open the door and vaulted into the street. The startled coachman gaped at him, but Daniel only lifted his hand to bid him wait. Running, he chased the stranger down the street, but the man had too much of a lead. He reached the far block, ducking between two houses. Daniel finally came to a stop in an alley. He had no idea which way the man had gone. He swore under his breath and turned back the way he'd come.

That same night, Grace sat in the bathing tub until her skin grew wrinkly and the water chilled, yet still her mind whirled around from one thought to another. She could still hear the words she'd used to convince herself to accept his seduction. She'd told herself she would just go a bit further, that she could stop whenever she wanted.

That sounded just like what her mother used to say about a game of faro.

Grace shuddered and closed her eyes. So she had stopped herself before Daniel could take things too far. Her mother had once been able to stop her compulsions, too.

Grace was gambling now, gambling on her own control. And she was gambling with her only future: possession of the violin and the chance to rent another house.

Was losing that worth experiencing Daniel's kiss, his touch? So he made her burn—hadn't she done this before? And it had almost led to her ruin. She had trusted Baxter Wells, too, and he'd proved unworthy of it.

She knew she was letting her sympathy for Daniel's history affect her. She wanted to help him get over the trauma of his youth.

But couldn't she just behave like his friend instead of a woman auditioning for the part of his mistress?

For just a moment, she imagined being his mistress in truth. She would have security and a place to live, the attention of a handsome man, and certainly she could help her brother.

But having a notorious sister would further harm Edward's chances at a decent marriage. And Daniel would eventually tire of her. She realized that she could never live with the uncertainty of a mistress's life.

Grace had had a difficult time falling asleep, and then slept in late in the morning. She didn't want to think about her next step in Daniel's "education." She needed to forget about him, for at least the day, because she had a dinner invitation for the evening, and she had a suspicion that he might be there.

After a solitary luncheon, she tried to read a book in the library, but kept reading the same paragraph over and over again. Then she heard the front bell, and everything inside her stilled.

Woodley found her, bowed, and said, "Lady Standish to see you, Miss Banbury."

"Show her in." She sank back on the sofa bonelessly, which was how Beverly found her.

Hands on her hips, Beverly looked about the library, and Grace realized that her friend was seeing for the first time the bare walls and empty tables. There were even some empty shelves, as if Edward had sold a rare book collection.

Grace smiled. "Good afternoon, Beverly. It's so good to see you."

"You might not think so. I want to know what is going on."

"About what?" Grace patted the sofa beside her, but Beverly didn't sit down.

"The condition of your home, for one."

"You know I don't regularly live here," Grace said evasively.

"But Edward does. And it seems he's in trouble."

"Strangely, not too bad," Grace said, wearing a rueful smile.

"Then it's you who's in trouble."

When Grace hesitated, Beverly took her hand and brought her to her feet.

"We can't talk in here," Beverly said. "Let's go outside."

Realizing that she was not going to escape this time, Grace followed her outside into the little flowering courtyard, to a bench past the fountain but not all the way to the stables.

Beverly looked at her expectantly. "Well? And don't try to lie. Your freckles stand out in your red face when you do. That hasn't changed since we were girls."

Looking into Beverly's sympathetic eyes, Grace found herself telling her everything, from her mother's gambling and losing their homes and Grace's hand in marriage, to the challenge over her seduction.

Beverly's mouth fell farther open with each revelation. Grace was so embarrassed that she couldn't even look at her after a while and had to stare into the fountain. But its peaceful gurgling wasn't helping her. Was Beverly disgusted? Had Grace lost her only friend?

Suddenly she was wrapped in Beverly's arms, her breath almost choked from her.

"You poor dear," Beverly murmured, patting Grace's back as if she were her child.

Grace let out a relieved sigh. "It's all right, but thank you."

Beverly held her by the upper arms and stared at her. "How dreadful that that man thinks he can just seduce you—an innocent!"

"I can resist him." Grace was convincing herself as well as Beverly. "He's playing by the rules we set down, and he stops when I tell him to."

"And all you have to do is resist for how much longer?"

"Eight days."

"And then the violin is yours."

"And it's worth so much money, Beverly," Grace said in a low voice. "I can rent us a home, give Edward something with which he can approach a woman in marriage. And it's not costing me much."

"Ah, but your pride, my dear," Beverly whispered.

To her surprise, Grace found herself blinking back tears. "When I found out what my mother had done . . . when I realized that we meant so little to her that she'd wager our homes . . ."

Beverly nodded, holding Grace's hand, sniffing.

"She lost our only place to live," Grace continued, pulling her handkerchief from her sleeve.

"There is no excuse for her behavior, Grace.
Thank goodness that Mr. Throckmorten did not
try to force you into marriage."

"How could he? I would have resisted, and he
would have embarrassed us both. He's not like
that."

"This is a man who wants to take you to his
bed," Beverly said doubtfully, "though you're a
virginal miss."

Grace looked away. She couldn't reveal everything about her past. It was too humiliating.

"So it's simple. You resist him, and you win."

"Don't forget about the redemption."

Beverly groaned. "You made this so much more
complicated than it needed to be."

"I had to! What else was I going to tell Edward?
He would—*challenge* Daniel! And I can imagine
who's the better shot. That's all I need."

"Now I understand why Mr. Throckmorten
appeared at a charity picnic. The ladies are still
atwitter. Don't be surprised to hear about it at
dinner tonight."

"Don't worry. It will work perfectly, I promise
you. With some guidance, he'll fit right back into
Society. Maybe he'll even find a woman to marry
someday."

Beverly eyed her doubtfully. "Not you?"

"Oh no!" Grace said too quickly. "He's only
considering me as a mistress. And I would never
want to marry him. I was raised by a gambler and

watched her make my brother into one as well. Daniel is a man who finds life so boring that he needs to take risks. No, I need a quiet man whose only compulsion in his life is books—or me. Until then, all I have to do is resist."

Beverly frowned. "You don't seem so certain."

"You don't know how well he kisses."

"Oh, my dear, it is a good thing you explained everything to me. You need my help in the worst way."

Grace smiled. "And how will you do that?"

"He needs to marry, does he not?"

"He's his cousin's heir, at least until the duke marries and has a son of his own."

"Then I shall make sure he has so many ladies to choose from that he'll be too busy escaping them to have time for you. It'll all be over by the annual Madingley Ball, you mark my words."

Obviously, Beverly didn't know Daniel very well, but Grace refrained from telling her so.

That evening, Daniel stood in Lord Cheston's drawing room before dinner, speaking with his lordship about a bill to be read before the House of Commons. His cousin Madingley was also there, watching Daniel too closely. No one else would recognize the suspicion in his gaze. Daniel knew he wasn't exactly behaving the way his family expected of him. They, too, must have heard about Daniel's good deed for charity. He didn't want to answer Chris's questions, so he avoided talking alone with his cousin—at least for now.

Daniel didn't need to look up to know when Grace entered the room. To his surprise, he felt it, as if a lavender-scented current moved through the room. She was with her friend Lady Standish, and though they didn't look his way, a path seemed magically to appear between them. Various guests looked back and forth as if waiting to see what would happen.

How had one waltz with Grace made them of such interest?

Well, it wasn't just a waltz. She'd made it seem like he'd rescued her from a runaway horse. She'd dragged him to work at a meal for the poor. Some might have thought a marriage pending, but most understood the sort of man he was. They all probably believed that Grace was deceiving herself about him. And that made him feel the first twinge of guilt, which was ridiculous.

Grace understood their relationship. He just had to stop thinking about her so protectively. He had spent last night in her parents' suite, watching for a man in the shadows of the street who had never appeared. Feeling ridiculous, he had vowed to hire an investigator and find out what was going on once and for all.

Lord Cheston harrumphed and rocked back on his heels. Daniel realized that he'd completely forgotten about the old man. Sometimes it was hard to read his expression beneath his heavy muttonchop whiskers and thick mustache, but for once, Daniel knew sympathy when he saw it.

"Never thought it would happen to you, Throck-morten," his lordship said gruffly.

"And what would that be, my lord?"

"You're being manipulated by a woman."

Daniel smiled, almost wishing he could explain that it was really the other way around, that Grace was doing her best to keep him off guard so that she wouldn't have to admit how much her control was really slipping.

"I saw you waltz with her," Lord Cheston continued.

Daniel arched a brow at him. "Your point?"

"You were far too intent on her. And then that meal at the park in Bethnal Green—how did you let yourself be talked into something that is a woman's domain?"

Daniel realized he could hardly explain that he'd been tricked. But then all the pieces seemed to fall together, and he finally realized how all this was connected.

Was Grace's plan to make him appealing to the *ton* once again? Was she trying to change him, to make him better in their eyes? He almost laughed aloud.

Daniel was directed to escort Grace into dinner, and the seating plan had them dining beside one another. Lady Cheston—and everyone else— obviously thought that Grace was manipulating him for herself and were going to go along with the plan. Or at least see what sparks flew, satisfying their insatiable demand for gossip.

So Daniel decided to give them a show. Instead of occupying himself with Grace, as they all expected, he monopolized the dinner conversation of the lady on his left and the gentleman across from her.

If everyone thought he needed improving, let them all give it a try.

When several courses of the meal had gone by, and he hadn't even looked at Grace, he saw the whispers and the disapproving stares sent his way. They all thought that he owed Grace his attention. But he was still faintly annoyed that he'd taken so long to discover her plan.

To his surprise, he suddenly felt Grace's hand on his right thigh. Plenty of women had done such a thing clandestinely, but somehow, knowing that it was innocent Grace, whose delights he'd only just begun to taste and explore, made him go instantly hard, instantly tense.

He laughed a bit too loudly at something Miss Alton said on his left and received even more curious stares for it, although the lady herself blushed and batted her lashes at him.

Grace's hand began to move, fingers lightly trailing a sensuous path down to his knee, then up again, all at a slow, deliberate pace.

He began to perspire.

What was wrong with him? Plenty of women had thrown themselves at him.

But not innocent young ladies who talked enough to their friends to know what drove a man wild.

He wasn't going to give in to her bid for attention. He asked Miss Alton to meet with him again after dinner, when the ladies and gentlemen rejoined one another in the drawing room.

Grace's fingers did not go all the way to his groin, and he was only partly relieved, the other part frustrated. He could have laughed at his own dilemma.

He whispered his most devilish suggestion in Miss Alton's ear. She gave a little gasp, her face went white, and she began to cough, as if she'd swallowed something the wrong way.

Grace's fingers slid down between his thighs, and he closed them on her hand.

The man on Miss Alton's left patted her back as she got herself under control. The stares he received were appalled yet unsurprised, as if he'd done what they all expected. Miss Alton's stare was both unsettled, which was only natural, and . . . curious.

"Mr. Throckmorten," she said in a soft voice, "there's no need to say such an outrageous thing simply to prove to Miss Banbury that she can't tame you."

"Tame me?"

But she'd already turned away, and he was left staring at her upswept blond curls. He turned to Grace, who'd finally pulled her hand free and was now frowning at him as much as everyone else.

He leaned toward her. "Forgive me for not going along with your plans for me."

"I don't know what you're talking about," she said softly, then lifted a glass of wine to her mouth.

Had she meant to improve him for all the women? Surely then she couldn't be upset by his conversation with Miss Alton. Wasn't that the whole point of Grace's plan? Or was she just trying to drive him crazy wondering what she was up to?

But her hand didn't return to his lap. If he had just gone along with the game, who knew what she might have done to get his attention?

Chapter 11

After dinner, when all the guests were reunited in the drawing room, Daniel decided to finish with the family questions by approaching Chris himself.

When a man talking to Chris saw Daniel coming, he looked between the two and excused himself.

"You are good at scaring people away," Chris said dryly.

Daniel sipped his brandy. "It's one of the more useful family traits."

"Hmm." Chris eyed him. "Interesting show you put on with both of your dinner partners."

Daniel shrugged. "I had to live up to everyone's expectations."

"Then why were you deliberately ignoring Miss Banbury? I understand from certain people that she's decided to make you her project."

Daniel grinned. "So they think."

"That's not the truth? Because if you were ignoring her, it certainly looked like there was tension between you. But then I'm your cousin, and I know you better than others do."

"Making me her project is part of the truth, but it's only her attempt to counter me."

"I don't understand."

Smiling, Daniel eyed him. "You don't need to."

"She seems to have chosen you deliberately, Daniel. I've done some investigating."

"Aren't you the thorough duke."

Chris ignored his interruption. "Her family has little money, although she does have a dowry. Perhaps she's targeting you because—"

"She knows I don't want to marry her, and she doesn't want to marry me."

"You're deluding yourself. You have money and connections, and now that you're attending more of these events, they're going to see that you're available. Miss Banbury is simply the most recent to express interest."

"Interest?" Daniel echoed with amusement. "I wouldn't call it that."

"Stop being so mysterious." Chris rolled his eyes.

"Very well, here's the answer to some of your questions. Miss Banbury is trying to change me, yes, but only to win back an antique violin that I won from her . . . family."

"Ah, that brother of hers who doesn't know when to quit."

Daniel didn't correct him.

"It's a sentimental heirloom?"

"An expensive one."

Daniel had said too much, for Chris's eyes lit with understanding.

"She needs to sell it," Chris said slowly.

"So she's trying to best me. I think the way to counter her is to get her away from her audience. I'm thinking about taking her out of London for several days."

"You'd be playing into her hands if she wanted to trap you," Chris said.

But Daniel knew he would also have a better chance to win their private challenge if he could get her alone all day—and all night. And he'd be keeping her away from the stranger outside her town house while Daniel had him found.

He was looking at Grace, who was seated on a sofa with her friend Lady Standish. They were talking together as softly as Daniel and Chris, and suddenly Daniel had to know what they were discussing.

He inclined his head to his cousin and began to move unobtrusively about the fringes of the drawing room. That was difficult to do when one had a duke in tow, but they managed it. When he'd positioned himself behind the sofa, he pointed to a sculpture there as if discussing it with Chris. Chris frowned at him but dutifully examined the piece of art.

Grace, intent on her conversation, hadn't seen them.

Lady Standish said in a low voice, "You've been bringing attention to yourself, Grace. I just heard Lady Cheston say she plans to pay a call on you."

"I had hoped to avoid that," Grace answered.

Though Daniel wasn't looking at her, he could hear the weariness in her voice.

"I didn't think anyone would want to visit someone of such a low social stature," Grace continued. "You know how bare the town house is. What will she think?"

Lady Standish spoke kindly. "Perhaps there are furnishings in other rooms that can be moved downstairs."

Before Daniel could hear any more, Chris suddenly took his elbow and pulled him to the next piece of art, a painting on the wall.

"I told you she was after you for your money," Chris said quietly.

"None of this is her fault. Both her mother and brother have a problem with gambling. She's only trying to save herself and her brother. It's not about marrying me."

"How else does a young lady save her family?"

Daniel wavered, but only for a moment. Grace could have what she wanted from him by restraining herself for another week. She wouldn't want to jeopardize that. And she didn't strike him as the kind of woman who would try to marry a man she didn't love.

"Look, I've already helped make her a more attractive prospect for any of these young bucks," Daniel said. "She's grateful enough."

"What do you mean?"

"I've shown interest in her, which makes other men notice her. And I could hardly meet up with her at all of these events if she couldn't prepare herself for them. So I hired two servants for the house."

"*Her* house?"

Daniel winced and looked about to make sure they weren't being overheard. "Technically, my house. I won it from her mother. Grace would have been out on the street."

"So you're her savior," Chris said grimly.

"Hardly. I'm her challenger. She thinks she can defeat me. I'm letting her think it."

"I think you're deluding yourself and that there's more to the story."

Daniel said nothing. What could he say without explaining private details he had no intention of sharing with anyone but Grace?

"She could have meant for you to overhear this latest plight of hers," Chris added.

"Then it worked. I'm going to hire a decorator to refurbish the town house."

Chris winced. "If anyone else finds out, you'll have ruined her. And then you'll be forced to marry her. Perhaps that's her strategy."

"It's not. She knows I would never let anyone force me to marry. But I can't mount a true challenge if my opponent is weaker than I am. She has to meet me equally, especially in Society. It will make winning all the more satisfying."

"So what happens if you win the violin? She'll have nothing, and you'll feel sorry for her."

"I'm going to give her back the town house. I don't need it."

With a groan, Chris ran a hand down his face.

"Surely my masterpiece is not so terrible," said a woman's voice behind them.

Daniel turned to find Lady Cheston looking at them both coldly.

"I did paint this, you know," she added.

Chris recovered with his usual good nature. "Lady Cheston, you misunderstand us. My cousin and I were betting on the artist's identity, and I was insisting we already had something by the artist in Madingley House."

Lady Cheston blushed. "Something of mine? You silly young man. I'm not talented enough for the honor of hanging in a duke's home."

And once again, Chris had taken care of another tricky situation. Smiling to himself, Daniel let his gaze drift around the room.

When Grace later made certain he knew that she'd accepted a ride home from Lady Standish, Daniel felt that everyone seemed to be conspiring against him this evening. He would not be kidnapping her tonight.

After the dinner party, Daniel went looking for Edward Banbury. Someone at the club told him two of Banbury's favorite gambling haunts, and Daniel found him at the second one, a gaming house for Society's fashionables, decorated in rich reds and blacks, with crystal chandeliers gleaming above.

At least Banbury hadn't sunk to one of the city's infamous gaming hells where he could get himself killed if he couldn't cover his bets.

Here, among the wealthy, he would only lose his honor. Daniel sensed that Banbury was holding on to it by his fingernails.

He watched Banbury for several minutes as the man stood by the hazard table. Banbury couldn't seem to stand still—he kept moving to get a better angle to watch someone else rolling the dice, but he didn't bet himself.

Daniel finally approached him. "May I speak with you, Banbury?"

The man stiffened, but finally nodded and followed Daniel to the lavish supper table. They helped themselves to a selection of cheesecakes, and then stood in a corner of the room, eating and watching the play around them.

"So what do you want?" Banbury finally asked.

"I'm going to send a decorator to look at the town house, listen to his recommendations for furnishings, and then have those items delivered."

Banbury set his fork on his plate with controlled deliberateness. "Until you are rid of us, you need to keep away."

"It's my town house, and I wish it to look just so."

Banbury opened his mouth, but Daniel continued talking before he could be interrupted.

"Your sister is beginning to make calls in Society, and that means they will be returning her calls, some out of plain curiosity."

Banbury stiffened, his face slowly flushing red. Daniel felt reluctant compassion, knowing how

Banbury and Grace had grown up. And she loved her brother, flaws and all.

"And that will help her find a good man to marry," Banbury said with belligerence.

"I know."

Banbury ran a hand through his hair, not looking at Daniel. "What I did with the furnishings never mattered," he said in a low, hoarse voice. "I was just a bachelor in that house. And then Grace came, and not only has she been hurt by our mother, but by me."

Daniel didn't know what to say. Though he'd thought himself burdened with a crazy, scandalous family, at least they'd always been there, worrying too much about him and giving him a decent upbringing. After their father's death, Grace and her brother had never had any kind of stability. And now their mother had taken even the safety of a home from them.

He sensed that Banbury was on the edge of a precipice, and one wrong decision could send him plummeting. And then Grace would suffer even more.

"I'm not like you, Throckmorten. You seem to control the game. But it controls me."

Daniel said nothing for a moment. "Did you think about what I said about the railways?"

"I read a book," Banbury said wearily.

"That's good. Research is important. I could tell you what I did when I first came of age, the best markets to concentrate in. I have some experience taking a small amount of money and investing it wisely."

"You didn't have much money?" Banbury said, his curiosity obviously reluctant.

Daniel shook his head. "An allowance. My father may have been famous, and my mother will never want because of that, but for now the money is hers. And there's the duke, of course, but you know where the bulk of his estate will go."

"But you're his heir."

"Only until he has his own child. Poor fellow has to marry."

Banbury nodded, still looking so intently at Daniel.

"Are you offering to tutor me?" Banbury finally asked.

Daniel met his gaze. "I suppose so."

"Then I'll take you up on your offer."

His voice was neutral, controlled, without betraying the surrender that Daniel knew he must be feeling.

"Good. I have an office at the Southern Railway. Meet me there tomorrow at two o'clock."

Daniel handed his plate to a servant and left without a backward glance. He didn't think Banbury would gamble, at least not tonight.

Grace paced long into the night. If she didn't start getting a regular night's sleep, it was going to show in her complexion. But sleep continued to elude her as she thought over and over again about her conduct toward Daniel at the dinner party.

She must have been jealous.

What other explanation could there be?

He'd deliberately snubbed her, she knew, paying attention to another woman. And that was supposed to be all right with Grace; she wanted him to be a normal Society bachelor looking for the perfect wife.

But she couldn't understand why he'd ignored her—surely such a strategy wouldn't result in her seduction?

So she'd ignorantly fallen right into his plot; he'd wanted her to notice him, to be the one needing his attention, instead of his always pursuing her.

And she'd pursued him.

She'd touched him quite . . . scandalously, felt the long hard muscles of his thigh. Heavens, if anyone had seen what she'd been doing to him—

With a groan, she started wandering the darkened house. Every so often, she looked out the front windows but saw no one loitering across the street.

She opened the door to the master suite, but it was dark and empty. Exhausted, she went back to her room and fell onto the bed, not even bothering to crawl beneath the coverlet.

And that was how Daniel found her, on her back in slumber, her long braid trailing across the pillow.

He put an arm around her bedpost and just watched the rise and fall of her breasts, the way her nightgown fell in folds between her thighs.

He stepped close and whispered her name, but she didn't stir. He removed the tie from the end of her braid and spread her long brown hair out across the pillow. It was soft and luxurious, and he imagined it sliding across his skin.

Would she awaken if he touched her?

He ran his finger from her ankle to her knee, the only thing revealed from where she'd stirred in her nightgown. And although she twitched, she was too deeply asleep to respond.

And without her participation, he couldn't enjoy her. She wasn't just a body he had to possess. She was a spirit, a presence, and he wanted to look in her eyes when he aroused her. He wanted to know that at last, she could resist him no longer, and that she'd taken him with her own free will. He didn't need her trust; he only needed her passion.

So he wrote a note at her desk, left it on the bed table, and went to finish his nightly vigil in the master suite.

When Grace awoke late in the morning, she was flustered and confused—and then she realized that her hair was tangled all around her. She pushed it out of her face as she sat up, sighing over all of the brushing she'd have to do to untangle it. In her sleep, the tie must have come loose.

And then she saw the note on the table, in a man's strong handwriting: *I resisted.*

She covered her face and, with a groan, fell back among the pillows. Daniel had invaded her room, and she had no memory of it. What had he done, besides release her hair from the braid that annoyed him?

But . . . he'd resisted. And he hadn't awoken her.

Had he come for what her wandering hand had promised him last night? Did he think she was ready to surrender? He'd find out soon enough that her armor was dented but not broken.

She tore up his note before anyone else could see it.

After an early luncheon with Edward—during which he barely spoke to her, so engrossed was he in his book on railways—Grace went shopping with Beverly. She didn't buy anything but ribbons for her hair, but it felt good to do nothing but talk about lighthearted concerns, fashion and hairstyles and who might become betrothed to whom.

But when she returned to the town house, Ruby met her in the entrance hall.

"We had visitors today, Miss Grace," the maid said ominously.

"They must have left their cards," Grace answered. "It was a good thing I wasn't here, or I would have felt obliged to see them. Have you started moving some of the paintings from my bedroom and the master suite?"

"I'm not sure that'll be needed anymore."

Grace lifted the bonnet from her head and frowned, even as the maid absently took it. "What do you mean? Lady Cheston says she's going to call on me—"

"A decorator visited today. It seems Mr. Banbury hired them to fix up the place."

"Mr. Banbury?" Grace said faintly, already knowing who was responsible and trying to figure out why.

"They're all excited, because they can do whatever they want—long as you approve."

"Of course." Grace plopped into a chair.

"Did Mr. Banbury win a lot of money?" Ruby asked suspiciously.

Grace opened her mouth, about to answer with uncertainty, but all she said was, "I don't think so."

"Supposedly Mr. Banbury hired the Woodleys, too," Ruby continued in a softer voice. "But he didn't do either of these things, did he?"

Grace shook her head.

"That man ye're challengin' thinks he can win ye," Ruby warned.

"He just wants the house ready because he thinks he'll take over soon."

"Is your quest to make him a better man workin'?"

Grace remained silent.

"The decorator said he'd bring his men and start workin' tomorrow. It'll be messy for a while."

She felt angry and defensive. "So is he trying to remove me from the house early?"

"No," said a male voice.

They both turned around to see Daniel standing in the front doorway.

"Might I come in?"

It was on the tip of her tongue to say that he owned the place, but she only exchanged a meaningful glance with Ruby.

"Do come up to the drawing room, Mr. Throckmorten," Grace said, mindful that the other servants might be listening. "I'll ring for refreshments."

Ruby didn't leave them alone, and Grace was grateful, even though Daniel glanced at the maid impatiently more than once as they waited for tea and iced cakes. Ruby sat in a window seat mending Edward's shirts, while Grace sat on the sofa, and Daniel paced. He looked too big for the drawing room, filled with energy that couldn't be contained. When the refreshments had been served, he pointedly took a seat beside her.

Ruby gave a disapproving sniff.

Grace stirred her tea and stared as the color lightened with the cream.

"Can't look at me?" he asked softly.

She gave him an arch smile. "How silly. Of course I can."

After a long sigh, he glanced at Ruby, then lowered his voice. "I'm looking at you because I'm remembering where your hand was last night."

She set the cup in the saucer with a rattle that splashed several drops onto her skirt. To her surprise, he quickly wet his handkerchief in a pitcher of water and dabbed at the spot over her knee before it could stain.

And she let him, knowing she'd touched him in a far more intimate way, her fingers dipping

between his thighs. She felt overheated with em-
barrassment. Why was it so difficult to accept her
own eager participation in their challenge?

She heard Ruby get to her feet and couldn't
even look at the maid. "It's nothing, Ruby. You
can return to your sewing." She had to get off the
topic of her scandalous conduct. How better than
to remind him of his? "You came to my bedroom
last night," she whispered disapprovingly.

"I had to, after the promise of your touch."

She inhaled sharply, and finally admitted, "It
was foolish of me to pay you back for how you'd
touched me."

"So that's why you did it?"

"Why else?"

"I thought you wanted my attention."

That was too close to the truth.

"No, I wanted you to see how it felt to be teased
in public, knowing there was nothing you could
do to stop it."

"I enjoyed it," he said simply.

She sighed, taking another sip of her tea. "I'm
surprised you did not press your advantage in my
bedroom last night."

"I tried to wake you, but you seemed
exhausted."

She frowned but didn't answer. Then she finally
murmured, "What else did you do?"

She was growing so used to his moods, to the
way his mind worked, that she could tell he'd
stiffened. She was curious as to why but didn't
ask.

"So you think I would abuse you?" he asked in a low voice.

She glanced up at him quickly. His expression was strangely impassive, and she wondered momentarily—had she hurt his feelings?

"I didn't say *abuse*," she answered, still studying him. "You know how I react to you. Were you trying to wake me up?"

"Not really."

"Then what were you doing?"

"Just looking at you," he said, his voice gone low and hoarse.

She was caught in the passion she saw in his heavy-lidded gaze. They weren't even touching, yet he aroused her, made her yearn for him. She was feeling overwhelmed and unprepared, and she wondered if she could hold out against the onslaught of her own needs.

With a start, she sat back, turning away from him. What was wrong with her? How could she even think about losing to him, when her future— and Edward's—was at stake?

He cleared his throat. "I'm leaving tomorrow for Hertingfordbury."

She gaped at him. "You're going to my home?"

"I want you to come with me."

She opened her mouth to protest, but he held up a hand.

"I thought you could introduce me to the steward and servants. I'll go without you, if I must."

Ruby had said that the servants back home had no idea that the family no longer owned the manor. Much as Grace didn't like the intimacy of traveling with him, she owed them the consideration of explaining what had happened. And perhaps she could talk Daniel into retaining them.

"I'll go," she said resolutely.

His eyes widened a bit. "That didn't require much persuasion."

"I should be the one to tell them, not a stranger."

"And what will your brother say?"

"He'll know that I'm accompanied by a proper chaperone," Grace said, gesturing to Ruby.

She hid her smile at his look of resignation.

"I am not a naive girl fresh from the schoolroom, after all," she continued.

He leaned back on the sofa and rested his arm on the back. "On the way, I'll be able to show you my charitable endeavor."

She gave a small smile. "And what would that be? The racetrack where you keep the jockeys employed?"

"Now, Grace, I already told you that I read to the blind. I'll demonstrate it on this trip."

She stared at him suspiciously. "I can't wait to see what you come up with."

When he leaned toward her, she glanced pointedly at Ruby, then back at him. "Mr. Throckmorten—"

"Remember, Grace, we have only eight days left in our challenge. I have to somehow find an advantage over you."

She leaned back, bracing herself on one hand.

"And if kisses alone won't work, I'll find your soft side with charity and my good nature."

She bit her lip to keep from chuckling. "I guess you'll need all the luck you can get, because I don't plan to lose."

Out of sight of Ruby, he moved his hand about her hip, cupping her backside, long fingers pressed and caressing.

Grace caught her breath, shocked at how quickly her desire for him could flare up.

His face too close, he murmured. "You have my promise—I'll be the winner in this game between us."

Chapter 12

Grace was worried about how both she and Daniel could disappear from the city—and Society guest lists—at the same time without causing suspicion. But all of that was taken care of at Lady Putnam's ball that evening.

She had hoped that Daniel would avoid the event, since he said he always did—before their challenge. But then she felt she was being a coward. She just would not allow herself to be alone with him. That was the secret to surviving his intimate persuasions and her own loss of control. There was only a week left. In a week of knowing him, she hadn't *quite* removed all her clothing in his presence.

Oh God, what had she come to when *that* was something to praise herself with! And how could she be proud, when she had allowed some of her clothing to be . . . rearranged. And too often she could remember his mouth on her, what he'd done with his teeth and tongue. It was amazing that she could still function whenever she thought of his effect on her.

At the ball, held in a suite of three large drawing rooms, Grace found Beverly and told her that she was leaving for home, and with whom she was traveling.

"I need your help to disguise that I'm leaving on the same day as Daniel," Grace said in a low voice, smiling at an elderly man who nodded as he passed by.

"Oh, Grace, this is not a good idea."

"I know, but I can't let our servants meet him with no explanation."

"You could write a letter."

"But then I couldn't persuade him to keep them all on. I'll be able to point out everything each one does to benefit the household."

"Then if I can't talk you out of this, what can I do to help?" Beverly finally said.

With her glass of lemonade near her lips, Grace said, "Let the occasional person know that I'm visiting home in two days. If anyone calls tomorrow, I'm going to have my servants tell people I'm out shopping with you. Will you mind the lies?"

"They're for a good cause," she said with a sigh.

"Speaking of a good cause . . ." Grace began, when she spied Daniel entering the room.

As usual, heads turned his way, and a wave of whispers went out from around him. Surely they weren't used to seeing him so much at these events. And then the heads began to turn one at a time to her. Everyone was waiting to see what they'd do together.

But it wasn't supposed to be about the two of them as a couple. He wasn't going to marry her, so it served no purpose for him to dance with her. Except that she liked his attentions, liked feeling the center of his warm regard. But there were other young ladies deserving of his time.

She turned back to Beverly and smiled. "Remember your vow to help Daniel meet prospective brides?"

"Yes?" she said brightly.

"There are so many beautiful, accomplished young ladies here, and he must already know most of them or their male relatives."

"Probably," Beverly said, looking a little confused.

"Then let's introduce him to the women he wouldn't normally meet."

Grace whispered her plan, Beverly clapped her hands, and they both managed to appear politely smiling when Daniel finally reached them.

He bowed. "Ladies, you both look lovely this evening."

Grace felt a little breathless just looking at him, all dark and handsome in his black evening clothes. He looked at her a bit too long, a bit too closely. It was time to distract them both.

"Thank you for your compliment, Mr. Throckmorten," Beverly said. "Forgive me for getting right to the point, but I could use your assistance this evening."

Grace saw him shoot a suspicious glance at her, but she kept a serene smile on her face.

"Do look at the corner closest to the main entrance," Beverly said, not bothering to point.

Daniel looked, but not Grace, who didn't want to appear too obvious. But she already knew that there were two rows of chairs set up in the corner, facing outward, for the chaperones and wallflowers.

"There are several eligible ladies there who are never asked to dance," Beverly said, "except by elderly gentlemen."

Daniel looked at her. "And it is your mission to have me find men to dance with them?"

"Why no," Beverly said lightly, "I would like you to do them the honor."

Grace bit the inside of her lip so that she wouldn't laugh out loud at the impassive way he glanced once more at the single ladies, then back to Beverly.

"Lady Standish," he began patiently, "there are many ladies there. I surely could not—"

"Don't be silly, Mr. Throckmorten. Some of them are chaperones and would refuse to dance with you anyway." Beverly blanched. "I didn't mean that they'd refuse to dance because it's *you*, but because they're chaperones."

"Of course." The dry tone of Daniel's voice expressed his doubts.

"Then you'll do it?" Beverly asked with obvious excitement.

"I would do anything for you, your ladyship."

"Then allow me to go over first, so I can begin chatting. After several minutes, you can come and request an introduction."

"So it won't look so deliberate?" he asked with amusement.

Beverly nodded and sailed away, holding on to her skirt, bowing slightly at the occasional person who crossed her path.

Grace felt Daniel looking at her.

"This was your idea, was it not?"

She smiled, keeping her gaze trained on the dancers performing the intricate steps of the quadrille.

"You can ignore me all you want," he said, "but I'm beginning to recognize how your devious mind works."

She frowned at him. "It is not so devious to want young ladies to enjoy themselves at a ball."

"Aha, it *was* your idea." He lowered his voice. "You no longer wish to dance with me yourself?"

His question hung in the air a moment, and she didn't know quite how to answer it. "You know you dance beautifully," she finally said with reluctance. "And I enjoyed myself. But I don't want people to . . . come to the wrong conclusion."

"And what would that be?"

"That you are pursuing me."

"But I am."

She sighed, still not looking at him, though she was aware of his warmth and his scent. "Pursuing me for a noble reason."

"Desire is not noble?"

"A wager is not noble," she said in a low voice, wincing that she'd even said the word aloud. She felt flustered and uneasy. A young lady should aspire to marriage—instead, she was aspiring to avoid an illicit seduction.

"So I can't dance with you?" he said, setting down his goblet.

"I didn't say that."

"Then I propose that I will do this favor for you—and Lady Standish, of course—and in return, you will owe me a private dance."

She took an unsteady breath, her eyes fluttering shut at just the thought of being held again in his strong arms.

How many days left until she won?

"Very well," she agreed. "You wish to dance out on the terrace?"

"No, it will have to be another night, where no one can disturb us."

His gaze could have melted her into a hot puddle of passion. She should have looked away, even as some distant part of her mind warned that someone could be watching.

At last he left her, and she could only think starkly that they would be in constant contact for at least the next two days.

Thank God for Ruby, or she couldn't imagine enduring endless hours in a rocking carriage with him staring at her with smoldering brown eyes.

As Daniel danced with three different young ladies, he knew he was once again the focus of whispered speculation. But he had to admit, it was for a good cause. It was a shame that these women had so few dance partners that they could only stumble over their words of gratitude.

Every so often, he caught a glimpse of Grace, smiling at him with pleasure. Such a simple thing made her happy?

She danced with other gentlemen, and he found he had to force himself not to keep glancing her way. He didn't need to be jealous. He knew he was the one who would be alone with her in the dark, who was the first to show her passion.

After several dances, he took a glass of champagne from a passing waiter and stood alone near the open terrace doors. A faint breeze penetrated the stifling oppression of the overheated ballroom. His gaze was drawn to Grace, who danced the waltz with another man. He watched the graceful way she moved across the floor, her skirts twirling with each turn, her face alight with happiness, as she temporarily forgot her cares.

Other men watched her as well, and he found himself studying their expressions. Most seemed curious or interested, or even wore a smile of admiration. But one man, who stood alone, let slip an expression of rapt adoration before suddenly looking about as if he was worried someone had seen him.

Daniel suddenly recognized him. He was one of the other two men who'd played the infamous card game with Grace's mother. He'd been the one who wanted Mrs. Banbury to sweeten the pot with the hand of her daughter.

Feeling a cold thread of danger, Daniel began to

move, skirting through the edges of the crowd but staying near the wall, step by step getting closer to the other man. He was the right height and build, short and thin, for the stranger who'd been lingering in the shadows outside Grace's town house.

But what was his name?

Daniel kept him in sight, even when a gentleman or two struck up a conversation. At last, by casually inquiring, someone was able to identify him.

Horace Jenkins was apparently a gentleman of property in Hertfordshire. He must have at least seen Grace from afar—but mostly likely he had met her, for how else would he have decided he had to marry her? But Daniel didn't want to ask Grace and arouse her suspicions too soon. He would have his investigators look into the matter. He didn't want a word to leak out that might compromise Grace's reputation, and he was certain he could convince Jenkins and the other man, for the right sum, to remain quiet.

Besides, Daniel was about to take Grace away from London, away from danger, away from her ability to retreat from him. With the days dwindling, he needed every spare hour to woo her.

He admitted he'd underestimated the difficulty of her seduction. But he had a trick or two left.

At dawn the next morning, Grace felt like a character in a novel. She had already had her trunk of clothing sent down to the stables, where Daniel's carriage was waiting for her. Then she and Ruby walked through the dew-glistening garden, through the stables, and then the gate in the wall that led to the alley. She felt nervous, as if she were doing something that might change her life.

Everything she did with Daniel Throckmorten had that potential, she thought. It should bother her, but instead it gave her a little thrill. Then she reminded herself that Daniel's coming into her life had changed everything, and not for the better.

She saw him standing beside the sleek, black carriage with its four matching horses, all snorting and tossing their heads as if anxious to go.

And suddenly Grace wasn't so nervous since she had Ruby to lean on. He had known she would not travel with him unchaperoned, yet his dark eyes lightened with amusement and a silent challenge, as if a mere maid could not stop him from taking what he wanted.

And that was Grace.

Even though she told herself not to be flattered, she felt it clearly, an almost feminine satisfaction. For whatever reason, he desired her. She was only his current challenge, a prize to be won. He was a gambler; it's what he did. She'd opposed gambling her whole life, had been on the receiving end of the terrible consequences too many times.

Yet she was participating in this indecent challenge—and enjoying it. Surely it was only the flattery of a man wanting her. And her certainty that she could win, denying him his ultimate prize. She would never again allow a man such control over her.

And then Daniel opened the door to the carriage and reached for her hand to help her enter. For just a moment, it felt like she was entering into a perilous trap.

She lifted her chin, took his hand, and stepped up inside.

Even though the hour was early, the traffic was brisk. Many wagons were heading into the city with their goods from the surrounding farms—milk and strawberries and everything London cooks purchased each day. Grace sat in silence, listening to the calls of vendors, because she kept the nearest window blinds closed.

"It will get rather uncomfortable in here if you keep the window up all day," Daniel said dryly.

"I'm not warm." The first drip of perspiration slid down the center of her back, and it was only early morning.

"Don't worry about appearances. Everyone will think we're married."

She frowned at the amusement he so readily displayed. "Not the people who know us—the people who believe that you're leaving town alone today, and I'm simply shopping." She hesitated, then gave him a bold look. "So why have you not married?"

He arched a brow, but surprisingly, he answered, "It never seemed the right time."

"You never met the right woman."

"I never tried. Before you, it was rare that I

attended balls, and only when my cousin insisted I look over the latest crop of debutantes. My current mistress took care of any other needs." He grinned and allowed his gaze to roam down her body.

She gritted her teeth, ignored his indecent reference, and said, "Your cousin, the duke?"

"He long ago adopted the function of caretaker for the family. He thinks marriage will settle me down and make me happy."

"But not for himself?"

"A duke has to be absolutely certain he's found the correct, presentable woman who's prepared for the position."

"Is that how the Cabots have always approached marriage?"

"The opposite, in fact. My grandfather, God rest his soul, believed that he married my grandmother for all the wrong reasons, wealth and beauty."

"You can't tell me that His Grace believes you should marry a poor, plain woman."

He laughed. "I am to marry a woman who suits me, one I can talk to. Madingley reminds me that our grandfather made so many mistakes losing his inheritance as a young man that he ruined his marriage by spending too much time away, rebuilding his fortune. So my grandfather was a firm believer in the proper marriage for his descendants."

"Did he believe his own children lived up to his expectations?"

"I don't know. But I don't have to bow to his memory like Madingley does. When you're a duke, your marriage affects so many people."

"Didn't the duke's father marry a Spaniard?"

He glanced at her with amusement. "So you already know."

"People like to talk about your family."

"His father married for love, and though Madingley loves his mother, I think sometimes he dwells too much on the scandal. When his father died nine years ago, he died after a happy, contented life."

"And what do you see when you think of marriage?"

He gave her a curious glance.

"Surely you have an opinion," she continued. "Your own parents seemed to love each other, although altogether, I hear that your aunts and uncle can be quite volatile."

"I think that one had better be deeply in love to make the commitment worth it."

She stared at him in surprise. "You believe in love? Not simply marrying for the betterment of your family or your fortune?"

He lifted a hand. "I didn't say I believed in it for me. Such a risk might be too great even for a gambler like myself."

"Because marriage is a gamble," she said slowly, realizing that she agreed with him, at least about that. Being with a man in any way was a gamble, and she'd lost the first time she'd entered the game.

As the carriage left the city, Daniel found himself watching Grace rather than looking out the window or reading the newspaper he'd brought. He didn't want to drop the subject of marriage, which surprised him. And her maid had obligingly drifted off to sleep, her head at an awkward angle near her shoulder.

"What about you?" he asked.

He thought Grace looked uneasy.

"Me?"

"Marriage."

She cocked her head, visibly startled.

"Why haven't you married? And don't relate it to gambling."

She gave a crooked smile, and her fingers plucked at a stray thread on her reticule. She was actually nervous, he thought in surprise, and his curiosity strengthened.

"You have a dowry," he reminded her.

"I do." She put on a cheerful smile. "But that doesn't make it easy to find the right husband. If I had a fortune, I could have my pick of any man, but I don't, so I have to be particular. And living in a small village has its limits."

"But surely there have been suitors."

"There have," she agreed. But her gaze slid away.

He found every bit of her fascinating, and he leaned forward, forearms resting on his knees. "Well?"

With a loud sigh, she said, "Because you yourself fear intimacy, must you pry into mine?"

"I don't need to tell you that I don't fear intimacy," he said in a soft, low voice, giving her a meaningful look.

She glanced quickly at her maid, who still slumbered.

Daniel eased his boot beneath Grace's hem.

She held her skirts down and glared at him. "Stop it!" she hissed.

A damp curl fell over her forehead, and to his surprise, it took everything in him not to slide his finger along it, easing it back into place.

He grinned. "Then answer my question."

"Yes!" she whispered. "Yes, I've had suitors, and yes, one became close to me. Yes, I thought we would marry, but he had other ideas and broke my heart. But it has mended. Are you happy now?"

She flounced back in the seat, arms crossed below her breasts.

What other ideas had this suitor had? Perhaps he, too, had only wanted a mistress. Daniel's conscience gave a slight stir.

"I'm sorry to resurrect the memories," he found himself saying.

She shot him a curious glance, and he wondered what he'd accidentally revealed.

Ruby awoke before they could say anything else, and he let his eyes almost drift shut. Grace let down the windows, pointing out the scenery to her maid as if neither of them had ever been on a farm.

Daniel guessed it was all to keep from having to pay attention to him.

It was far too easy to talk with Grace, who was more interesting than other women. At least she wouldn't be able to complain, as his last mistress had, that he didn't talk to her.

If he subscribed to his cousin's worries, he'd think that Grace was trying to lure him into marriage. And she had just asked about it, of course. But he thought her motives were more to keep him distracted in conversation. They would be sleeping in the same house, rather sooner than she thought. He'd warned her he was going to show her his "charitable endeavors." And that meant a stop at Enfield Manor, where Viscount Wade was visiting his grandmother, just outside London. Though Simon Wade was engaged to be married, Daniel thought it must be rather easy to sneak about Simon's family home—after all, he was about to marry his grandmother's companion, and must have done some sneaking of his own.

If Daniel remembered correctly, there was a balcony that ran the length of the house, with a door for each bedroom.

Chapter 13

B efore midday, Grace noticed that the carriage was turning off the Great North Road. She sat up straighter, then with her elbow nudged Ruby, who'd been dozing. Both of them looked with suspicion at Daniel.

He smiled.

"Are we stopping for luncheon?" Grace asked.

"No."

She frowned. "Then where are we going?"

"You look as if I'm about to abduct the both of you to the Orient and sell you to the highest bidder."

"No, because that would only bring you money, something you don't need more of."

"And how do you know that?"

"One hears things."

"But a gambler always needs money."

She narrowed her eyes.

He gave a great sigh. "Very well. Allow me to remind you that I did promise to show you my charitable contribution to Society. Unlike most people, I give more than money. I give of my time."

Grace thought she heard Ruby cover a snort of laughter, but when she glanced at her, the maid was staring serenely out the window.

"You said you read to the blind," Grace said with skepticism.

Ruby was now silently quivering, covering her mouth.

"I do," he said solemnly.

Shaking her head, Grace sighed and looked out the window. It wasn't long before they turned off the road onto a narrow lane that led up to a pretty country mansion three floors high.

"Where are we?" she asked.

"Enfield Manor," he said, "home of the Dowager Viscountess Wade."

Then he waited, as if for her reaction. But the name wasn't familiar.

After directing Ruby to the kitchens for refreshment, the butler showed them inside to a sunny drawing room where sheer draperies billowed with the breeze coming in tall windows. A woman rose to her feet.

"Miss Shelby," said the butler, "may I present Mr. Throckmorten and Miss Banbury."

Both women curtsied while Daniel gave a brief bow. Miss Shelby was an attractive young lady, tall, with the reddest hair Grace had ever seen.

Miss Shelby gave a glad smile and came forward, letting Daniel take her hand. "Daniel, it is so good to see you. I'm certain that the butler went off to tell Simon of your arrival. He'll be here momentarily. Do sit down."

Grace followed the two and took a seat in a comfortable wingback chair. Miss Shelby turned to her.

"Miss Banbury, how nice to meet you," the other woman said. "I admit my surprise that Daniel is visiting accompanied by a lady."

"Thank you for the gracious welcome, Miss Shelby," Grace said. "Mr. Throckmorten and I are on our way to inspect property of mine that he has recently acquired."

"Inspecting property?" said a deep voice from the doorway.

Grace turned and held her breath in surprise. A tall, handsome blond man stood alone, and although he wore a genial smile, the amusement did not carry to his eyes. And then Grace saw the cane he held in front of him, and she realized that the viscount was blind. She felt sorrow move through her, but from his winning smile, she imagined he would not want her to feel that way.

Unaccompanied, he walked farther into the room, and to her amazement, he neatly avoided a chair and a table. They all stood up.

Daniel said, "Lord Wade, may I present my traveling companion, Miss Banbury."

"My lord, it is good to meet you," Grace said, sweeping into a curtsy. She felt awkward when it seemed that the viscount was looking right at her, but of course, he could tell where her voice was coming from.

Viscount Wade reached out a hand, and Miss Shelby took it, drawing him smoothly forward. To

Grace's surprise, Miss Shelby leaned against him briefly, and he placed a kiss on the top of her head. Then he sat down at her side, and tilted his head toward Daniel.

"So, now you have ladies inspecting property with you?"

The two men smiled, and Grace felt uncomfortable, as if those words implied a different meaning.

Miss Shelby eyed her with sympathy. "You two gentlemen are always giving a woman reason to ignore you, are they not, Miss Banbury?"

Grace nodded, feeling relieved at Miss Shelby's open geniality. "I guess they cannot help themselves—at least Mr. Throckmorten cannot."

"I will let you in on a secret," Miss Shelby said, leaning toward her but not lowering her voice. "Lord Wade has a terrible habit of saying one thing and meaning another. It is amazing I agreed to marry him, with all the flaws he has."

Grace smiled. "Congratulations on your engagement."

"Thank you," she said, glancing her fiancé, who could not see her.

But Lord Wade was smiling with such fondness that it was obvious who was the focus of his attention.

"I wish my employer could be here to meet you," Miss Shelby continued.

Grace frowned with confusion. The lady was a servant?

Lord Wade said, "My grandmother, who is in

London for several days with my sister, dotes on Daniel. Thinks he's a good influence on me."

If Grace had been sipping tea, she'd have spit it out. As it was, she took a breath and risked a frank question. "Miss Shelby, you work for the viscountess?"

"I am her companion."

"Was," Lord Wade added. "Now she's a future granddaughter-in-law."

Grace looked on Miss Shelby with a new light. Obviously working for her living had not ruined the lady. She had made a good match. "Miss Shelby, did you enjoy your employment?" she said, hoping the question sounded like innocent conversation.

But she saw Daniel's quick frown.

"Lady Wade was an excellent employer," Miss Shelby said. "So kind and gracious."

"She has to say that now," Lord Wade said, one corner of his mouth quirked up in a smile. "But her first situation was not as favorable."

"You mean because I didn't spend it with you," Miss Shelby answered.

Though her tone was light, Grace sensed that the lady masked her real feelings. There was always a risk that an employer could treat an impoverished woman with little respect. Grace glanced at Lord Wade. But then again, these two were engaged, and had met under such an unusual situation. She decided to talk to Miss Shelby in private when she had the chance.

Grace turned to the viscount. "Lord Wade, I

hope you can clear up a misunderstanding for me. Mr. Throckmorten made you seem like a man who needed his attention. To make himself more impressive in my eyes—"

Daniel coughed.

"—he claimed that you needed him to read to you."

Miss Shelby grinned as she looked askance at Daniel, and Lord Wade turned the focus of his gaze on him as well.

"Did he?" Lord Wade said. "It seems to me that he visits in an attempt to best me, which is destined to fail."

"To best you?" Grace said with curiosity.

"At rowing," Daniel offered. "He's a master at it, and the rest of us are just pretenders."

Rowing? she thought with surprise.

"I think it's time to give you a demonstration," the viscount said, getting to his feet.

Miss Shelby rose as well and slid her arm through his. "I think it's time for luncheon first. After that, you boys may show off to us admiring females."

Grace found herself relaxing the longer she was with Lord Wade and Miss Shelby. They were obviously very much in love and very happy. It made Grace sigh with a pleasant sort of envy. She studied Daniel as surreptitiously as she could, because she didn't think she'd ever seen him so relaxed and full of amusement. It made her realize that he kept a reserve about him in London, as if he didn't want people to get too close. She had seen that armor lower briefly around his cousin the duke, but now she was getting a better view.

And . . . she finally admitted to herself that she liked him like this. And she liked his choice in friends.

But did they know about his gambling habits? Did they know that he not only won large properties but people, too? She would not be the one to disappoint them with such news. They didn't need to know the depths her family had sunk to.

After luncheon, all four of them went out onto the terrace, where they were joined by two menservants. Grace could see where the ground sloped down away from the house with a sprawling garden. Beyond that was a small lake, gleaming every time the sun peeked out from behind the clouds.

Grace watched as Lord Wade used his cane to help himself down the stairs. Then to her surprise, she saw a raised wooden banister leading the way down a path. Lord Wade put his hand on it and began to walk, not stopping his conversation with Daniel.

"Do you like my little addition to the garden?" Miss Shelby asked, as they followed the men.

Grace turned to smile at her. "So the banister was your idea? I'm impressed."

"Simon maneuvers the house so well that I always thought it a shame he had to rely on other people to walk about his grandmother's estate. I had these installed at his home in Derbyshire, too. We're going there after the wedding in a few months."

At the lake, Miss Shelby guided Grace to a bench, where they watched the four men get into two boats tied up to the pier.

"Simon can row by himself," Miss Shelby said, "but of course he needs someone to navigate. Daniel also has a servant, to make the weight even between the boats."

"Ah." Grace sat back to enjoy the race, and found herself pleasantly surprised when Lord Wade moved out almost immediately into the lead.

Miss Shelby sighed. "He never lets anybody else win."

"And he shouldn't."

They were quiet for several minutes, and Grace received the impression that Miss Shelby was trying to think how to broach a delicate topic. Grace found herself feeling more and more tense. Would she have to explain how she and Daniel had met? She hadn't even thought about a story for that.

"Miss Banbury," Miss Shelby began slowly, "you seemed very interested in my former occupation."

Grace relaxed. "I am, for I am considering the same thing."

"Though I do not know your situation, please accept my sympathy. You were obviously raised a lady, and resorting to employment is a difficult— and brave—thing to do."

"Thank you, but as I'm sure you already know, we do what we must. I do have a small dowry, but due to legalities decided by my late father, I cannot touch it until marriage."

"And you find yourself in . . . dire straits?"

There was so much compassion in her blue eyes that Grace had to look away. "Yes, our family circumstances have changed. Though I can find employment, my brother is now left landless." Her voice trailed off, and the tears she'd thought she put behind her almost surfaced again. She would never get over this feeling of betrayal, this anger toward her mother.

"I understand. He is yet unmarried?"

Grace only nodded. She was so caught up in her thoughts that it took her a moment to realize that the boats were now headed back to the near shore, and Lord Wade would easily win. But Daniel was pushing hard, almost lifting himself off the seat as he tried to row with more and more speed. Then quite suddenly one oar entered the water on an unusual angle, the boat tipped, and Daniel and his servant fell in.

Grace and Miss Shelby surged to their feet, running down the gravel path and onto the pier.

Lord Wade was already tying up his boat, but he gave them a bright smile. "I hear there's a mishap. I do hope he can swim," he added with a chuckle.

Daniel and the servant were both swimming well. Thank goodness they had already shed their coats. They trudged out of the water onto shore, dripping wet. Grace didn't bother to turn her gaze away from Daniel's nearly transparent shirt. Whenever he tried to seduce her, he never re- moved any of his own clothing first. She hoped he didn't realize that might help his efforts because she was far too fascinated with his body.

Miss Shelby led Daniel inside to change, and Grace followed at a slower pace with Lord Wade. The silence between them was comfortable, and she remarked casually on the beauty of the estate. But here was an opportunity to talk to a friend of Daniel's, to learn something about him.

"My lord, might we sit together in the sunshine for a moment?"

His expression remained friendly as he nodded, and she realized how much emotion she usually read in someone's eyes by its lack with him.

She hesitantly asked, "Shall I tell you where the chair is?"

His cane tapped the table in front of him, and he said good-naturedly, "Is there a chair to the right?"

"There is."

He found it with his cane, positioned himself before it, and sat down.

"We do not know each other well, my lord," she said, "but I must tell you how impressed I am at your ease with your blindness." She hardly dared believe she was speaking so forwardly to a vis- count, but there was something about Lord Wade that encouraged openness.

"It wasn't so, at first, I'm afraid. It was a recent injury. Louisa—Miss Shelby—made me realize that I could do more on my own than I thought."

"You are lucky to have one another," she said softly.

He turned his head toward her, and she had the strange feeling he was studying her.

She spoke quickly. "My lord, how long have you known Mr. Throckmorten?"

"Since boyhood. We were at school together."

She hesitated, and then decided that Lord Wade would end her questions when he wanted to. "My father died when I was young, just like Mr. Throckmorten's. It must have been terribly difficult for him."

Lord Wade said nothing for a moment, and Grace gave a soft sigh, knowing that she would learn nothing personal about Daniel.

"I didn't know him before that," Lord Wade finally said. "He came to school so determined to do well, perhaps to prove to his father's memory that he would be fine. It wasn't until he was with the other boys that he heard the rumors."

She winced. "Children can be so cruel."

"And it's particularly terrible when all you have left is one parent, and the world thinks she's a murderer. By then, he'd already given up his music, so I think he was looking for a way to cope."

Given up his music? Grace thought in surprise. What did that mean? "And how did he cope?"

"He fought. He fought every boy, no matter how big, who maligned his mother. Finally, they reassessed the situation and backed down."

"But he made sure, even when he was an adult, that they kept talking about him," Grace said slowly, as if to herself.

Lord Wade arched a brow, a faint smile on his face. "You know him well."

"No, I cannot profess that. But in some ways Mr. Throckmorten's behavior makes sense. I did not realize that he composed music like his parents."

"No, not that. He once said to me that they heard the music in their minds and tried to make it work on paper. Music only came out through his hands and fingers, through playing."

"The piano?"

"Yes, and many other instruments. His cousin told me he was quite gifted for one so young."

Grace thought about a little boy losing his father, throwing away what he loved best to do. He had gone off to school, leaving his grieving mother, and finding himself in a world of bullies who made him fight.

"Simon, you make it sound so dramatic," Daniel said in a bland voice as he left the house.

Grace felt a guilty shiver move through her. He wouldn't appreciate her gossiping about him. But she lifted her chin and stared at him, challenging him to say something about it.

He studied her for a moment, before he lightly said, "Simon, do you mind if I take Miss Banbury on a walk through your garden? She's fond of plants."

He barely bothered to make a legitimate excuse.

Lord Wade sat back, tapping his fingers on the table, smiling. "By all means. We'll see you both at dinner?"

"Of course," Grace said as she rose. "Have a good afternoon, my lord."

"And if you're bored, Daniel, I do have a few books that need to be read to me."

But Daniel had already taken her arm and was leading her down the stairs. Their feet crunched on the gravel path; the scent of roses wafted over her. The birds chirped in the garden, and somewhere in the distance horses whinnied to one another. It would have been a lovely afternoon if she hadn't been able to feel the heat of anger radiating off Daniel.

"I can't seem to bring you anywhere, can I," he said smoothly.

She laughed. "I don't remember being given much of a choice."

"And so this is your punishment?"

"Punishment?" She took a deep breath, trying to disguise her annoyance. "I was entertaining your friend while you were gone. Was I supposed to ignore him?"

"Then why did you talk about music?"

"I asked him how long he knew you, and things progressed from there."

She watched his handsome profile, the slim

blade of his proud nose, the way his eyes seemed so unreadable. She was used to seeing desire there—he did not even try to hide that from her. He had allowed her to know such intimate intentions.

But she was not supposed to know other details of his life? How could she help him if he shut her out of so much that made him who he was?

"You could tell me about your music," she said boldly.

At last his expression thawed, and he glanced at her. A lock of his brown hair fell forward over his brow, still wet from his tumble into the lake. She found she wanted to brush it back, a tender gesture that disturbed her.

"There's nothing to tell. I was a little boy with two musical parents. Of course they tried to make me love it, too. Apparently it didn't work."

"So it isn't just your mother who wants nothing to do with music. I think you misled me."

"I disagree."

She sensed the rising tension in him, knew she was asking for trouble, forcing his attention. And the only way he wanted to give it to her was—

He suddenly dragged her off the path and into a copse of trees.

"Daniel!" she cried softly, pushing at his chest when he pulled her against him.

"Since you're so interested in me, you must be interested in this."

And then he kissed her, and as usual, heat and need merged until she wanted to cling to his clothing to pull him closer. He opened her mouth with skill, forced her head back. Somewhere nearby they could hear the low murmur of gardeners talking.

And the threat of discovery only fueled the fire raging between them.

He pulled back a bit, nipping at her lips with his, nibbling a path along her jaw, and then tugging at her earlobe.

"We'll be staying in the same house tonight," he murmured hoarsely.

She closed her eyes, trying to remember how to think. "You would not dare something scandalous here in the home of your friend."

He lifted his face and smiled down at her, all smooth sensuality and boldness. "Wouldn't I?"

He moved his hips, and she felt the thrust of his thigh between hers.

She pushed him away. "You wouldn't!"

"But I only have so many days left. You cannot believe I would waste such an opportunity."

"But Lord Wade—"

"Is a man. Do you think he avoids his fiancée, who lives right here with him?"

Grace blinked in surprise. She'd always felt that such indecencies were her own flaws.

"But his grandmother, his sister—"

"This is a big house, Grace. When one is willing . . ." He trailed off suggestively.

She felt his hand slide from her waist downward, curving over her hip. When she pushed hard against him, at last he let her go. She turned and bent forward to peer out between the shrubberies.

"Oh, yes," he murmured.

To her shock, he pulled her back against him, his hips into her backside. She covered her mouth against a gasp, heard voices even closer, and by squirming she at last convinced him to let her go. Only a moment later, she was walking serenely on the path as if she'd never left it.

Daniel caught up to her. He looked amused and aroused and—

How did he so easily know how to appeal to her? She was falling under his spell, under everything he did to her, and she had to find a way to distract him.

"Would you mind telling me how Lord Wade became blind?" she asked.

"Yes, if you'll tell me why you were so interested in Louisa's former employment."

"That is easy," she said lightly. "Surely you must know I have to find a way to support myself."

When she glanced at him, he was frowning, and he looked away as if he didn't wish her to see his expression.

Did it bother him to remember his part in bringing her family down?

And why was it so easy for her to forget?

Chapter 14

Daniel knew she'd been making plans, unlike other women who might have the vapors over the thought of a precarious future. He knew something of what Louisa Shelby had gone through as a companion before she'd come to the Wade household. He didn't want to think about Grace facing the same thing—young men who thought they owned their servants and could do as they pleased.

"Or perhaps I don't need plans," she said conversationally. "Because of course I will win the violin."

And then, while he was still trying to sort through his own confusion, she blindsided him.

"Did you not say the first night we met that you only wanted the violin?" she asked. "For a man who has given up music, the possession of a violin seems strange."

"It's not. I told you that my father once owned the same instrument."

But he didn't think she believed that as his motive.

"We have covered two subjects that neither of us is comfortable with," she said, swinging her arms briskly as she walked. "Let's agree to avoid them and discuss Lord Wade."

"I'm surprised you didn't hear about his injury," Daniel said mildly. "It was the talk of the *ton*, especially since Simon cut a swath with the ladies before that."

"You forget that I seldom left Hertingfordbury."

"He was thrown from his horse and hit his head. Within a couple of days, his sight was gone."

"He is a very brave man," she said. "And he was here, staying with his grandmother, when he courted Miss Shelby?"

He nodded, narrowing his eyes as he wondered about her purpose.

"Then perhaps I shall be just as lucky."

Though he hadn't noticed, the house was before them, and she was able to quicken her pace to reach the stairs before him. Though he watched the sway of her hips as she ascended, even that could not distract him from his thoughts.

She could not possibly believe that Louisa's luck wasn't rare.

He didn't want her thinking about making a living. He felt foolish, but he found himself wanting to distract her, so when they both reached the empty terrace, he caught her arm and leaned near.

"Don't forget about the private dance you owe me for my charitable dances last night."

She caught her breath. He was so in communion

with her body that he felt the fine trembling in her arm.

"Certainly Enfield Manor is not the place—"

"I'll decide the place." And then he moved ahead of her. "I'll see you at dinner."

That evening, Grace was no longer surprised to see how easily Lord Wade had overcome his disability as he ate freely with them. He and Daniel and Miss Shelby discussed the people they knew in London, and it was obvious they had all moved smoothly through the circles of Society. They always made her feel included, as if they told their stories for her amusement and not just for their own reminiscing.

"And how is Martindale since his father's death?" Lord Wade asked.

Grace remembered immediately that Martindale was the young earl who'd sold his family's ancestral land to Daniel. How would Daniel feel when he had to tell his friend what had happened?

"Struggling," Daniel admitted.

"You've done all you can for him," Miss Shelby said softly.

Grace frowned. Did they not know the truth? Though Martindale needed to sell his land, there were many in London who thought Daniel took advantage of that.

"He had no one else he could trust to hold on to the estate for him," Lord Wade said.

Daniel shrugged. "His father put the family

through hard times with his wasteful spending. At least young Martindale deserves a chance to dig his way out."

And Daniel's money would help, Grace thought. But hold on to the land? Did Daniel mean to . . . sell it back to the young earl when Martindale was ready?

Daniel had acted out of kindness, not as a man only looking for a good investment. And he would never tell anyone the truth of what he'd done.

Except for his friends, of course.

But not her. For the first time she felt left out. Daniel didn't owe her any explanations for the way he conducted his life. She was a challenge to him, a new amusement that he had yet to grow tired of.

It was she who kept changing how she saw him and their relationship, and it couldn't be good for her. In the end, when he didn't receive what he wanted from her, she probably wouldn't see him again. She didn't know how she felt about that.

Grace very carefully locked her door, waiting until Miss Shelby had gone, so the woman wouldn't be offended. There was already a bath steaming before the bare hearth, with towels and soaps laid where she could reach.

Then she realized that Ruby was waiting for her.

Grace smiled. "That bath looks wonderful, Ruby. Thank you. How has your day been?"

As she helped Grace undress, Ruby chatted for

several minutes about the people she'd met and
the way the household worked. But Grace kept
getting the feeling that Ruby had questions that
she didn't feel comfortable asking. She *had* been
alone with Grace and Daniel all morning in the
carriage.

After several moments of silence, when Grace
was finally down to her chemise, Ruby said, "Ye
haven't won the violin yet, miss, since ye're still
bein' with him."

Grace paused in the act of testing the water.
Straightening her shoulders, she gave her maid a
smile. "Not yet. But I'm closer. He won't be able to
hold back a family heirloom for long."

"I hope it all turns out as ye wish, miss."

When Ruby hesitated as if she would say more,
Grace pleasantly said, "I won't need you anymore
tonight, Ruby. Sleep well."

Ruby's look was worried, and Grace felt guilty,
but she only kept smiling until the maid had left
the room. And then Grace turned the key in the
door.

With a groan, she let her chemise fall to the
floor and stepped into the bathing tub. The water
was the perfect temperature, and she leaned
her head back against the rim and sighed with
pleasure.

She heard the faintest click.

"Ruby, did you forget something?" She opened
her eyes and turned her head toward the door, but
of course it hadn't opened. She'd locked it.

"No, but you did."

Her head turned so fast she was surprised she didn't injure her neck. Daniel stood just inside the tall glass door that led out onto the balcony.

She thought he would smile in triumph, but his look was more intense, more brooding than she would have imagined, as if he'd thought about her all day—and he hadn't liked the distraction.

"I didn't realize that was a door," she said between gritted teeth, even as her mind raced frantically. What could he see from across the room? She hadn't even begun to soap herself yet, so there were no bubbles to hide her. She wanted to fling the facecloth over her breasts, but that would only show how vulnerable she felt—as if she thought she had something to fear. And she didn't. All she had to do was say no.

Sometimes it amazed her how easily she trusted his word.

But could she trust his control? Or her own?

Ever since she'd first found him in her town house at night, she had worried when he might next walk in on her. Every bath had been rushed, and she'd only felt safe changing when Ruby was in the room.

But she'd never imagined that he would dare such a thing in the home of his friend.

He began to walk toward her.

"Daniel, stay there!"

But he ignored her, and at last, she pulled two facecloths from the stand beside her and tried to arrange them over her breasts and loins. They floated precariously, and she had to wedge one between her thighs and hold the other down with both hands.

And then he was above her, looking down.

She couldn't breathe. She felt foolish covering herself from him. He'd already seen her bosom—goodness, he'd even licked her there.

He leaned over and rested his hands on the rim of the tub. He didn't try to disguise the way his gaze moved from her wet knees above the water, across the expanse of her body, and up to her face.

"You're not going to scream," he said softly.

To her dismay, it had never even occurred to her. "I might if you don't leave this instant."

"But Grace, I have only days left."

"A week," she quickly amended. "And that's long enough for you to find some other way to attempt your seduction. You've invaded my privacy!" She wanted to sound angry and cool, but her voice was hesitant because she had to work so hard to think of things to say.

Instead of thinking that she was naked in front of him, and it was far too exciting.

"Do you want me to leave because you trust yourself so little?" he asked softly.

Smooth man that he was, he knew just what to say to rouse her defenses. "Of course not." She forced herself to speak coolly and hoped her expression was relaxed. The challenge would be to pretend he did not affect her.

How could she win at that?

Everything he did affected her now. She could

not remember what it was like to despise him for his flaws—his gambling, his scandals.

"If someone finds you here," she said, "your own strategies will fail you. And I won't find myself forced to marry a man I don't love."

"That won't happen. No one saw me enter."

He began to move, circling about the tub as if he wanted to see her at all angles. When he was behind her, she tensed, wondering if he was about to let her hair down, as he preferred. She looked over one shoulder and then the other, but all he did was lightly tug her earlobe.

"You could pretend I'm not here," he murmured. "I won't mind."

"So I'm supposed to wash myself in front of you? I think not."

As if he hadn't heard her, he continued, "But of course I might get wet. And I wouldn't want my clothing ruined."

He walked to the end of the tub, and to her dismay, he shrugged out of his coat and laid it across a chair.

"Stop that this instant!" she demanded, although just the sight of his broad shoulders covered with only light linen made something ignite deep inside her, a tiny flame that wouldn't be ignored.

"I think it would look far more suspicious if someone saw me with wet clothing." He sounded as conversational as if they faced each other across a tea tray in a drawing room.

He untied his cravat and slid it from around his neck. His gaze never left hers, and she found her mouth too dry to form words. He loosened his collar and opened the buttons at the top of his shirt. His bare throat was strangely erotic, but that was nothing compared to when he suddenly pulled his shirt out of his trousers and over his head.

Her mouth sagged open before she somehow remembered to close it. He was perfectly formed, all smooth muscle and skin. In her only previous intimate encounters with a man, they'd been so rushed that most of their clothes remained on. This was the first time she'd laid eyes on a man's naked chest, and she could now see why it was such a forbidden thing. He was magnificent. All she could think about was touching and exploring. She had a wild need to press up against him and—

She realized that the facecloth at her bosom was floating away. She made a hurried grab for it, trying to spread it wide, and then suddenly he took it from her hand and lifted it away.

She tilted her head back and stared up at him, and what she saw in his face made her forget about covering herself. Hunger, stark and needy, as if he would die without what she could give him.

A distant part of her warned that this was what he wanted her to think; another part of her remembered that he could only do what she allowed him. Couldn't he?

But there was a traitorous wanton inside her, who reveled as his hot gaze moved across her naked breasts. The water was no cover, although it distorted as it lapped at the upper slopes.

He reached for the soap, not taking his eyes from her, and lathered the facecloth.

"What are you doing?" she asked faintly, already knowing, already scandalized and aroused.

"You need to be washed."

His voice was hoarse, and it rasped along the edges of her nerves, as if he scraped his nails across her flesh. She gripped the edges of the tub, knowing she should stop him but feeling a rising thrill at the risk.

He was her weakness, and she could not deny herself his touch. Just his touch, nothing else.

She sounded desperate, even in her own mind.

He lifted her left arm from the rim of the tub and began to wash it in slow, gentle circles. She closed her eyes and held back a moan. His ministrations felt wonderful and gentle. He worked his way up her arm, and she gave a little gasp as the facecloth brushed the side of her sensitive breast. He moved to the other arm and did the same thing, then to her shoulders and neck. Inside, her emotions swirled together, pleasure and awareness and rising passion.

"Lean forward," he whispered.

Without questioning him, she did, expecting to feel the cloth scrub her skin. After a pause, she stiffened as she realized that his soapy hands were bare. He rubbed and stroked, sliding his large hands up and down her back. His strokes went wider and wider, until he just teased the edges of her breasts. She gave a moan and a shiver.

She couldn't think of any reason to stop him. That should have alerted her, but any silent alarms in her mind had long since faded away.

He pulled her back, and as she stretched and arched with satisfaction, his hands slid from her shoulders and down over her breasts. The shocking pleasure of it eased a groan from her. His head was next to hers, and he nipped along her neck and shoulder. His hands kneaded and cupped her breasts, and when his fingers gently rubbed her nipples, she felt desire spread out through her body, racing along her skin, sensitizing every part of her to his touch. She leaned her head back against his shoulder, arched until her breasts were even deeper into his hands. His breath on her cheek was a hot caress, and it seemed only natural to turn her head and meet his lips with hers.

Passion spiraled through her as his tongue invaded her mouth. She met it with her own, dueled and won her own entrance. He tasted of brandy and himself. She had a wild urge to pull him closer to lick more of his skin.

He broke the kiss and slid his hands away from her breasts. "You're still quite dirty," he said, his expression serious.

To her shame, she whimpered at the loss of his touch.

But she didn't have long to wait. He moved

to the far end of the tub, and now she was able to watch him from beneath lowered eyelids. He soaped his hands, then took one foot and began to rub. She had not thought that her feet could feel such pleasure. He worked his way up her ankles and calves, but it wasn't until he reached her knees that she could summon any intelligent thought.

He wasn't going to stop.

She didn't want him to stop.

What kind of woman did that make her?

With heavy eyes, she watched his concentration. Not every man would care about her pleasure, she knew from experience. As his fingers began to trail up her right thigh, she wanted to press her legs together, but they felt boneless and heavy, no longer at her command. All of her concentration and awareness was centered on the feel of his fingers, her burning skin, and the way the depths of her body felt on fire with need for his touch.

Her legs sagged open, the cloth covering her floated away. His fingers combed gently through the hair covering her womanhood, and she bit her lip to stop her cries of pleasure. She rolled her head back and forth, body quivering, tense with waiting and wanting. At last his questing fingers moved deeper, circling, stroking, finding the center of her and stoking the fire. She had never imagined such pleasure, could not control her need to be ever higher.

She was on the edge of a new sensation when something insistent intruded on her thoughts. She couldn't push it away, couldn't let herself relax until she knew.

She opened her eyes and tried to close her weak limbs.

He looked up at her in surprise. "Grace?"

"This—this pleasure you give me . . . it doesn't mean you've won," she whispered hoarsely.

His mouth quirked up in a tight smile. "No. When I'm inside you, you'll know I've won."

She narrowed her eyes, gasping, even as he continued to gently stroke and tease her. "Never."

"You dare much," he said, his smile widening into a grin.

And then he came down over her, lifting her up so that he could take her nipple deep into his mouth. His fingers picked up the rhythm at her core, the water churned around her as she stiffened and gasped. An explosion seemed to go off inside her, and Daniel's mouth was suddenly on hers, swallowing the cries she could not control. The shudders of pleasure moved through her, were part of her. She didn't want them to end, so overwhelmed was she by how he could make her feel.

At last she was able to open her eyes and truly see him. He didn't look smug or victorious. He reached to brush a damp curl out of her eye, and she thought she saw . . . tenderness.

It was gone only a moment later. She wondered if she had imagined it, because now he was wearing a faint smile, though there were marks of strain bracketing his mouth.

"Have you been well pleasured, my lady?" he asked in a low voice.

"You know I have." She felt awkward, unsure of herself, because he had not received the same pleasure.

She stared at him solemnly, and it took every ounce of shattered control not to reach out and touch him, feel that smooth skin. She knew he'd be hot to the touch, and she longed to press herself to him and experience more.

But this was what he wanted. He was waiting for her to give in. With her mouth set in a grim line, she said nothing. His eyes grew shuttered, impassive, and at last he rose to his feet. In the instant before he turned back to his clothing, she saw the long ridge of his arousal, so obvious in his tight trousers.

She told herself she would not feel guilty—she hadn't asked for his attentions. As she silently watched him dress, he completed every button and tied his cravat impatiently. She knew he did this in case someone saw him strolling on the balcony. He did this for her, because she'd asked him to keep their challenge a secret from the beginning.

Because if they were discovered, he would not marry her.

She had always had a thread of cynicism moving through her; it came from having a mother who let her down so frequently. But she hated to feel it in herself now. She couldn't trust him—but she wanted to.

Impeccably dressed once more, he turned back to her. "Shall I help you out?"

"I still have to wash my hair."

He bowed deeply, as if she'd done him some kind of honor rather than just allowed him the liberties she had. He walked to the balcony door, opened it, and closed it behind him.

With a groan, she closed her eyes and sank beneath the water, wetting her hair. She felt tender and tingly and new inside, as if the insight into what could happen with a considerate lover had changed her. Now she knew what true unselfish intimacy was all about.

What would she do tomorrow night if he came to her again? She would be in her own home—now his home, she thought with a start of sadness—but that wouldn't stop him. He was determined, and time was counting down. She told herself to feel relieved that she'd rebuffed him again, but she knew better.

Every time they were alone, she gave up more and more. If he pressed her harder, if he laid her down on the bed and rose naked above her, would she surrender at last? If she glimpsed that look of tenderness on his face again, the one that made her feel special to him, what would she do? The drowsy, pleasurable haze he inspired with his hands and mouth made her confused and certain of only one thing—that she wanted him. She wanted to burn like this again, and to know that he was consumed by the flames as well.

Chapter 15

Daniel knew he wasn't himself in the morning. He ate breakfast in the dining room with Simon, Louisa, and Grace, and the three of them chattered away like old friends. He could barely pay attention to the conversation, so consumed was he by thoughts of Grace.

Except for avoiding his gaze, she acted . . . completely normal.

And he was terribly frustrated, in both mind and body.

He had thought teaching her the pleasures she could experience would finally make her lose control. For just a moment when he'd stood above her bathing tub, he'd thought she would at last surrender to him.

But she'd drawn on a deep reservoir of strength and sent him away.

Fool that he was, afterward he had stood outside her room and tortured himself more by peering through the draperies to watch her washing her hair. And then she'd risen gracefully to her feet, all glistening nude beauty, and poured a bucket of water over her head to sluice away the soap. Her body had still blushed pink where he'd caressed her.

He had groaned aloud, there in the dark, separated from the light and warmth that was Grace.

He had returned to his room and paced for several hours, feeling for the first time that he might not win this challenge. He had satisfied her, but he'd been the one left wanting and needing her.

He gave a start at the table, realizing that Louisa was speaking, although not to him.

"I'll be visiting London next month," she was saying to Grace. "Please pay me a call. We can attend the symphony together, and I'm certain I can introduce you to many gentlemen you'll approve of."

Simon cleared his throat but remained silent. Louisa pointedly ignored him. Daniel barely kept himself from frowning. Now Louisa was matchmaking?

"How kind of you," Grace replied, looking delighted.

Daniel distanced himself from his confused thoughts, watching Grace's look of interest. He should be happy for her. She had a dowry, and she needed a husband. Louisa would certainly find her someone nice.

Someone Grace could trust. Because he knew he was not that kind of man.

It was more difficult than normal to hide his bad mood when they took their leave of Enfield Manor. Rain was pouring down as the carriage began the day's journey north. Keeping the windows raised made the carriage hot and stuffy, and Grace fanned herself occasionally, but there was also a restless nervousness to her that had her tapping her toes and fidgeting. She kept giving him curious looks, and he finally pretended to go to sleep. It wasn't difficult because he'd had a restless night dreaming about her. He was finding himself vastly annoyed with this challenge and the difficulty of winning it.

But hadn't he been bored with his life before Grace fell into it? Hadn't easily winning everything he tried proved no challenge at all?

And now Grace was livening up his days, challenging his evenings, wandering through his dreams at night. Why was he even complaining?

He found his temper improving through the morning, and by the time they reached the village of Hertingfordbury, nestled amidst rolling hills by the river Maran, he was looking forward to seeing where Grace was raised. But as his demeanor improved, hers wilted. What did she think would happen? Or was she afraid of how it would look to her staff for her to appear in company with a man?

Her family property, Maran Park, was a prosperous farm that bordered the river and spread across acres of sheep pasture and grainfields. The manor itself was rectangular, two stories with a columned portico in the front, which made it handy to drive the carriage beneath to escape the rain.

Daniel descended first, and then turned to help the women down.

As Ruby started up the stairs, Grace took her arm. "I have not alerted the household to the new owner. Please allow me to do so before you say anything."

"Aye, miss," the maid said, and disappeared inside.

Daniel stood alone with Grace, trying to read her expression.

"Is it good to be home?" he asked softly.

She gave him a quick frown. "You mean your home?"

He winced inwardly as he realized his stupidity. Of course for her this place would have good memories—and bad, because it was no longer hers.

But he could not regret having been involved in a card game with Mrs. Banbury. It had brought Grace into his life. And Mrs. Banbury might have lost the properties to someone who wouldn't care about preserving them for the family, like he did.

But he couldn't tell her that, for the game would be over.

Daniel gave her a moment to collect herself. He had wanted to have her safely away from London while he had Horace Jenkins investigated. Daniel had also wanted to be alone with her as much as possible—which had worked well at Enfield Manor.

But he had foolishly underestimated her reaction to Maran Park. He had taken it away from her, left her homeless, and she would be even more reminded of it here. Her sadness and his regret would not lead to seduction, not tonight.

"I'll introduce you to the steward and the housekeeper first," Grace said with a sigh. "Their offices are in a corridor near the kitchens."

The meeting with the servants went as well as could be expected, Grace thought. The steward seemed unsurprised at the change of ownership, as if it were long anticipated. Her fears that someone would discover the wager hadn't materialized, probably because they all just assumed that her mother had finally had to sell the property for the money. The weight of relief that lifted from Grace made her breathe easily for the first time all day. Her secrets were still safe.

Daniel was competent and authoritative as he agreed that the staff should remain the same. After that, everyone breathed easier, and a cheerful kitchen staff served them luncheon in the dining room.

Daniel sat at the head of the table, and Grace at his right. When the footman set down their plates and left the room, she forked through her mutton cutlets, and then finally looked up at him.

He was chewing slowly and watching her.

Something tugged deep inside her, a heavy feeling of budding pleasure, but she forced herself to ignore it. They would be alone in the house tonight but for the servants, and she needed all her powers of resistance.

And all she could think about was that he had
seen her completely naked.

It had been difficult to spend the morning facing
him, and she'd been relieved when he'd slept. But
now, looking into his knowing eyes, she felt like
she might never stop blushing. His hands had
been between her legs, his mouth on her breasts.
Even though she'd experienced all of these embar-
rassments with Baxter Wells, it had felt different.
For one thing, she'd thought she'd been in love
with Baxter, and he with her. With crudity, he had
disabused her of that notion.

"Are you going to look at me?" he asked softly.

She glanced worriedly at the door to the kitchens, then back at him. "Of course."

"I am sorry that my being here hasn't been easy
for you."

She arched a brow in surprise. "It is difficult."

"I thought you might want to speak with your
servants without me present, so I'll take the carriage to visit my mother this evening and return
for you tomorrow."

She blinked at him. He was leaving? She told
herself she would be alone, at peace, in one of her
favorite places.

But it wasn't hers anymore. Her mother had
taken care of that. Her family wasn't here, and
she suddenly felt a loneliness that took her by
surprise.

But his home would be full of people—more
of his family, whom she wanted to meet. It was
the seat of the duke of Madingley, a palace, so

she heard, with at least a hundred servants, and grounds that stretched out as far as the eye could see.

Daniel had grown up there, with two happy parents, until a tragic accident. Then he'd been thrust into a world of mean little boys and rumors he'd had to defend against.

He could have turned out to be a much different man, colder, cynical. And on the surface, that was the image he let people see. But she saw below that, to a man who defended his mother, who helped a friend in a desperate situation. Perhaps she could better understand how to redeem him by meeting the rest of his family.

Daniel smiled at her. "You have no comment about my leaving?"

"I am . . . simply surprised. I will think on it and come up with the perfect response."

"Of course you will. Or perhaps you wish I wouldn't go."

She realized that she didn't want him to go without her. "I think you may go, but I will go with you."

His smile faded, and he studied her as if looking for a motive.

"You don't need to be so suspicious," she said. "Why would I not want to see where you grew up, now that you've seen the same about me?"

"I will consider it, but only if you tell me about your family and living here."

"And why would you care about that? It's not as if I can tell you anything about running a small country manor. I'm sure you already own dozens."

"Not quite," he said dryly.

"Then how many?"

With a smile, he said, "Five, including this one."

"And did you win them all?"

"Only this one. The rest were honestly purchased. So now I've answered your questions, and you need to answer mine. How old were you when your father died?"

"Nine."

"And that made your brother . . ."

"Eight. Not old enough to learn much from my father, but still, we were able to benefit from his influence. The memories are good ones. Edward wasn't able to go away to school, but he was tutored. Perhaps you'd think he wasn't missing much."

"I made valuable friends at school, which I've always appreciated," Daniel said neutrally.

She didn't ask him about the enemies he'd made. "Edward's tutoring led to my own education. He always made sure I could learn anything he was."

"And your mother didn't interfere?"

"No. I don't think she much cared, one way or another." She hadn't meant to say so much about her mother's shortcomings as a parent.

But at least Daniel didn't give her a look of pity, only interest. Though both of them had lost their fathers at a young age, their mothers had handled their grief in vastly different ways.

"Edward is still educating himself," Grace quickly said to change the subject. "I even saw him reading a book on the railways."

"Good, he's doing his assignment."

"Assignment?"

A brief look of annoyance crossed Daniel's face, and she knew it was directed at himself. She was beginning to know him well. "Too late, Daniel. You've already revealed it. What is going on between you and my brother?"

"Just some advising. I'm teaching him about wise investing, and I recommended he read up on the railways because that's where so much money is being made right now."

She put down her fork and stared at him in surprise. "You're trying to help my brother?"

"'Guide' would be a better word. You don't have to look so surprised," he added dryly.

"And why shouldn't I be surprised? Most people would be."

"Because you—and everyone else—seem to think I'm only out for my own betterment."

"You don't show the world much else, Daniel," she said gently. She felt . . . a softness deep inside her when she thought of him helping her brother. It wouldn't affect her relationship with Daniel, so surely he didn't do it because of her.

"I don't *have* to show the world such things." He wiped his mouth with a napkin, as if he suddenly couldn't wait to leave her.

"You encourage people to think the worst of you. You seduce young ladies," she admonished him.

"Every man does that."

"They do?"

He gave her this gentle smile that made her feel . . . strange, and then he lightly cupped her cheek. "You are an innocent, Grace."

He did not know the truth about her innocence. She pulled away. "What time are we leaving?"

His smile faded. "What if I don't wish to escort you?"

"Then I guess I'll have to return to London alone. Perhaps Edward has discovered the identity of the man watching the town house." She gave him a bright smile, knowing that he would not want her where he could not watch over her. It was a safe feeling, and it had been a long time since she'd felt safe.

He narrowed his eyes. "Your education held you in good stead. We'll leave in an hour, so that we can make it to Madingley Court before dark."

She pushed back her chair and rose as well. "Then I better hurry. Poor Ruby will have already begun to unpack."

When Grace would have turned away, he caught her arm and pulled her closer. She nervously glanced at the entrance to the kitchen corridor, but the door remained closed.

"No one is coming," he said softly, his breath lightly touching her ear.

She shuddered. "Why would you say that?"

"Because I am a duke's cousin, and they're all hoping that I'm courting you."

He was, but for the wrong reasons. She felt a sadness she didn't want to examine too closely.

"I think you just can't bear to be away from me," he said.

Then he nibbled her earlobe, and though she trembled, she didn't pull away.

"I think I'll be even safer under your mother's roof." She wished her voice were steadier.

"It's a big house."

"More places to escape from you."

"But you still owe me a private dance. I have not forgotten."

She looked up into his dark brown eyes, full of a warmth that made her feel too good. "Then I suggest you release me, so that we can get on with the chase."

Chapter 16

That evening, just after the sun had set, the carriage turned down a lane guarded by imposing stone columns on each side, signaling the entrance to Madingley Court.

Grace watched Daniel's face, but he betrayed no expression. He'd been almost reserved on the drive to his home, as if he were regretting bringing her. She had known this would happen. After all, his family might think that he was interested in marrying her, which was far from the truth. But perhaps she could use this to her advantage. How could Daniel be truly redeemed if not in the eyes of his family? She would let them think what they wanted about her, let them think that he was actually considering marriage. It would give them hope for his future. And perhaps he would see that his marriage would give his mother so much pleasure.

"So what should I know about your family?" Grace asked.

Daniel turned his impassive gaze from the window and back to her. Ruby was ignoring them, staring at the grounds of the ducal estate. Grace figured it must be so huge that it would be a while before the mansion came into view.

"Many of my family will be in London for the Season," Daniel said.

"But not your mother." She felt excited and nervous, and didn't understand why. But she would be seeing a side of Daniel that he'd kept hidden from her, and she was looking forward to it.

He tilted his head. "No, not my mother. You seem most curious about her."

"Of course! I've admired her symphony for much of my life—but I will not mention it," she added before he could speak. "Who else will be there?"

"My aunt Isabella, the duchess. She is not one for London."

Grace remembered that she was a Spaniard, and not of royalty. Her life could not have been easy among the *ton*.

"Her daughter Elizabeth is just out of the schoolroom, so she'll be with her mother. My aunt Rosa and her husband Professor Leland have just emerged from a year of mourning for their son, so they, too, are in London with both their daughters and daughter-in-law."

"You have a cousin who died? I am sorry."

"Matthew was killed in battle in India. They never found his body in the midst of a fire, so my aunt has had a difficult time worrying that he is not at peace. When I last saw them in town, I thought perhaps it was still too soon for her, for she had accepted only a few invitations."

"So only your mother, an aunt, and a cousin will be at Madingley Court."

"Disappointed?" he asked, while his mouth tilted in a half smile.

"Of course not. Fewer names for me to remember." And it was his mother whom she most wanted to meet. "Will they be bothered that you bring a woman home? Or is it a regular occurrence?"

He chuckled. "Not so regular, but you already know that. It's why you wanted to come."

She wished she didn't blush so easily. "Do not take for granted my curiosity. So how will you explain my presence? You'll of course want to make clear that you are not courting me."

"I'll make it clear," he said easily.

She felt a bit disappointed. "How?"

"We were looking over your property. How could I not visit my own mother when I'm nearby?"

She sat back, feeling satisfied. Though his face became shadowed in gloom as the light faded, they did not bother to light a lantern. When they took another turn, the woods on either side suddenly seemed brighter with a faint glow. Grace frowned and let her window down.

She couldn't hold back a gasp as she saw Madingley Court. It was a towering castle of pointed turrets and battlements and hundreds of windows, many of which were lit from within. The castle stood out against the blackness of the night, as if it had always protected Cambridgeshire from the dawn of knighthood.

"Rather large, isn't it?" Daniel said with amusement.

"Surely you must have gotten lost in there." Grace was unable to tear her gaze away.

"Only a time or two. Then I discovered it was far more fun to *pretend* to be lost."

"And worry your mother unnecessarily."

"Remember, she grew up here, too. She was not easily fooled. But others were."

"Your father."

He didn't answer, although his faint smile remained in place.

It took a long time for the carriage to drive past the castle, and then they turned into a courtyard and pulled up beneath a columned portico.

Daniel helped them out, and he must have seen Ruby gaping upward at the many floors, for he said, "Do not worry about finding your way around, Ruby. The housekeeper will take good care of you."

The entrance hall soared two stories above their heads, with statues in recessed alcoves along the walls, and a marble inlaid floor.

An older woman in a black dress, white apron, and a lace cap waited for them, and her plump face broke into a smile at the sight of Daniel.

"Master Daniel," she said, "it is so good to see you."

"Mrs. Townsend, you look radiant, as always."

He took her hand and kissed her knuckles, and her face went as red as an apple.

"Master Daniel, you are too cheeky." She turned to Grace and didn't bother to hide her curiosity.

"This is Miss Grace Banbury and her maid, Ruby," Daniel said. "We had business in Hertfordshire, and she agreed to allow me to visit my mother before we returned to London."

That hardly satisfied the housekeeper, who looked between them with interest. And *that* satisfied Grace. Let the staff believe that Daniel was finally settling down.

"When we saw the approaching carriage," Mrs. Townsend said, "I informed the family, who agreed to delay dinner. Now they'll be happy they did. It will be served in an hour. Miss Banbury, will that give you enough time to prepare?"

Grace looked past the housekeeper to the next room, a great hall with groupings of furniture scattered about and swords and shields decorating the walls. "Surely it will take us that long to reach a bedroom." She smiled.

"Not at all, miss," the housekeeper said. "By the time we reach a guest room, your luggage should already be there. Master Daniel, you can see yourself to the family wing."

"Of course. Miss Banbury, I shall see you soon."

Daniel was almost expecting his mother to appear in his bedchamber, but somehow she contained herself until he reached the drawing room. He paused in the doorway before she saw him, and he was glad that she seemed unchanged in the three months since he'd last seen her. But the mourning gown she'd been wearing since her husband's death always made her look more pale and drawn. She was alone in the grand room, and she gazed pensively into her wineglass. Probably wondering what he was up to by bringing a woman home with him.

At last she saw him, and her loving smile was the same as always. He went in and kissed her cheek, and she pulled him down beside her for a hug.

"Oh, Daniel, it has been too long," she said, smiling up at him.

"You only have to come to London, Mother. It is not far."

She waved a hand. "I don't miss it a bit. There is always too much going on here. I was going to tell you about Miss Wadsworth, who has just come out this Season, but I guess I don't have to now."

"You would deprive me of gossip?"

"As if you cared about that. But no, I can see you've managed to find a lady all by yourself. Will wonders never cease."

"She is not my lady, Mother," he explained patiently. "Her name is Miss Grace Banbury, and she was showing me the property I recently purchased from her family."

Something flickered in her eyes. "Oh, Miss Banbury. The duke mentioned her."

"What did Chris have to say?" he asked warily.

"Only that she seems taken with you. I hope you are not leading the girl on."

"I'm not, Mother." He wondered what Chris had *really* said.

Before he could say more, his aunt Isabella entered the room with his cousin Elizabeth. They both gave glad cries upon seeing him, and he was hugged and kissed thoroughly. Though Aunt Isabella was a duchess, she dressed in the conservative clothing she preferred. She was never one to draw attention to herself, probably because her dark Spanish skin and black hair, now touched with silver, did it for her. She had never blended in with pale English beauties, and he had always felt a kinship with her.

Elizabeth had her mother's deep black hair, but her skin was the paler color of a peach, and she blushed with happiness on seeing Daniel.

When Grace entered the room, she stopped uncertainly in the doorway, staring at the happy reunion. The immediate family was already so much larger than hers that she had a hard time imagining what it must be like when they all got together.

An older woman dressed in mourning was the first person to notice her and sent a curious, subdued glance her way. At first Grace thought that Daniel's aunt, the one mourning her son, must have been in residence, but then she realized that this must be Lady Flora, Daniel's mother. She was a tall woman, like her son, and there was a resemblance in the cheekbones and the same chocolate-colored eyes.

"You must be Miss Banbury," said the woman suddenly, and the other three people all turned to look at her.

Daniel came to her, and she found herself absurdly grateful that he would not leave her to explain herself. He held out his elbow, and she put her hand on it, letting him lead her into the largest drawing room she'd ever seen. She tried not to gape at crystal chandeliers spaced over her head amidst classical paintings, or the intricate carving along the hearth she could have stepped into.

"Mother, Aunt Isabella, Elizabeth, this is Miss Banbury," Daniel said, "Miss Banbury, meet my mother, Lady Flora, my aunt, the duchess of Madingley, and my cousin, Lady Elizabeth."

Grace curtsied to the ladies, almost surprised when they all did the same. She had never met such a group of exalted people before, and she felt like the simple country girl that she was. How had Daniel kept from laughing when he saw her small manor at Maran Park?

Lady Flora smiled although Grace still saw the reserve shadowing her eyes.

"Miss Banbury, how good to meet you. I understand that you grew up near our part of the country."

"Not a day's journey away in Hertingfordbury, my lady. Although that property now belongs to your son."

"Ah yes, how good of you to show it to him."

Though Daniel's mother was the height of civility, Grace sensed that she was being weighed, and knew that traveling with Daniel had not helped her in their eyes. She calmed herself by remembering that if Lady Flora knew what her son was truly doing with her, he would be the one suffering her censure.

Daniel led her into the dining room, and Grace tried not to gape at the table, which stretched down the length of the room to seat at least fifty people. They all sat at one end, the women grouped around Daniel at the head of the table.

Everyone was so polite to her, and Grace was able to relax and watch the interplay between mother and son. Though this was a different Daniel than the relaxed man he'd been at Enfield Manor with Viscount Wade, there was still an ease, a comfortableness about him now that he was home. He had been raised much as his cousin, the duke, who was also born of scandal; why had Daniel turned his life so differently? She was getting glimpses of the depths of him.

"Miss Banbury?" Lady Flora said after the bowls of Julienne soup had been taken away.

Grace smiled at her. "Yes, my lady?"

"So your family home now belongs to my son," she said directly.

Lady Elizabeth, several years younger than Grace, coughed into her napkin as if her food had gone down the wrong way.

"Yes, my lady," Grace said, tensing.

"You sold it to him?"

Before Grace could speak, Daniel said, "I dealt with her mother."

Lady Flora gave her son a measured look. "Miss Banbury, if you are her only child—"

"Oh, I am not, my lady," Grace interrupted. "I have a brother, Edward Banbury. He lives in London now."

"So your family has property there, as well."

May God forgive her for lying, but all she could say was, "Yes, my lady."

"Please forgive my forthrightness," Lady Flora said with a sigh, "but does your mother know you've come here?"

Grace didn't understand the undercurrent flowing through the room, although she imagined her unorthodox journey with Daniel to be the reason. "She is traveling in the north, my lady. But my brother knows."

"Mother, Miss Banbury is not a young girl," Daniel said impatiently. "And we traveled with her maid attending us at all times. Now can we please enjoy our dinner? You were about to tell me of Mr. Abernathy's outdoor dinner party. Surely it was ruined by the rain."

Grace felt a bit nauseated. Daniel's young cousin was sneaking fascinated glances at her as if Grace were an established courtesan. Lady Flora was nothing but polite and continued occasionally to draw Grace into conversation with the others. Grace had known she would be a curiosity to Daniel's family, but had never imagined it would be so grueling. But, of course, they were in a so-

ciety so far above hers. They must believe her a
terribly inappropriate match for Daniel. After all,
until the duke married and had a son of his own,
Daniel was his heir. She'd come here thinking she
could redeem him in the eyes of his family, but
had now realized that seeing her partnered with
Daniel did not appease them.

After dinner, she felt a moment's panic when
Lady Flora suggested that Daniel could meet them
later in the drawing room after he'd smoked one
of his terrible cigars. But Daniel had demurred,
insisting that as the only gentleman, he would
remain with the ladies. Grace should have been
grateful that he was looking out for her, but she
also found herself annoyed. He had surely known
how his mother would react to her presence. Why
hadn't he warned her, so she could change her
mind about traveling farther with him?

But of course, she'd given him the perfect opportunity to find more time alone with her. She
had thought that being home might make him
more conservative, but on seeing this palace—this
castle—now she knew they could get lost together,
and no one would ever be able to find them.

At last she could end the evening without seem-
ing like she was frantic to escape. A maid arrived
to show her to her room, and Grace curtsied to
Daniel's family and left them to their private conversations. Although she was in a hurry for some
sort of sanctuary, she could not resist looking into
any open doorways she passed. Most of the rooms
were unlit, too dark to see anything, but they

passed one more, and the maid's candelabrum lit a ghostly whiteness. Grace came to a stop, and the maid came back for her. The candlelight revealed a room scattered with furniture covered in sheets. It seemed rather strange for a room in the main part of the house.

"What is this?" Grace asked.

The young girl glanced into the room and gave an absent shrug. "'Tis the music room, miss. But no one uses it anymore."

Of course not, Grace thought, intrigued and far too curious. As she followed the girl, she paid attention to where she was so that she could find her way back. Ruby was waiting in her bedroom, and when the housemaid left them alone, Ruby gripped Grace's arms.

"Have ye ever seen such a place, Miss Grace?" Ruby cried. "I can't even find the kitchens from here. And there's bells that tell us what room is ringin'—"

"Ruby, I'm having my own trouble remembering a particular room, so I have to find it now."

Ruby frowned at her. "Now Miss Grace, ye'll get yerself lost, and then what will Mr. Throckmorten think of ye?"

"Believe me, he'll stay far away from the music room. I promise I'll be back soon."

Grace took up the candelabrum left by the maid and hurried back the way she'd come, going down one floor, and taking two left turns where corridors met. But at last she found the music room. She knew for a fact that the family wing was on the opposite side of the house, so no one should disturb her. She had time to see where Daniel had spent much of his boyhood.

She took the sheet off the piano and admired its beautiful lines. There were sheets covering cases along the wall, and she found a miniature version of the violin and several other instruments. Lord Wade had said that Simon could play many instruments as a boy. Had he spent hours here happy with his parents?

But he'd given it all up after his father's death and his mother's notoriety.

She sat down at the piano. Maybe she was going about their challenge all wrong. Why did he need to be redeemed by her? He was a good man, helping his friends—helping her brother, though certainly Edward was a risky proposition. Daniel had deeply felt his mother's scandal and fought everyone who abused her. He was not a man who needed redemption. Yet she still wanted him to have a better life.

Was it music he was missing, and not even realizing it? Was this what she needed to give back to him, to make him whole? Perhaps only then would he give up his gambling, risking too much when he had so much to live for.

And could she then leave him and think he was a better man for knowing her?

She ran her fingers lightly over the keyboard but did not play.

The thought of never seeing him again except socially gave her a pang in her heart. Their rela-

tionship was becoming more than she'd anticipated. She was getting wrapped up in Daniel's
life, and it was difficult not to let herself fall gladly
into his bed. When he left her, regardless of who
was victorious, there would be a new emptiness
in her life. Her days and nights were all about him
now, and when he was gone—

The imagined bleakness took her breath away.

Without realizing it, she accidentally pressed
down too hard, and a single note rang into the
silence. The sound echoed like a ghostly, happy
memory of better days. She froze as it died away.
She'd thought she'd heard someone in the hall, and
she quickly ran to the door and peered outside,
but she was alone, thank God. She didn't want to
have to explain to Lady Flora that she was abus-
ing her hospitality by nosing into private areas of
the mansion.

And if Daniel found her, he might either be
angry at her intrusion, or he would yet again attempt his seduction, and she would be far too sus-
ceptible now.

As she had been from the beginning. She'd
known she had a weakness for him, and now it
had grown into an urgent need.

Taking up the candelabrum, she made her way
back quickly to her room.

She didn't see Daniel, who silently watched
her.

Chapter 17

Daniel knew he could have gone to Grace's bedroom, pursued her, and experienced even more of her passion, but he watched her disappear down the dark corridor and didn't follow.

Instead, he went into the music room.

He'd come here without volition, and he should have known she would somehow be able to find the exact room in the mansion that most called to him.

How did she know these things when even he himself didn't?

He did not have a candle, but there was a lamp in the corridor that cast the faintest glow inside. The draperies had not been drawn over the tall windows, and that helped him to see. Grace had forgotten to cover the piano. He did so to spare his mother.

He had never asked his mother why, after so many years, music still so distressed her. Perhaps it was habit now, like it was for him, to humor her.

He realized there were many things about the past he never spoke of with her. Like why she'd really stopped composing, like how it felt to have the world think one a murderer.

He couldn't think such things around Grace, who was beginning to see into his thoughts. He was spending too much time with her, letting her see too deeply into him.

And he couldn't stop, as if he were riding a carriage down a hill with the reins dragging on the ground rather than securely in his hands.

Grace spent a pleasant morning in the company of Lady Elizabeth, Daniel's cousin. Earlier, at breakfast, Daniel had told her that he had several meetings scheduled with the steward and staff, acting in the duke's place, and that he would join her later.

Grace had been glad for the distance. She had spent a humiliating amount of time awake in her bed the previous night, wondering if he'd come to continue his seduction. When he had not, she'd been more upset than relieved. What did she want—for him to win this insane challenge?

Or was she looking for every possible chance to be with him?

This wasn't how she'd thought the challenge would turn out.

So to distract herself, she'd gone riding with Lady Elizabeth and had a tour of the incredible park surrounding Madingley Court. There were more gardeners here than the sum of her entire staff at Maran Park. When at last they'd returned to the stables, a house servant was waiting for Lady Elizabeth.

"My lady, Mr. Baxter Wells is here to see you."

Grace's heart gave a sharp thump, and she saw the pleasure the young woman took in having a suitor. But Lady Elizabeth had no idea what kind of pleasures Mr. Wells wanted from her.

Grace knew how he took advantage of a woman's innocence, how smooth the lies could fall from his lips. Grace had fallen for it all, at the same age as this young lady. How could she remain silent?

When the maid had left, and the groom had led away both horses, Lady Elizabeth walked back out into the stable yard with her.

"Miss Banbury," Lady Elizabeth said, "would you mind if I leave you now?"

"Of course not, my lady, but first, could you listen to a word of warning?"

The girl's happy expression clouded over. "I don't understand."

"You don't know me well, so perhaps it is not my place to speak of this to you, but I cannot remain silent. I know of Mr. Wells's reputation. He can seem the most genial of men, but take care that he does not want more from you than you want to give."

Lady Elizabeth blushed. "Really, Miss Banbury, I don't know what you mean. He's always been perfectly polite."

Grace felt like the biggest fool, but she didn't

want the innocent girl to suffer. "Some men will try to make their advances on you in private. I—I just want you to be aware."

Lady Elizabeth gave her a nod of thanks, then took her leave and went up to the mansion. Grace remained behind, knowing she'd made herself look suspicious. But she just could not stand by and watch that man do to someone else what he'd done to her. She still remembered how he'd dismissed her after they'd been intimate, the way he'd accused her of trying to trap him into marriage. She shuddered in remembered pain. She didn't want to go up to the mansion and risk seeing him again, so she turned back to the stables, wondering if the grooms would allow her to go riding alone.

"Miss Banbury?"

The sound of Daniel's voice lifted her spirits, and she turned to face him, holding back an absolutely welcoming grin that he might misinterpret.

"Are you doing anything right now, Mr. Throckmorten?"

He arched a brow. "Talking to you."

"Would you care to go riding?"

"There is a guest up at the mansion. I thought you might wish to be with the ladies."

"No, thank you, it might be awkward. Now about that ride . . ."

He agreed to accompany her, and Grace could practically hear his curiosity as if he'd spoken aloud. She knew he would gladly get her alone, to ask questions and to advance his own pursuit.

She was relieved when a groom followed them as chaperone. Daniel just frowned when she gave him a smug smile.

When Daniel and Grace returned from their ride, Grace went to her room to prepare for luncheon—or to don her armor against his mother's questions, Daniel thought. As he passed near the entrance hall, a man was striding down the corridor as if he'd come from the drawing room.

The man nodded to him. "You must be Throckmorten."

Daniel stopped, curious. "I am. And who are you?"

"Baxter Wells. I was paying my respects to your cousin."

"Good to meet you." Daniel was about to nod and be on his way, when Wells looked about as if wondering if they could be overheard. Unease made Daniel stiffen.

"Lady Elizabeth tells me you're traveling with Miss Banbury," Wells said, his voice lowered, his expression knowing.

Daniel found himself wanting to reveal that a maid was also traveling with them, but he hardly owed this stranger any details. "Do you have a point?"

"Only that traveling with her can be quite an adventure."

The man was openly leering now. Daniel remembered the look on Grace's face when she'd said that a man had broken her heart.

Swiftly, he punched Wells hard in the stomach once, then took the man's arm when he doubled over, groaning.

"I suggest that Miss Banbury's name never pass your lips again," Daniel said, his voice a growl of warning.

"Of course, of course," Wells said, bobbing his head as he pulled away and staggered toward the front door.

A footman stood there, his face expressionless, as if he hadn't seen the duke's heir accost another man. After the door had closed behind Wells, Daniel nodded to the footman, who nodded back.

And then Daniel went to track down Elizabeth. He found her alone in the drawing room, writing a letter.

She looked up with a smile. "Good morning, Daniel."

He didn't smile back. "Is Baxter Wells courting you?"

Her smile faded, and a look of confusion surfaced. "You are the second person today to take offense to him. I have only recently met him, but he seems a kind man."

"He's not. Who else spoke to you about him?" As if Daniel didn't know.

"Miss Banbury. She said he was not to be trusted."

"He's not."

She opened her mouth but seemed to think better of her question. "Very well. I must say that

Miss Banbury did not owe me a warning. It was very kind of her to try to help me, when she could not know how I would accept her help. She seems nice, even though Chris's letter said—"

She broke off, her face a study in regret at what she'd revealed.

"What letter?" Daniel asked, sitting down beside her and speaking in a low voice. "And who did he write it to?"

Elizabeth sighed. "To Mama, of course, but she shared it with Aunt Flora."

"Don't make me pry every detail out of you," he warned, as if she'd ever believe a threat from him.

She rolled her eyes. "Well, if Mama felt free to share it with us, I should share it with you. Chris is worried that Miss Banbury is trying to . . ."

Her voice trailed off, and Daniel found himself thinking, "seduce you," as if that was what Grace had in mind. It was almost amusing.

"Trying to what?" he asked.

"Trying to trap you in marriage," Elizabeth finished, looking uncomfortable.

"That is the most ridiculous thing I ever heard," Daniel said. "And you may tell the rest of them for me."

"Chris is worried because she's not exactly of the finest family."

"And do you of all people believe that family is more important than the person?"

Her own parents had fallen inappropriately in love, and she wouldn't exist if her father had done as Society would have wanted.

"Daniel, do not involve me," Elizabeth said. "You made me tell you all this, and I don't know what to think—and I don't want to."

"You said my mother knew about this letter. No wonder she was interrogating Grace."

"You call her by her Christian name?" Elizabeth said, wide-eyed.

As if that was the worst familiarity a man could be accused of. Elizabeth was so young, Daniel thought fondly.

"A slip of the tongue," Daniel amended. "Now promise me you'll discourage Wells and that you'll never be alone with him."

"I promise." She huffed a breath. "And to think, I thought that making my coming out would have everyone treating me as an adult!"

Grace stood outside the drawing room, having overheard more than she meant to between Daniel and Lady Elizabeth. Her heart was doing painful flutters in her chest, and to her horror, she felt like she might cry.

Daniel's family thought she was trying to trap him. It was the same thing Baxter had accused her of. She would have thought she'd hardened herself to such untruths, but obviously she hadn't because she could barely swallow past the great lump in her throat.

She had been a fool. How had she not seen this coming, especially after her experience with Baxter? She had taken a chance traveling with Daniel, even when accompanied by her maid, but

she'd thought any scandal whispered would have
been about his quest for his newest mistress, and
her supposed naïveté about his motives.

But *her* motives were the ones in question.

She could not believe that the Cabots would
ever spread such a rumor on to others, but still,
it hurt. If they only knew how she was resisting
their precious son, she thought bitterly.

Daniel couldn't believe such a thing of her,
not after the way she resisted him every chance
she got. She folded her arms tightly over her
stomach. But of course, she hadn't been resisting
so successfully lately. He couldn't possibly think
she was devious enough to . . . mislead him,
could he?

After dinner, Grace said an early good night,
hoping that the family accepted her excuse of
needing sleep for the early-morning departure
for London. When in reality, she just had to
get away from their unfailing politeness. Now
that she knew what they all thought of her, her
stomach twisted every time someone spoke to
her. Daniel seemed suspicious of her too-quiet
behavior. He was staring at her far too much.
Would his mother begin to think he was already
smitten with her?

She felt exposed, vulnerable, lost amidst what
others thought of her. Was she losing her own
self-worth?

Sleep would not come easily, she knew. She
asked the maid guiding her through the man-

sion to take her to the library, then after the girl explained the directions to return to her room, Grace was mercifully left alone.

Lamps lit several tables, and she lifted one, half-heartedly perusing the titles lining the shelves, looking for something to attract her interest.

"Grace?"

She almost dropped the lamp at the sound of Daniel's voice. She whirled around to see him closing the doors behind him.

"Leave those open!" she hissed. "If someone sees us in here together—"

"It's a drafty castle. I'll tell them a breeze blew it shut."

Her mouth dropped open, aghast. "As if you should give your mother any other reason to believe the duke's—"

She broke off, knowing she'd said too much. She ducked behind a sofa as he stalked toward her.

"So what did you overhear?" Daniel asked, his eyes fixed intently on her.

"Nothing!" Frantically, she looked around her, spotting the second set of closed doors at the far end of the library. She began to back up toward them, step by step.

"I don't care what Chris thinks," Daniel said, "and you shouldn't either. This is just a game between us, correct?"

"Not a game, Daniel," she said, unable to match his amusement. "This is a challenge. To you it's a game for your private amusement, but to me . . ." She trailed off, not wanting to reveal too much.

"And I don't care about the duke as much as I do your mother. Her opinion is important!"

"She would never speak to others about you."

He came around the sofa, and she was forced to retreat behind a table.

"But if she can believe such things about me, then anyone can." She didn't like the uncertainty in her voice, and she glared at Daniel as if it were his fault.

"I have explained things satisfactorily to my mother."

Her back came up against the doors. "What do you mean?" she demanded. "What did you say to her?"

"I said I was working with your brother on another investment. That's the reason we're spending so much time together."

"More lies!"

With a groan, Grace fumbled for the door latch behind her and opened it. Immediately the warm, earthen smell of a conservatory wafted over her. There were no lights within, but the moon shone through the glass roof, enough for her to turn and flee down a dark path. She had no idea where she was going. There had to be another door. She had to escape Daniel before he did something without thinking. If they were caught alone here—

She shuddered even imagining the consequences. His family would think her the worst sort of woman, and she'd never recover her standing with them. Much as Daniel made her feel safe, forcing him into marriage had never been her intention. And he probably wouldn't marry her anyway, leading to a schism with his own family.

He was coming behind her, moving closer and closer. She was pushing long fern leaves out of her way and heard him doing the same. She could swear she felt his breath on her neck, and she walked as fast as possible, afraid to run for fear she'd trip and fall headlong into the shrubbery.

The path curved away from the house, deeper into the conservatory. Never had she been in one so large, but trust a duke to have only the best. The moon cast strange shadows, and she almost thought Daniel had somehow gotten in front of her. Why hadn't he caught her by now?

The path suddenly ended where the glass met in a corner. She'd missed a turn somewhere. The view must be spectacular for the path to end here, but at night, there was only inky blackness outside.

She gave a start as she felt him come up behind her, crowding her forward until her hands pressed up against the cold, moist glass.

"It's been days since I've touched you," he murmured hoarsely.

She felt the length of his body all along hers, especially the thrust of his hips into her backside. "Only two days!" she whispered, grasping the threads of her composure.

"Two days too long."

He nipped at the point where her shoulder met her neck, and she bit her lip to hold back a groan.

But her shuddering body surely told him what he needed to know.

"Daniel, please, don't. Not here."

"Don't you remember how I can make you feel?" he whispered, licking along her ear.

The glass was cold against her cheek as she moaned, closing her eyes. She would never forget a moment of his interruption of her bath, the way his hands played her like she was his instrument.

She felt a sudden draft at her feet and realized those hands were fisted in her skirts, lifting them.

"Anyone could walk by outside and see us!" she hissed.

He was ignoring her. She felt his hands on her bare thighs, her skirts and petticoats rising in a bunch on both sides of her waist. She felt his hips, and the bulge of his erection against her backside. Her drawers were little protection against the heat and hardness of him.

His hands came around her torso and cupped her breasts, kneading them as if the corset weren't there. And though she couldn't feel the exquisiteness of his fingers on her skin, the powerful envelopment of his big hands made her moan.

She was falling under his spell, and she had to stop him before he turned his life upside down for her. It was one thing to be pursued in the night, when it was just between them, but now she could not forget who else would be affected.

"Your seduction won't work, certainly not here," she gasped.

"I find it daring." He tugged at her earlobe with his teeth. "The chance of scandal brings a certain excitement."

"This isn't a scandal, it's my life!"

Her silly voice revealed too much, too much pain and confusion and despair.

Chapter 18

The heat of passion had overtaken Daniel's mind, consuming all rational thought—but there was something in Grace's voice that he couldn't ignore. She was trembling beneath his touch, her body so soft, a welcome respite and resting place to the aching hardness that was his erection.

But he let her skirts fall, separating himself just enough from her body until she was safely covered again. He reluctantly lowered his hands, circling her waist from behind and just holding her for a moment, comforting her with his touch, because he didn't know the right words.

He remembered that she had seen Baxter Wells today. All the memories she'd probably tried to forget had flooded back to her, along with her fears of being thought a desperate woman out to seduce a rich man.

Daniel didn't like that another man had hurt her, had probably taken her innocence. Daniel had thought he was the first to show her passion, but now he knew differently. She'd been used and discarded, and he could only imagine that part of her blamed herself. A woman was too vulnerable in matters of the heart.

Her pain made him want to do violence to the man who'd used her. His body stiffened with it, for she now stirred uneasily, where only a moment ago she had rested like a wounded bird in his arms.

"Shh," he murmured against her hair.

She hadn't lied to him—she'd told him she wasn't so innocent, but he had not understood. How could he ask her about it, when she'd never trust him enough to tell him something so personal, so painful?

He realized that he wanted her trust, but didn't know how to achieve it. He wanted her to freely tell him her secrets, all of them. Instead, she equated him with Wells. Could he blame her?

"Let me go, Daniel," she said quietly.

He stepped away, and she turned to face him. She gave him a searching look, and he wondered what she saw. He made no amusing comment, did not give her his famous half smile. He just wanted her to see . . . him.

There was a vulnerability, a stillness to her features that moved him. He thought he could look into her emerald eyes forever.

By the devil, where had that foolish thought come from?

He cleared his throat. "I'd show you back to your room, but I imagine you don't want to be seen wandering the corridors alone with me at night."

"And you shouldn't want to be seen alone at night with me either—especially not at Madingley Court."

He arched a brow. "You make me seem like I quiver at the sound of my mother's voice."

She gave a ragged sigh. "You know I believe nothing of the sort. Good night."

She stepped around him and started up the path.

"Don't veer left, or you'll end up at the door outside."

She hesitated, looking at him over her shoulder. "You must be very familiar with the layout of the conservatory."

He shrugged. "That's why I was able to hunt you into a corner."

"Did you hide here when you were a child?"

"Of course."

An expression of sadness and softness came over her.

"Grace, do not make more of it than it was. All little boys like to hide. It gives us a feeling of control. But not little girls?"

"I couldn't hide. Who would have looked out for Edward?"

Now he felt like his eight-year-old self was a coward. He'd had no one to take care of but himself—and his mother. He'd done all he could.

"Good night, Grace."

With a nod, she turned and marched away, her back straight.

*   *   *

The journey back to London took most of the day, and Daniel allowed Grace to have her peace. Even when Ruby dozed, and he could have enjoyed himself teasing Grace by trying to lift her skirts, he didn't. Consequently, she gave him many suspicious glances as he kept his expression bland.

When she insisted he leave her off in the alley behind her town house, he did so, giving her an intimate smile that promised more. He held up four fingers. Her brows lowered in confusion.

He mouthed, "Four days left."

By lanternlight, he saw her understanding, the blush that followed, and the way she lifted her chin in defiance. He was still confident—but so was she.

Though she didn't know it, he followed her until she was inside, even saw her reunion with her brother through the windows. He returned home, and although it was the dinner hour, he had his investigator send over his report. Daniel settled down at his desk in the library, a brandy in his hand.

There were two men who'd played with him and Mrs. Banbury on that fateful night. The first, Clive Radford, had been on his way north, and was still in York. Most likely, he was not the man they were looking for. The second gambler, Horace Jenkins, was a man of some property in Hertfordshire who'd come to London for the Season. When he was in town, he rented a room at his club and conducted his business efficiently. His only habit—one Daniel shared—was a liking for games of chance. There was nothing here to implicate him as anything more than a man who thought himself in love with a woman he didn't have the courage to court. There wasn't even any proof that he was the one watching the Banbury town house, but even making that assumption, the man had done nothing suspicious except run away when chased.

But . . . Daniel had always trusted his instincts, and something about this seemed wrong. Jenkins might be shy, but if Daniel was being objective, Grace was hardly the kind of woman who could turn a man of property away. Her dowry was small, and her relations were not noble. So why didn't Jenkins simply ask to be introduced?

Daniel decided to continue having him followed just in case he did something suspicious. If he had the chance, he would offer Jenkins an introduction to Grace and gauge his response.

When Beverly came to call in the afternoon, Grace watched her friend's expression when she saw the refurbishing that had been done in only three days. Though the town house was small, there was now an elegance to it, with framed paintings of endless landscapes that somehow made each room look larger. There were new draperies in the main rooms, and several new pieces of furniture that accented the best of their well-made older pieces. Even the dining-room sideboard now had several new silver platters and tureens on display.

"Grace, how lovely," Beverly said, when they finally settled in the drawing room. "You'll be ready to accept the attentions of any man."

"Or any Society matron," Grace added.

"I would normally say that I'm so glad you were able to put your own touches to the place."

Grace winced.

"But of course, you were not involved with this, because neither you nor your brother has the money for such expenditures."

Grace sighed.

"It was Mr. Throckmorten again, was it not?"

"It was. How could I refuse? It is his home, after all."

"Which he could easily wait to redecorate—*if* he can claim it."

"Thank you for not saying *when*."

"Is he simply trying to soften your regard for him?" Beverly asked, eyes narrowed as she thought. "Or—oh please, Grace, tell me you did not lose the challenge, and you're already his—"

"Mistress?" she interrupted with a shocked whisper. "Of course not. But . . . it is getting more difficult."

Beverly patted her hand. "Of course it is, my dear. He is a handsome man, with a reckless charm that even I, a married woman, find attractive. And now he's using his wiles—decorating, for heaven's sake!—to recommend himself to you."

"As if his kisses weren't enough," Grace added with a sigh.

"Ah, you've let him kiss you."

She covered her face. "I can't bear how you're looking at me, Beverly! Your sympathy is too kind. This should be easy! But why can't I resist him?"

"Surely your attempts to redeem him have had some effect in keeping him away from you."

"Not much. He is a very determined man."

"A gambler always is."

"I don't think he's used to failure. I'm a . . . a challenge, and I'm resisting."

"And so you're saying that you yourself have nothing to do with the attraction?"

"I don't know," Grace whispered, twisting her fingers together in her lap.

"Well then, it's a good thing he's a gambler."

"What do you mean?"

"Because otherwise I think you'd succumb to his charms far too easily."

"Beverly, I—" But she broke off because she knew her friend was right.

"He doesn't seem to want to marry, Grace," Beverly said gently. "Or at least his intentions toward you are not honorable. I don't want you to get hurt. Unless of course"—she paused, her head tilted in thought—"you decide to set your sights on marrying *him*."

Grace could only gasp. "But . . . then I would be a woman out to entrap a man! I would never do that because I've been accused of it once too often." At Beverly's confusion, Grace said quietly,

"I thought I was in love once before, and in the end, my suitor thought I was trying to . . . force him into marriage." She left out the truly humiliating details.

"I cannot believe such a thing! Surely he did not know you well."

"I didn't think so either, after that. But I met Daniel's family, and I learned that the duke is concerned about my intentions toward Daniel and warned his whole family."

"The duke is a protective sort of man, my dear. Family is everything to the Cabots because so often it is them against the world. You cannot fault him for worrying about his cousin—his heir, after all."

"I know."

"But truly, Grace, can you not look on this logically? If your reservations about his gambling are gone—"

"I didn't say that."

"Well did he display any compulsion to gamble these last three days?"

"No . . . although he and Lord Wade did challenge each other to a boat race."

"The Blind Baron?" Beverly said in surprise.

Grace felt confused. "But he's a viscount."

Beverly waved her hand airily. "The barony is one of his titles, and people can be so cruel. But I am glad to hear he's doing well. Getting married, too."

"I met Miss Shelby. She was his grandmother's companion."

"So you see, I am certain she was a woman accused of trying to trap a blind man. Yet are they happy?"

"Very—and very much in love."

"Then just because one party decides to initiate marriage doesn't mean it can't end well."

"Oh, Beverly, my head is spinning."

"You must make a decision, Grace. I was going to put marriageable ladies in his path, after all."

Grace hesitated. "Wait a few days," she finally said in a small voice. "I'll think about what you've said."

"That's my girl. By the time of the Madingley Ball—only a few days past the end of this challenge of yours—you'll be able to tell me what Mr. Throckmorten is to you."

After Beverly had gone, Grace sat like a lump on the sofa, her mind full of conflicting thoughts. Daniel didn't want to marry—yet he was obviously attracted to her. They had no trouble conversing with each other, and she found him very humorous—which was dangerous, because it was so appealing.

And never did she feel forced in his seduction. When she asked him to stop, as she had last night, he always did. In some ways he respected her. He could have tossed her and her brother into the streets.

But was all this a good basis for a marriage? Could she love a man she had never thought she could trust? When the allure of her seduction was gone, would he not turn back to gambling, which had provided the exciting risks he liked to take?

But it all came down to—love. Did she love him? And did she want his love in return? Or was she as his family and Baxter had painted her, a woman who would settle for security over love?

When Grace saw Daniel at Lord Hammersmith's dinner party that night, she looked at him with the eyes of a woman considering marriage. He didn't know what she was thinking because he met her gaze openly, smiled, and turned away, safeguarding her reputation. If only he knew the crazy thoughts whirling about in her brain.

Marriage. *Marriage!* To Daniel Throckmorten, rake and gambler and scandalous child of a scandalous family.

She couldn't even imagine how to go about such a thing. She didn't want to give up on their challenge; she needed that violin for Edward and his future chance at marriage.

Edward had escorted her to the dinner, and now he gave her arm a squeeze before going off on his own to speak to two young ladies. Grace couldn't pay attention to him, so busy was she with her dilemma.

When the challenge was over, did she just continue to encourage Daniel's visits, hoping something tender flourished between them?

As she watched him across the room talking to an elderly widow, she knew her own tenderness toward him had already happened. She found herself making excuses for his gambling, telling herself he could be like most normal men and stop it when he wanted to.

But he'd competed in a game involving the right to marry her—how was that being in control?

She moved through the drawing room, talking and being drawn from group to group. At last she and Daniel stood in the same crowd of five guests. She couldn't help but notice the speculative glances one elderly lady kept giving the both of them.

Grace's stomach began to tighten with nerves. Her plan had been for everyone to notice Daniel's attention to her, to assume that he was finally ready to marry. Of course, she had not meant that he might marry *her*, but now she was only confused.

During a lull in the conversation, the elderly lady, Mrs. Walker, turned to Grace and said, "Miss Banbury, I was disappointed when both you and Mr. Throckmorten could not attend my breakfast two days ago. And neither of you attended Lady Thurlow's ball that same night."

Grace felt suddenly hot and wondered if her face was on fire. Surely her smile was frozen; surely everyone was looking between Daniel and her, knowing that they'd spent three days together. She'd just begun to relax among Society, and now her self-respect, the only thing that was hers, might be damaged.

"Mrs. Walker," she began gravely, not even sure what she was going to say.

"Miss Banbury," Daniel interrupted, "I told Viscount Wade that his small house party was too exclusive, did I not?"

Grace blinked at him. "Yes, you did."

"You were at Lord Wade's home?" Mrs. Walker asked in surprise.

"His grandmother's home," Grace was able to say.

"Miss Banbury and I were guests of Lady Wade's. We had good weather. You did some riding, did you not, Miss Banbury?"

Grace smiled. "Miss Shelby, Lord Wade's betrothed, was kind enough to show me about."

The conversation veered to the surprise of Lord Wade's engagement, and Daniel began telling the guests in detail about Lord Wade's rowing challenges. Daniel seemed . . . perfectly fine.

Grace felt like throwing up.

How was she supposed to keep track of so many secrets? And what would she say if people had heard they'd visited Madingley Court as well? She could only pray that the duke's servants were too loyal to spread gossip.

But Baxter Wells had been there, too! She could barely stop herself from frantically staring around the drawing room to see if he was here, spreading rumors of his own. And if Edward came across him, there might well be bloodshed. She looked around for her brother and saw that he was standing alone, staring pensively out the window, before he gave a smile to a gentleman who came to speak to him.

During dinner, Grace realized how Lady Hammersmith viewed her relationship with Daniel when she had him escort Grace in and sit beside her. The table was long and wide, with high centerpieces of flowers blocking much conversation. The man on Grace's right was talking to the woman on his right, leaving her to turn to Daniel on her left.

He was looking at the framed menu between them, but he glanced her way.

"You have to learn to be a quick thinker," he said softly.

She wanted to groan. The room was noisy enough that no one could hear them, but still . . .

She wanted to ignore him, but as she put her napkin in her lap, she murmured, "I haven't had as much practice as you. And the journey was a terrible risk to take. Of course people would wonder if we were together."

"But we deflected their questions with the truth."

She spoke between gritted teeth. "And what about our next stop? What if Mr. Wells decides to tell everyone that I've been to Madingley Court with you?"

Daniel nodded to the footman who set before him a plate of "Fried Smelts with Dutch Sauce," according to the menu. When everyone was preoccupied with their food, he softly said, "He will say nothing, or the blow I landed in his stomach will be followed by more."

Grace quickly turned her wide eyes back to her own plate. "You *hit* him?"

"He deserved it after how he treated you."

She blinked in disbelief. "Oh. I didn't realize you knew he was the man in my past."

He tapped the side of his head. "I'm smart."

Had Daniel Throckmorten appointed himself her defender now?

Throughout dinner, Grace spoke to the man on her right, smiled at the people on the opposite side of the table, and did everything to prove she was not focused on Daniel. Afterward, when the men rejoined the ladies in the drawing room, she saw her brother once again standing alone.

She went over to him and smiled. "We have not had much chance to talk since my return."

"And we didn't talk before you left either, or I'd have talked you out of taking that melancholy trip to Maran Park."

"I needed to speak with the staff, Edward. You know they are like family to me."

"And he's keeping them all?"

She nodded and quickly changed the subject. "What have you been doing while I was gone?"

"Not gambling, if that's what you're implying," he said darkly.

She winced and touched his arm. "Edward, you know me better than that. If I thought you were gambling, I would ask about it."

He heaved a sigh. "I apologize. I have been . . . on edge. I attended a breakfast and a ball."

"And how were they?"

"Since my newest goal is to marry, it did not go well."

"Oh, Edward," she murmured with sympathy.

"These women still think I have property to bring to marriage—which is now a lie, of course—but that does not sway them into staying long enough to even speak about the weather."

"You'll have property again, Edward, I promise. And your investments will surely begin to grow."

He shrugged and put on a false smile when their host, Lord Hammersmith, came to say hello.

Daniel watched the Banbury siblings from across the room. He'd always been good at reading faces—it was part of what made him a talented gambler and businessman—but he didn't need skill to understand Banbury's frustration and Grace's worry. Banbury's being Grace's brother had somehow made him part of Daniel's presence in the family.

Daniel had seen the cool reactions to Banbury's presence among the young marriage-minded ladies. He found that he cared about the younger man, who hadn't had the guidance of decent adults when his father died, like Daniel had. Daniel wanted to help Banbury meet the appropriate marriageable women, but he first had to trust that Banbury could control his old demons.

When Grace left her brother, Daniel approached him.

"Throckmorten," Banbury said with a nod. "Did you see all you needed to at Maran Park?"

There wasn't even a trace of bitterness in

Banbury's voice. He must be hiding it well. "The estate is flourishing. It has been well managed."

Banbury shrugged. "The steward is excellent. I hope you keep him on."

"All the staff will be retained."

"Good." His stiff shoulders relaxed.

"I have a proposal for you."

Banbury glanced at him curiously. "A business proposal?"

"It's personal. I know you've been trying to earn back money to buy the violin from me."

Banbury's expression turned wary. "Yes."

"What if I give it back to you in exchange for complete access to Grace?"

The man didn't even take a moment to think. "No," he said flatly.

Something inside Daniel eased. "No?" he repeated lightly.

"I am only Grace's brother, and what she chooses to do with her life is up to her. But she has my guidance and my protection, and I would never give that up to any man." He didn't bother to hide his glare. "Do you understand me?"

"I understand." Daniel took a sip of his brandy, and said mildly, "Are you still coming to Southern Railway tomorrow for our next meeting?"

Banbury gave him a surprised look. "I—don't know."

"You should come. It's a meeting of all the directors. You'll learn much."

"I'll be there."

* * *

When the dinner was over, Daniel went to his carriage, where his coachman waited for instructions. The night was dark, with a mist of rain blurring the view of the gas lamps lining the streets. It was still early; normally he would have gone for a game of hazard.

But he thought of Grace, going home alone. Gambling had altered the very course of her life in so many ways, and to Daniel's dismay, he almost couldn't enjoy it anymore. Certainly the lure wasn't there for him.

The only lure that drew him lately was the thought of Grace alone in a bedroom, waiting for him.

Even though he knew he was having her house guarded, and that Jenkins seemed to be in retreat, he told himself he had to watch over her personally. After all, there were only three days left in his seduction, and he certainly hadn't given up. In fact, he thought he was closer than ever to achieving his goal.

Long after midnight, he let himself in the rear door of the town house and crept quietly upstairs. He went to Grace's bedroom first, silently opened the door—and found an empty bed. A cold, unfamiliar feeling swept through him, and it took him a moment to recognize it as fear. Had Jenkins somehow breached the security of the house?

He almost went to Banbury next, but decided to search the house first, finishing with the other bedrooms on the floor. He found her sound asleep in the big bed in the master bedroom, as if she were waiting for him. The tight knot in his chest eased as he looked at her lovely face, so innocent and vulnerable in sleep. Her nightclothes were covered by a dressing gown that was tucked clear up under her chin. But her small, bare feet were exposed, and he did not resist the urge to run his fingertips from her ankle to her toes. She twitched in her sleep and rolled over, exposing flesh up to her calves. This could be interesting.

But she'd been waiting for him, he thought, slinging an arm around the bedpost as he looked down at her. It was getting more and more difficult to seduce her with abandon, when he was thinking about her too much, caring too much. He was already protecting her reputation at parties while at the same time trying to take it for his own.

He carefully sat down beside her, resting against the headboard. There was a peacefulness in being with her that he'd never felt with anyone before. He was almost . . . content, and he didn't know how to analyze that.

Grace rolled again, this time right up against his outstretched legs. She stirred and lifted her head, eyes still half-closed with slumber.

"Daniel?" she murmured.

The sweet, softness of her voice did something strange to him that he couldn't name.

He brushed back the hair from her eyes. "I'm here."

She came up on her elbow, a small smile playing about her lips, and tugged on his shirt. Surprised, he came down over her, and she reached up to kiss him. He wasn't even sure she realized what she was doing. Her lips were soft and gentle, caressing his mouth with a quiet, simple passion that moved him, confused him.

At last he pulled away and she sank back against the pillow, closing her eyes. "Luncheon tomorrow," she murmured. "You and me."

She fell back asleep before he could even respond, as if she knew what his answer would be. So he'd be a little late for his railway meeting. With a sigh, he sank down a bit in the pillows, she snuggled against him, and he lay awake, for the first time the recipient of some part of a woman's trust.

Chapter 19

Daniel pulled up outside Grace's door in an open carriage, jumped lightly to the ground and up the steps. Woodley, the butler, was waiting to open the door, and the man gave Daniel a quick wide-eyed stare before settling into his usual bland, pleasant expression. Daniel didn't understand—until he saw Grace.

She was standing just beyond the butler, hands on her hips, her glare full of disapproval. He couldn't imagine what he'd done; he was punctual this morning, and last night, he hadn't attempted to ravish her in her sleep, though it had pained him to return to his own cold, lonely bed before dawn.

"I take it I should not come in," Daniel said dryly.

"If I had not promised Beverly that I would attend this charity event, I would have had Woodley slam the door in your face," she said, obviously fuming.

But instead she marched past him, opened her parasol so quickly that he had to duck to avoid having his eye pierced, and stepped briskly down the stairs to the street. He thought she might vault into the seat to avoid touching him, but she disdainfully held her hand to him for assistance.

Only when he had the reins in his hands and was guiding the two-horse team away from the curb, did he say, "So, are you going to tell me what's wrong?"

"My brother told me what you asked for in exchange for the violin," she said in a tight voice.

"I see." He hadn't demanded Banbury's promise of secrecy, of course, but he hadn't thought the man would want to hurt his sister.

"He didn't want to tell me," she continued as if she could read his mind.

A frightening prospect, that.

"But I saw the two of you talking, and I demanded to know if it was about me. Edward is a terrible liar where I'm concerned. I can read his face like a book."

"I'll keep that in mind." He didn't look at her as he paid attention to the crowded city street.

Was it over now, the challenge that had consumed most of the last two weeks? He couldn't imagine not seeing Grace every day, pursuing her every night. But she would take his offer to Banbury in the worst possible light and had obviously condemned him without even questioning his motives. He shouldn't be surprised, but he was.

"How could you test Edward like that?" she demanded, throwing up her hands and almost losing her parasol in the process.

Daniel almost took a turn too fast in his confusion. "Test?"

"Of course I understood immediately what you were doing, and I told Edward as much. You were testing him to see if he could control his impulse to gamble. A true feverish compulsion would make him offer up even his own sister to help himself, and you'd know he was untrustworthy."

He opened his mouth, but she plowed on ahead.

"I can help Edward by myself, you know, if you feel you can't trust him. He's changed, and I can see that. I thought you could, too."

"I needed proof," he said slowly, "before I took the next step with him."

"And what's that?" she demanded, eyeing him like a mother hen protecting her chick.

"I thought I would invite him to the ball celebrating the new directors of Southern Railway. He'll meet educated, refined, and wealthy young ladies, not of the *ton*, it's true, but eager to wed a gentleman, regardless of his financial status. Their fathers are my friends and business associates, and I had to make sure I was entrusting their daughters to a man in control of his impulses."

She stared up at him, he stared down at her, and he saw again the soft tenderness sweep over her face.

"Hey, guv'nor, watch it!" came a shout from the street.

Daniel returned his attention to driving before they had an accident.

"Daniel," she said in a quieter voice, "that is sweet of you."

"Sweet?" he scoffed. "Give me credit for understanding a good business venture when I see one. When your brother begins to succeed, I will certainly take my share of the profit."

"Of course," she said, her face too expressionless.

He had the annoyed feeling she was fighting a smile.

When Grace entered Lady Fogge's spacious drawing room, she came up short. Men and women mingled as usual, but they did so amidst small tables and chairs set up all about the room.

She felt Daniel at her back. "Miss Banbury?"

She knew she had to say something about why she'd come to a dead stop. "Just looking to see who I knew."

But she couldn't focus on that because she was looking at the deck of cards at each table.

You're being silly, she told herself. There were often card games available for guests who wanted to amuse themselves. She had always made her excuses and conversed with others who didn't enjoy playing.

But this was an event to benefit babies in the worst districts of London. She had thought guests would be offering money for blankets, or hearing a speaker who would encourage them to donate to the cause. When she'd first come up with the redemption idea for Daniel, she had thought this would be the perfect event to exhibit his good qualities.

"Ladies and gentlemen," said Lady Fogge, the round-faced hostess who stood beside her blushing daughter. "We have decided to try something different to raise funds today. We can all enjoy ourselves—and benefit a worthy cause. So today we play Speculation, and I encourage you to bet freely, for the winnings will all go to the Ladies' Benevolence for Babies Fund."

Grace had spent her life avoiding what had been her mother's downfall—her family's downfall. Even playing for charity made her feel ill inside.

Beverly came toward her, smiling. "You'll play with me, of course, Grace."

If Beverly didn't understand that she had never played cards, how would Grace convince Lady Fogge and the rest without looking like a fool?

"She's a terrible cardplayer," Daniel said, coming from behind to stand at her side. "Why else would she bring me, except to win as much as possible for those poor babies?"

Grace felt something come unfrozen inside her. Daniel understood without her even explaining.

Beverly looked between them, and Grace thought her friend's face reddened in belated understanding.

"Of course, what a marvelous idea," Beverly quickly said. "Mr. Throckmorten, come sit at my table. Grace, you can encourage us."

Grace ended up standing behind Daniel, and rather than behave like his usual cool, enigmatic self, he charmed the ladies and made the men forget that he was beating them. At times she stood to the side so that she could watch his face, but never once did his expression reveal anything but joviality. But of course, she knew he was a master at keeping his emotions under control. It had obviously made him a successful gambler; she could not imagine him as a man who went past his limits.

Yet on the way there, when she'd confronted him about testing Edward, she had seen far too much in his face, from resignation to surprise to confusion. It was as if he could no longer hide what he was feeling from her. Was she more than a conquest to him? Was Beverly right—should she consider pursuing marriage to him?

At luncheon, Lady Putnam, a friend of Beverly's, looked at Daniel over the centerpiece. "And how is your mother, Mr. Throckmorten?"

Grace listened with interest, for she'd never heard anyone mention his mother to him.

"She is well, ma'am. I was able to visit her recently, and hear all about the charities she's sponsoring in Cambridge."

"It's a shame she does not visit London." The old woman leaned forward and spoke in what she must have thought a whisper, but was heard at the end of the table. "Surely everyone has forgotten the scandal."

There was an expectant hush, and Grace wished she could somehow rescue Daniel from this awkwardness, as he'd rescued her today.

"Thank you, Lady Putnam. I am sure she knows that."

Did he know how much he'd truly changed himself after what happened to his father? If only she could help him regain his music, return to a time when its pursuit soothed him, but she didn't have the first idea how to go about it.

She was getting too involved, falling deeper and deeper into Daniel's problems, Daniel's life.

And she couldn't stop—didn't want to stop. His feelings mattered to her. The way he cared about her seemed more important than anything else.

Oh God, she really *had* fallen in love with him. And it might be the biggest mistake of her life.

That evening, as Grace listened to the next well-meaning young lady attempt to play the piano at her doting mother's musicale, she thought of how Edward had whistled as he'd left the house to join Daniel at the Southern Railway ball. His optimism had returned, and she could only be grateful to Daniel for that. Daniel hadn't had to help her brother, but he had done so. She kept telling herself that it was only a means to woo her, but she couldn't believe that of him. He was a good man. He'd spent his life helping people in trouble though he would not think that.

When the music portion of the evening was over, Grace went to help herself to iced cakes in the refreshment area set up in a small drawing room. She smiled at a man who came in behind her. He was of average height and build, and his black hair was beginning to thin on top.

He stopped in front of her and cleared his throat. "Miss Banbury?"

"Yes?" It was strange of him to speak to her when they hadn't been introduced, but perhaps he was new to Society. And suddenly she realized that she hadn't seen him at dinner.

"My name is Mr. Horace Jenkins."

When he paused awkwardly, she smiled. "I hope your evening has been pleasant, sir."

He smiled back, and for a moment she thought he was nervous, but he only took a deep breath.

"It has, now that I've met you. You see, I've wanted to be introduced for a long time."

She blinked in surprise. "I'm . . . flattered, Mr. Jenkins. I have not been in London long, but—"

"I know. In fact, I know all about you. I, too, live in Hertfordshire."

"Oh." She felt the first hint of uneasiness. "I am surprised we have not met."

"I have seen you, of course, but I was not sure how a visit from me might be accepted."

What could she say to that? "I am a friendly person, Mr. Jenkins."

"You're kind and sweet, and I know you'd understand why I—" He broke off.

Kind and sweet? How could he know that? "You what, Mr. Jenkins?" she asked, trying unsuccessfully to hide the nervous edge in her voice.

"Why I played in a card game to win your hand in marriage."

Grace inhaled swiftly, and all her focus sharpened on this one man. Thank heavens, there was no one else in the drawing room but the two of them. "I—so you were one of *them*."

"I was the one most eager to win your hand, Miss Banbury," he said sincerely. "The others wanted the property, or even the violin, like that fool Throckmorten. I would have done anything simply for *you*. But I lost."

"What would you have me say, Mr. Jenkins?" she asked softly. "I wish that card game had never taken place."

"That's because Throckmorten won," he said coldly.

Grace felt a jolt of awareness and certainty. Jenkins had to be the man who'd been watching her house.

"You didn't marry him," Mr. Jenkins said, when she didn't reply.

"No, I didn't."

"Good. He's a bounder with no morals. You should have rejected him outright, but instead I see you with him at every event."

He was no longer bothering to hide the thread of angry jealousy. Another man came into the room and perused the refreshment table. Mr. Jenkins looked at Grace in a knowing manner, as if daring her to say something.

And what could she say that wouldn't reveal the whole sordid scandal?

And then what would Daniel's family think of her?

Oh God, she was worried about marriage with him more than the harm to her own reputation and family. How had this happened to her?

When they were alone again, Grace tried conciliation. "Mr. Jenkins, due to that card game, Mr. Throckmorten feels he has certain . . . rights toward me. I resist him at every turn, but I cannot show that in public."

"Is he going to marry you?"

"No." What else could she say? It was probably the truth. And she thought even the possibility would make Jenkins angrier.

Instead he began to fidget, and perspiration broke out on his forehead. She'd made a mistake.

In a low, heated voice, he said, "Then why are you consorting with him? If he is not going to hold to the terms of the bet, then you should be with me."

She eyed the door, but he was between her and it. "Mr. Jenkins, he won the bet, and I don't know what the future holds in regards to marriage with him."

"I would marry you, Miss Banbury. Say you will."

"I—I cannot, in good conscience, Mr. Jenkins. Please understand that I—"

"I don't understand anything! It is not fair! And I've seen the way you look at him. You've probably already given yourself to him!"

She gasped. "Mr. Jenkins! Such crudity doesn't even deserve the decency of a reply!"

"I would overlook your faults, Miss Banbury."

Angry and too reckless, she drew herself up. "If you had hoped to sway me, insults will not help."

"I am always willing to overlook a woman's faults," he continued, as if he hadn't heard her. "I told that just last year to Miss Wadsworth, but she still refused me. And Miss Sutton the year before that."

Grace simply gaped at him as he rambled.

"I am done waiting, Miss Banbury. I need a wife, and this time I shall have the woman I've chosen."

Coldly, she said, "Good day, Mr. Jenkins."

His eyes glittered as he looked down her body. "This isn't over."

He stalked out of the room, and Grace felt a heavy weakness come over her. She clutched the table, wondering for a moment if her legs would carry her.

But no, she was not going to let that man—or any man—defeat her. She didn't know what she was going to do about Mr. Jenkins, but she would think of something. Surely if he wanted to marry her, he wouldn't besmirch her name in public. That would only make him look worse.

Yet how many more near disasters would she have before the *ton* finally heard of her many hidden scandals? There was Baxter Wells's intimate knowledge of her, Daniel's seduction, and now the threat of her mother's terrible bet coming to light. Grace had spent so much of her life trying to be above reproach, to rise above her mother's uncontrollable behavior. And now it was all falling down around her.

She left the musicale with Beverly, and then

asked to borrow her carriage. Though Beverly looked worried, she did not protest. After Grace let her off, she proceeded to Daniel's town house. He was the one in whom she'd been confiding; he was part of this whole mess. He should be the one to help her out of it.

As they neared his home, she suddenly realized how it would look for an unmarried lady to travel alone through the London night to a bachelor's home.

She rapped on the roof and waited as the carriage stopped. When the driver opened the door, she said, "Let me out at the corner and then wait for me."

He looked at her uncertainly, and she knew what he was seeing. A woman dressed in evening finery, wrapped in a cloak, alone at night.

"Miss, are ye sure 'bout this?"

"Yes, I am," she said briskly, barely hiding the anger that burned through her. "I just need to walk, to think. Wait here for me."

She turned away from him and headed down the street. Daniel's house was only two doors down, and she was able to sneak down the stairs and slip around back.

As she stood on the back step of the servants' entrance and knocked once, she had a moment of clarity. What was she doing? Daniel could not solve this for her. If he discovered she felt threatened, he might do worse than punch Mr. Jenkins, like he'd done to Baxter. He couldn't keep attacking her suitors. Then there would be even more scandal for him, this time brought on because of her, and his family would think her the worst sort of female.

She turned to leave, hoping everyone was in bed and had not heard the knock.

But the door opened behind her, and she wilted.

An older man wrapped in a dressing robe stood there, his cap askew on his balding head.

She looked over her shoulder. "I'm sorry, this is the wrong house."

"Grace?"

She froze at the sound of Daniel's voice. He came out of the gloom from behind his servant and into the light of the candle. He was dressed in his evening clothes, all black but for his shirt and cravat. The servant looked curiously between them but backed away when Daniel reached for her arm. She didn't resist as he pulled her inside.

To the servant, Daniel said quietly, "You can return to your bed."

Not letting go of Grace, he pulled her through the dark house, down a corridor, and into a paneled library where lamps lit the night. It had the faint smell of smoke and leather, a thoroughly masculine place.

Daniel released her and put his hands on his hips as he loomed over her, his expression tight with anger. "Would you care to explain why you are wandering London alone at night? There's been a man watching your house!"

"I didn't go home," she said, feeling belligerent.

Though he had not been the man to threaten her, she was angry at him for being at the beginning of this whole disaster that had enshrouded her life—and angry that he'd been the first one she'd wanted to go to for help.

"He could be following you!"

"He's not."

"What are you doing here? It can't be because of the railway ball. You could have asked your brother about his success with the women."

She crossed her arms over her chest. "Was he successful?"

"He was."

"Thank you," she said curtly.

He gave a half smile. "That doesn't sound very grateful."

Fisting her hands, she advanced on him. "You—oh!"

She whirled away, and then came to a stop when she saw an antique violin mounted on the wall. Her father's violin, the reason she was in this insane challenge.

Oh, she should leave; she was feeling angry and reckless, an equal mixture of despair and confidence writhing through her.

"That's going to be mine," she said in a low voice.

He came up behind her and gripped her shoulders. "I don't think so."

She looked over her shoulder at him. "So you think I can't resist you."

"Not for long."

His fingers undid the clasp at her throat, and her cloak fell to the floor.

"I have resisted every day since the beginning," she said.

"And it's getting harder, isn't it?"

Her neck and shoulders were bare, and he trailed his fingers along her collarbones.

"You'd like to think that," she whispered, suppressing a shiver at the pleasure of his touch. "I can stop anytime I want, but I think men are different."

Oh heavens, what was she doing? She was in his home, baiting him, daring him to make her give in. But her anger and helplessness and desire were all coming together inside her, and she could no longer think about what would be the right thing to do.

"Let's see who can stop," he said.

And then he turned her around and pushed her back up against the wall. His mouth came down on hers, holding her trapped.

And she reveled in it. She kissed him back fiercely, letting emotion and passion wipe away all her conflicted thoughts, her worries for the future. In that one moment, all she knew was that she loved him, that she'd come to him for help, though in the end, she could not risk asking him. She had never found a man who excited her more than he did. And if when their two weeks were over, he left her—

She wanted to love him; she wanted to punish

him for making her feel this way. So instead of accepting his kisses and caresses, she instigated her own, exploring his mouth with her tongue, letting her eager hands roam over his chest and slide beneath his coat and unbuttoned waistcoat. His muscles were hot and hard, and when she found his nipples through the fabric of his shirt, he moaned into her mouth.

The coat and waistcoat joined her cloak on the floor, and she pulled his shirt out of his trousers and slid it up his body. As he struggled to take it off over his head, she did what she so enjoyed having him do: she took his nipple into her mouth and sucked on it. Beneath her hands, the muscles of his abdomen convulsed.

"Grace." Her name was a hoarse prayer on his lips.

She suddenly shoved hard, and he fell backward onto the sofa. She came down on top of him, but the sofa was awkward, and in trying to get as close as possible, she ended up straddling him. He stopped breathing on a groan as he arched his hips up against her.

Though his trousers and her drawers still separated them, they moved against each other, rubbing. He grabbed the lower bodice of her dress and tugged until her breasts popped free of the low corset. For just a moment, they hung above his face, and then he greedily took one in his mouth. She cried out and moved even more frantically against him.

He cupped her head in his palms and pulled her down until their lips met. Against her mouth he murmured, "Let me come into you, Grace. Let me love you."

Those words were like a rain shower of reality. He meant he wanted sex, but those words—the tenderness of his voice—

She reared back. "No."

Chapter 20

Daniel came up on his elbows. "No?"

Grace's hips were still molded to his. He could feel her dampness, and the way her body cradled his erection, so close to the center of her, where he ached to be.

He rubbed his cock against her, moving in a way he knew she would like. And she gasped for him, her face contorted for him, her head thrown back above her naked breasts, but her passion was being overcome by remorse.

She almost fell as she climbed off him. Turning her back, she tugged her bodice back in place while he narrowed his eyes at her. What had he done? How had she been able to stop herself when he had been lost with her in his arms? Never in his life had a woman been able to separate him from his thoughts, from his rationality.

But it had not been the same for her. She'd been able to stop as if he meant nothing to her.

And he finally had to admit that that hurt. And it wasn't because he wanted to win this crazy challenge.

He wanted her. He wanted her to want him, to need him.

"I can't give in, Daniel," she said huskily, then bent over to search through his discarded clothing for her cloak. When she straightened, the look in her eyes was bleak and determined, even proud. "Whatever you men do, I can't give in."

You men? What the devil did that mean? "Grace, you can't leave here like this."

"I have Beverly's carriage waiting down the street. I'll be fine."

"But the man watching you—"

"He's no longer watching me."

He didn't understand her sudden bitterness. "Just because you haven't seen him—"

But she was already fleeing down the hall, and he hadn't even had the presence of mind to get dressed so that he could chase her. All he could do was follow her progress through the windows as she ran out the back door and around to the front of the house. He saw the carriage not two doors down, and only when she was safely inside did he feel relief.

But there was no relief for the rest of his body. He yearned for her; but she did not feel the same for him.

Two more days left to the challenge. He sensed it might be all he had left with her. Was that what he wanted?

Grace spent the morning listlessly answering letters from friends back home. She didn't want to go out and risk Jenkins and Daniel coming face-to-face over her in public. The only bright spot to her day was Edward's obvious happiness. He was whistling whenever he walked by the library where she was working. When she'd asked him about the ladies he'd met, he said it was too early to discuss it, but the smile on his face almost brought tears to her eyes. At least one of them was happy. He left before luncheon, and she was miserably alone again.

As she'd known he would, Daniel came to visit her in the afternoon. With sudden inspiration, she left him waiting a long time for her in the drawing room. The piano took up much of the space, and she wondered if it drew him. She cautiously crept to the doorway and peered in. Daniel was standing at the window, but she saw him look over his shoulder at the piano. She leaned back against the wall before he could see her, and then a few minutes later, she looked in again. He was rifling through the sheet music that she'd left out.

Once again, she leaned out of sight, unable to keep a silly grin from her face. She'd been right about him and his music. But more minutes passed, and he didn't play. When she looked in again, he was pacing.

Disappointed, she took a deep breath, shook her skirts into place, and serenely walked in. "Good afternoon, Daniel."

He stopped and stared at her, and she found she couldn't remember what she'd meant to say. The awareness between them always caught her by surprise, as if she kept expecting it to lessen. He looked down her body, and she let herself look down his.

"I have not changed in just one night," she said softly.

He came toward her. "Which is a good thing. I don't suppose you'd close the door."

"No."

He shrugged and stopped before her. "I can still taste you," he whispered wickedly.

Heat rose inside her, and she knew she was blushing.

"I want to taste you everywhere." His voice was low and urgent, as if he hadn't meant to say those words but couldn't help himself.

She could have swooned. She had to stop this before she fell into his arms in broad daylight.

"I've sent for refreshments," she said, striving for a normal tone.

He arched a brow, giving her a slow smile. "Your defenses can't work."

She lifted her chin. "They have so far."

"True."

When he came toward her, she stepped away, toward the piano. "I saw you looking through the sheet music."

Wariness appeared briefly in his eyes, before his usual polite mask settled into place. It bothered her that he felt he had to hide what he was thinking from her.

Of course, she was hiding many things from him.

"And don't tell me you don't listen to music because your mother doesn't," she continued calmly. "That just doesn't ring true to me. Surely the fact that your father was a composer, and that he died when you were so young, makes more sense."

He opened his mouth, but whatever he meant to say, he seemed to think differently. "You'd think so," he began, "but that's not true. I was proud of my father's music. It was what I had left of him, and playing it made me feel closer to him at first."

She held her breath, and then finally encouraged him with, "At first?"

She kept expecting him to laugh away her concern, to pretend it didn't matter. But they stood facing each other in the center of the drawing room, and he didn't retreat.

"Is this what you need from me, Grace? Painful truths from my past?"

"I don't know why I need it, Daniel. But . . ." She trailed off uncertainly. How could she tell him that he needed to understand himself?

"Very well, then you'll hear it," he said without expression. "I think I gave up music because of Mother, not my father."

She frowned. "You've already said that your mother won't listen to music anymore, and that you—"

"Let me finish. When my father died, my mother didn't know how to handle her grief. She'd spent her married life at one with her husband's artistry, full of the same passion for creating music as he had. But where he succeeded, she never had, though she tried in so many different ways. And she seemed fine with that, as if someday she would learn enough to succeed at her dream. When my father died, I don't know if music provided a bridge to his memory, but for whatever reason, she immersed herself in it for months. I barely saw her, except at meals, and even then she would be distracted, as if she could not escape whatever feverish energy she'd created. This went on for months."

Grace barely breathed, so afraid of interrupting Daniel's confession. He hadn't given up music because he associated it with his father or because of the rumors of his mother being a murderer—music had taken away his mother at a time when he needed her the most.

"When at last she finished the symphony she was composing, she was exhausted and beginning to come to terms with my father's death. She hadn't necessarily meant for the symphony to be exposed to the world, but a friend showed it to a conductor without her knowledge, and suddenly she was being hailed as the next great musical genius." He smiled wryly. "And I was angry."

"You were young and confused," she said softly, touching his arm. "You'd lost your father, and I'm sure it seemed like you'd lost your mother, too, since she was so preoccupied."

He shrugged. "I didn't want her to go back to something that had hurt her—hurt us."

"You stopped playing because you didn't want

to remind her about music," Grace said, "in case she'd become caught up in it again. Were you worried she would?"

"For a while," he admitted. "And then I was sent to school. The first time I came home, I ran to the music room, but the sheets still covered everything."

"Like they do now."

He nodded.

"Do you ever wish that you—or she—would rediscover music?"

But that was one step too far. He only grinned and reached for her, pulling her against his body.

"I am an adult now. There are more pleasurable things to do with my time."

His breath on her face, his warm, hard body the length of hers was once again stealing away her will, her resolve to resist him. He leaned down to kiss her, and she let him, glad that he'd shared something so private with her.

"Get your hands off my sister!" Edward's voice thundered.

Grace stumbled backward and saw Daniel's face become impassive.

"Banbury," Daniel said, as if they'd just met pleasantly on the street.

Grace turned to face her brother, guilt and worry clogging her throat, making it hard to speak. "Edward, it was only a kiss."

"It's more than that, and I know all about it," Edward said, stalking into the room and passing her to face Daniel. "Jenkins approached me at my club."

Grace groaned, knowing that Mr. Jenkins had chosen his revenge well. "Edward—"

But he ignored her to say to Daniel, "I can't believe I was beginning to trust you and your so-called advice."

"I have never steered you wrong," Daniel said calmly.

"No, you were only trying to distract me while you pursued my sister. My God, did you even tell her what crude right you'd won from my mother?"

"No," Daniel said.

But Edward had turned away from Daniel in time to read Grace's expression and see the truth. A bleak sadness crossed her brother's face. "Grace, why didn't you tell me? Were you embarrassed?"

She raised a hand to stop Daniel from speaking. "I was hurt and humiliated, Edward," she said. "Daniel and I had agreed that we would not marry. I didn't think it mattered."

"Not mattered?" Edward cried. "Our mother tried to give you away like you were property!"

She put a hand to her mouth and felt the first tears leak from her eyes.

"It's like a sickness that even I can't avoid," he continued bleakly. "I have tried so hard to put it aside, and though some days it's easier than others, I still was able to do it. But Mother didn't even try."

"And can you trust your restraint so well already?" she asked. "I don't even trust my own."

"You don't gamble," he scoffed.

But then comprehension raced across his face, and he turned angrily back to Daniel. "It's you, isn't it? You are the man testing her restraint. My God, I trusted you, when all along you've been trying to bed my sister."

"Edward!" Grace cried.

Daniel stepped toward her brother, and suddenly she could see the terrible result if she let them at each other.

"Daniel, you must leave!" she said heatedly. "This does not concern you. This is about the lack of trust between my brother and me."

As she'd guessed, that made Edward turn back toward her, his expression affronted. "Grace, what are you saying?"

She took his hand and realized he was trembling. "Daniel, please leave."

He nodded to them both and left the room. Grace and Edward were frozen in place until they heard the front door close on the ground floor.

Grace took Edward's other hand, and she was at least relieved that he didn't pull away. "I haven't told you everything, it is true," she said, her voice shaking. "I didn't want you to know what I had to do to retrieve the violin."

"Oh, Grace." He winced and closed his eyes. "Not that damn violin again."

"It was all we had, Edward! The property was gone. I could find employment, but you—"

"You don't think I can work if I have to?" he demanded, trying to pull away from her.

She clutched his hands harder, needing to be connected to him. "But I didn't want you to have to! You're a gentleman, Edward, and I wanted you to be able to live the life you've grown up in, just like our father. The money from the violin would help."

"You told me you could persuade him to give it back to you," he said, his face paling. "Grace, what did you promise him for the violin?"

She took a shocked breath. "You think I would sell myself for it? Edward, I would never—"

"Then what? I didn't buy that balderdash about redeeming him from the beginning. I thought you were wasting your time. But that was only a convenient lie to mask the truth, wasn't it."

"It was desperation on my part, yes, but I truly believed it could work. He's a good man, Edward, and if I could have made Society see that—"

"Grace, tell me the truth!"

She jerked at his harsh tone, stung. Tears were flowing freely down her face, stinging her eyes, dripping to her bodice. "He didn't need a wife, but he wanted a mistress," she said raggedly.

Reddening, Edward turned toward the door as if meant to defend her against the world, but she had a death grip on his hands.

"Listen to me! I refused, of course, and he knew I would. He was trying to provoke me because it's what he does best. I told him he could never convince me to be his mistress. He thought he could.

One thing led to another, and we agreed on a—a challenge."

"A wager, you mean," Edward said.

The disappointment in his face broke her heart.

"Oh Grace, I thought you were immune to the terrible need Mother and I share."

"I am—or I was. But it . . . seemed so easy to win! He said that he could seduce me into willingly being his mistress, and I told him it was impossible. After everything that had happened to me with Baxter Wells, I thought this was too easy to win. And we'd have the violin, Edward. Its purchase would let us have our own home again."

"Are you saying that he has not—that you have not—"

"No! Tomorrow is the last day of the challenge, Edward, I promise." But right now didn't seem the best time to say that she wanted to keep seeing Daniel, that she loved him, that she didn't know if she even wanted to resist him anymore.

"Then don't see him again."

"I can't do that! It was part of the agreement, and we've both kept to the terms."

He covered his face with his hands. "Oh Grace, you're doing this for me. How can I bear it?"

"I'm doing it for both of us," she said softly. "Let me finish this, Edward. I know what I'm doing."

"You can't trust him. He's probably only assisting me with investments to soften you."

"But he never brags about it, or uses it to sway me. I drag those explanations out of him. He's an honorable man, Edward."

"And you've fallen in love with him."

She opened her mouth, but how could she lie anymore, when there were still other things she hadn't told him?

"Tell me, Grace, tell me what you feel."

"I *think* I love him," she whispered, then hurriedly continued, "but I am not so foolish as to think he loves me. I don't know what will happen. But Edward, let me finish this. Promise me you won't try to stop me."

He searched her eyes, and she saw him stiffen, his mouth flattening. "Very well. I promise. But he'll hurt you, Grace. You've thought yourself in love before."

"I know." She hugged herself. "I don't know how this will end, but Edward, I have to try."

Edward turned away and strode out the door.

Daniel was waiting for Banbury in the shadows of the town house. He felt responsible for Banbury's problems and couldn't just let him go off and do something thoughtless. He followed Banbury to his club, where, to Daniel's relief, Banbury drank but did not enter the gaming room. Daniel couldn't watch him all night, so at last he went home. He knew deep inside that Banbury wasn't finished, that there was still a confrontation to come.

Had Grace told him everything? Daniel had been relishing his pursuit of Grace, but when he put himself in Banbury's place, he knew the man would feel betrayed.

And after midnight, when someone pounded on the front door, he knew just who it was.

Daniel sent his butler back to bed and opened the door himself. Banbury launched himself into the entrance hall, and Daniel fell backward with him on top. They rolled around on the floor, knocking over a table, crashing a vase, landing a few punches, but Banbury wasn't exactly sober, and Daniel was holding back.

At last Banbury came up on his knees, his chest heaving as he struggled to breathe. When Daniel offered him a hand up, he ignored it and rose unsteadily to his feet. Blood dripped from the corner of his mouth, but there was little damage. Daniel moved his jaw experimentally, but it seemed in working order.

"Stop seeing Grace," Banbury said, his voice husky.

"I can't."

Banbury closed his eyes for a moment, his expression grim. "She told me about the challenge. How dare you use an innocent woman for your pleasure!"

"I can't talk about this with you, Banbury."

"Damn you, do you love her?"

Daniel froze, surprised that for a moment, he didn't know what to say. "No." But saying that one word made him feel hollow, uncertain. He couldn't explain what Grace was to him, what he wanted her to be beyond his mistress.

Now he'd lost Banbury's trust—and he'd never had Grace's.

"It's over after tomorrow?" Banbury asked.

"The challenge is."

"And will you stop pursuing her?"

"Don't ask me to lie to you, Banbury."

The other man stared at him grimly, then turned and walked out the door.

Daniel paced for two hours, and then went back to the Banbury town house. He let himself in the back door, moving through the dark halls until he reached Grace's door. When he went inside, she was sitting in the window seat, looking out over the courtyard garden.

The candlelight showed her pale face, the dark smudges beneath her eyes. But her voice was calm as she said, "Did he come after you?"

Daniel leaned back against the door. "He did, but we only exchanged a few blows. He wants me to stop seeing you—"

"As if that is his decision to make!" Grace interrupted.

"I refused."

She eyed him speculatively. "Can't let the challenge go?"

"One day from its completion? I think not. And you can't either."

But he found himself holding his breath. Would she end it? Was she so distraught over being discovered that she could not continue?

And what would he do then?

Before she could answer, he decided to distract her. "You heard your brother mention a Mr. Jenkins as the man who told him about what I'd really won."

She nodded, but warily.

"Then you've guessed that he's one of the men I gambled with against your mother."

She nodded again.

"For your peace of mind, know that I've had him—and the other man—investigated. The other man is in the north, and Jenkins himself, though he might have been waiting outside your house, does not seem a threat. I'm having him watched, regardless, so that you can rest assured that he won't harm you."

"There are other ways to harm a person," she said softly.

There was a distance in her eyes that he couldn't read, and she didn't explain.

"You mean by telling Banbury the truth?"

"Yes."

But she didn't meet his eyes.

"Do not worry—it will go no further," he said with conviction. "I'll have a talk with Jenkins."

She came up out of the window seat and approached him. "Daniel, I don't want you to do that. You'll only antagonize him. He's embarrassed me before my family. I'm sure that's all he wants."

"We don't know that, Grace."

"I do. If you stir it up, it will make things worse."

She seemed so desperate, so sincere, that he didn't have the heart to go against her. "Very well, but if anything else happens with Jenkins, you'll tell me."

She nodded, her expression relieved.

He didn't like seeing her this way, worried and sad. He wanted to renew the fire in her eyes. "To-morrow is the last day of the challenge."

A faint smile turned up the corners of her mouth. "I've almost won."

"I don't concede yet. And since you cannot avoid me tomorrow, we'll spend the evening together."

"One last chance?"

There was a definite softness to her, an amuse-ment, and he felt relieved.

"We're going to Vauxhall Gardens."

"I've heard of it of course, but I've never been there."

He had her interest now, and part of it was be-cause she thought he would not be alone with her. Little did she know what could go on in the Gardens, with its dark pathways, ancient Greek décor, and many people walking the line between respectability and chaos.

"But how can I go with *you*? Shall I bring my chaperones?" She was laughing at him now, as if she sensed victory in her grasp.

"No chaperones will be necessary. We'll be masked, of course, so no one will know us. I'll send over the perfect gown for you to wear."

"A disguise?"

He came closer and put his hands at her waist.

She trembled faintly, and he knew with surety that tomorrow night would hold the true test. "A disguise. You can pretend to be . . . anyone you want."

Her head was turned away from him, as if she were worried he might try to kiss her. Her lovely profile showed her contemplation.

"Say yes," he murmured against her temple, feeling the softness of a curl against his lips, inhaling the headiness of lavender.

"Yes."

Chapter 21

It was almost over, Grace thought the next evening as she waited in her drawing room for Daniel. Ruby waited with her, wearing the same disapproving frown she'd worn since they'd both opened the dressmaker's box and lifted out the gown that Daniel had sent to her.

Ruby shook her head and tsked softly. "'Tis showin' too much of your bosom, Miss Grace," she said for the tenth time.

"Every draft tells me that," Grace answered, trying to lighten the mood.

But she stared down at her breasts, pushed up high by the corset until they were almost overflowing the gown. And then she settled the feathered mask over her face, and she was someone else, someone dressed in the silver and white of a woodland fairy gleaming by moonlight. She felt light and beautiful and—bold, but it was how Daniel wanted her to look their last night together.

She would let him look, and she would revel in matching wits together. After this, with no challenge, he would probably lose interest in her, and she tried not to let herself despair.

How could she make him fall in love with her? She'd proved woefully inadequate with Baxter Wells, so she certainly could not trust her own instincts. And Daniel's family would be urging him to stay far away. Much as he enjoyed his role as rebel, he loved his family and would not hurt them.

But she had to be with him one last time.

She heard the knock at the front door, felt her nerves jump within her at the sound of Daniel's deep, smooth voice talking to the butler.

And then at last he was shown in, and he came to a dead stop in the doorway, his grin fading, and his dark eyes narrowing.

She held her breath, as he looked her over so thoroughly he might have been touching her.

How could she keep resisting him when she was in love? The warm look in his eyes made her melt—made her imagine emotions he didn't feel for her.

Ruby cleared her throat, and the spell between them was broken.

Daniel bowed. "Miss Banbury, you look lovely this evening."

"Thank you, sir. You have excellent taste in ladies' gowns."

When Ruby tsked again, he grinned. "But it is only a costume, and it disguises you well. Who would ever think the proper Miss Banbury lurked beneath?"

"I could ride in the carriage with ye, Miss Grace," Ruby said.

Grace shook her head, not even looking at the maid. "No, it's all right, Ruby. You don't need to wait up."

Whatever the maid thought of that, Grace didn't notice, because she took Daniel's arm and let him lead her out to the enclosed carriage.

They had to cross the river to reach Vauxhall Gardens, and the ride seemed too long, yet too short. The tension and awareness between them said it all—it was the last night of the challenge. She was thinking if she could just hold out until midnight, what she did with Daniel afterward would not matter.

She knew he had plans for what would happen this evening. *Let him try*, she thought, her face covered in the mask. She was someone else tonight, a woman who didn't have to fear blackmailers or poverty.

"Put on your mask," she said softly.

Without a word, he slid the black mask down over his eyes, leaving his sensual mouth bare.

The mouth she wanted to kiss.

The heat was rising too fast within her. She had brought a feathered fan, and now she waved it before her face. She watched his gaze dip to her half-covered breasts, and knew she was hiding and revealing them every time she moved the fan.

She was playing a reckless, daring game, but the results would affect the rest of her life.

At last they arrived at Vauxhall Gardens, and Daniel helped her down from the carriage. They joined the crowds, from noblemen to commoners, seeking entrance, and since so many people wore masks, she was just as anonymous as they. Who would know what she did this night but she and Daniel?

Together they went through the dark passage, their feet crunching on gravel, and emerged into fairy light. Thousands of globe lamps were hung in the tall trees and down the famous walkways. She had told Daniel that it was her first visit, so he followed the crowds and let her walk the grounds beneath the arches spanning the South Walk, past temples and pavilions and colonnades and the balloon-ascent tower. From a gaslit pond emerged giant Neptune and eight white seahorses. Grace clung to Daniel's arm and laughed and gaped at the fairyland all around her.

At last they settled in their supper box near the Gothic temple that housed the orchestra. Two other couples were seated in their box, and it was obvious they'd already been dipping into the wine, for their enthusiastic greeting made Grace giggle. No names were exchanged.

As the music swelled loudly, the globe lights at the front of their box did not quite reach the back, where Grace and Daniel sat side by side. He kept his hand on her thigh and she let him, feeling the pressure of each finger on her skin as if she wore no clothing. Their shoulders rubbed against each other, so closely did they sit. They shared thin slivers of ham and chicken, drank too much wine, and bought extra fruit from the strawberry girl. Daniel touched a berry to Grace's lips, and when she would have taken a bite, he slid it over her chin and down her neck, tracing a moist path between her breasts before meeting her eyes and taking a bite of the strawberry. Her lips were parted with his daring, and he fed the second half of the berry to her himself.

"Don't let your wife see how you treat your mistress!" guffawed a drunken voice from the front of their box.

The other three people laughed uproariously, and Grace saw Daniel's swift glance at her. Though his mask hid the upper half of his face from her, she knew what he was thinking: Would she take offense? Would she insist on leaving?

But she wasn't Grace tonight, and if they wanted to think her his mistress, well . . . let them. She could play the part.

Grace lifted her wineglass in a toast. "To his wife, who doesn't know what she's missing!"

Several glasses clinked together above the table, one broke, and there was even more laughter. Grace leaned into Daniel's lap so that their lips were but a breath apart.

"Are you pleased with me, sir?" she whispered.

He seemed to be having trouble speaking, and she leaned closer and nipped at his bottom lip. His hand came up and fiercely cupped her head to hold her against him for a true kiss. She had to brace her hand on his thigh to remain upright.

Their dinner partners hooted and clapped as if the entertainment were better than Vauxhall itself.

"Here is a bold lady!"

Grace broke away from the headiness of Daniel's kiss to see one of the brightly dressed and painted clowns standing at their table.

"We need an adventurous maiden to join our show," the clown continued. "Care you to come, my lady?"

She was out of her chair before Daniel could even express an opinion. She found herself dancing on the lawn, as the clowns and the acrobats performed their tricks all around her. She could see Daniel standing next to their supper box, keeping an eye on her, his mouth quirked with amusement. The night was lit with thousands of globes that twinkled like stars above her, and as she whirled, she threw her arms wide and tilted back her head to take it all in.

She wasn't the only guest frolicking with the entertainers. Another woman bumped into her, and they both laughed. But this woman was unmasked although Grace did not recognize her. The woman's face was flushed with dancing and perhaps too much wine.

The woman eyed her speculatively. "So are you Throckmorten's latest mistress?"

Grace knew her mask was firmly in place—there was no reason to panic. In fact, she felt strangely confident. "Who?"

The woman laughed and reached toward Grace's face, as if she meant to pluck the mask away. Grace reared back, laughing, and ducked behind another clown.

Someone caught her and lifted her off the ground, and she knew without looking that she was safe in Daniel's firm embrace. As he carried her away from the Grove and down the darker paths, people cheered and toasted with their glasses. It was a hedonistic night, and she reveled in being part of it.

She was kissing Daniel before the darkness even descended, their masks brushing. She knew other couples were furtively searching for their privacy, but she didn't care. She didn't know how he could even see where he was going, so thoroughly did she keep his face to hers. But at last she drew back to breathe, her arm around his shoulders, his strong arms behind her back and beneath her knees. Above her, Greek columns gleamed darkly against the blacker backdrop of the night sky. He sat down on a bench and laid her across his lap, leaving her open and vulnerable to him.

While their mouths did a mating dance, his hands traced every part of her body as if he couldn't get enough. She knew why he'd chosen the gown, for he was able to release her breasts with barely an effort. And then his hot mouth bathed her nipple, and she smothered a moan. Each tug of his lips made her feel another pull, deep in her belly. A whisper of cool air brushed her lower legs, and his palm slid up her calf. She would have let him continue his exquisite torture, but he suddenly lifted his head.

"Damn, but this isn't happening here," he growled, standing up and settling her on her feet.

She swayed and he caught her. When she put her arms around his neck and shamelessly pressed her body against his, his only response was to tug her corset and neckline back in place.

He took her hand. "Come on!"

And then he started to run, at a slow enough pace that she could keep up with him. They swerved between crowds of people, past the Rotunda, where everyone was heading to watch the equestrian show. The lit trees faded behind them, and they pushed past the crowds still coming in for the second show.

As he signaled for their carriage, he pulled her up next to him.

"Aren't we staying for the fireworks?" she asked, out of breath yet laughing because she knew his response.

He nuzzled her cheek. "We'll make our own fireworks."

When the carriage arrived, he didn't wait for the coachman to descend. Daniel dropped down the stairs, picked her up, and swept her up inside, where she fell back on the padded bench, propped on her elbows. A lit lantern swayed above her. After he folded back the step and closed the door, the carriage lurched, and he practically fell on top of her.

His mouth came down on hers, and he dropped to his knees on the floor. In between frantic kisses, he slid the mask off her face and tossed his own over his shoulder. She pushed his coat off his shoulders, so she could feel the heat of him through his shirt. His tongue entered her mouth, his hands began to strip her, and she lost the last of her sanity, forgot about wagers and challenges. All that mattered was the explosion of passion between them, the excitement, the way she felt about herself when she was with him. Even when he wanted her body, he made her feel cherished and worshipped. She loved him and wanted to show him.

She pulled his shirt out from his trousers, reaching under to run her hands up his hard stomach. When she tweaked his nipples with her fingernails, he shuddered, making her feel as if she had the same power over him that he wielded over her.

He had somehow managed to reach beneath her and unbutton her gown, because it spread loose across her breasts. He sat her upright against the back of the bench, as he began to pull the gown up over her head. After her corset and chemise and drawers went flying, she was sitting there naked but for her stockings.

And she wanted him naked, too. With desperate hands she helped pull off his shirt, then watched with excitement as he unbuttoned his trousers. He couldn't stand in the carriage, so he fell back on the far bench to remove them. Two naked people were soon sitting across from one another in a carriage. All she could look at was his engorged penis. She and Baxter had been furtive in their lovemaking, so she had never gotten such a vivid look as she did now. She felt hot and tremulous and needy just imagining being one with him.

And then Daniel was on his knees before her, hands on her face to bring her to his kiss. They were greedy, devouring each other's mouths, hands skimming and caressing and grasping. His erection rubbed intimately against her womanhood, her thighs clutched his hips, and she leaned back against the bench so that he could bring his mouth to her breasts. He held them reverently and licked her nipples with long strokes that made her shudder with rising pleasure.

At last she felt his erection probe deeper, and when he hesitated, looking into her eyes, she knew nothing else but the need to give in, to feel the pleasure that swept her away from herself. She loved him. She nodded and wrapped her legs about him as he began to ease gently inside her.

Too gently, too slowly. With a moan she tightened her legs, welcoming his sudden deep thrust. The pleasure was almost painful, so deep and pure and urgent. On his knees he surged and retreated, each undulation sending her higher and higher. He bent over her to take her nipple into his mouth. She strained and quivered until at last, her pleasure broke over her, and she rode it with a cry of bliss. He groaned against her breasts. She felt him shuddering as his own climax poured through him.

He leaned against her, holding her safe in his arms. Her legs slowly slid down from the grip they'd had on his hips. He was still inside her, full and hard, filling a place in her soul she'd thought empty.

And then she heard a distant tolling of church bells ringing through the city. Daniel stiffened in her arms, as they counted out twelve tolls.

He had won the challenge.

"Those bells are always wrong," he said mildly.

Though her amusement was out of place, she burst out laughing. "All of them? All over the city?"

"Of course. I know for certain that you won our challenge, that you held out and defeated me."

He straightened above her, hands beside her hips on the bench. She looked up at him, at the fine perspiration on his brow that dampened his dark hair at his forehead. Their bodies swayed with the movement of the carriage through the London streets. They were still most intimately joined, but that had no part in the soft way she regarded him, the tenderness she knew was showing on her face. The violin had been a link for him to his father. Surely he would not so easily surrender it to her if she didn't mean something to him.

But what now? If he wanted her to win, was it all over? For after all, hadn't he just taken the ultimate prize, her surrender?

Chapter 22

Daniel stared down at Grace in bemusement, watching as her breathing finally
eased. She had to be uncomfortable, sitting on
the bench as she was with him still between her
legs.

But there was no virgin's discomfort, as he had
guessed back at Madingley Court. Baxter Wells
had been here before him.

His anger at the man returned. She'd been led
to believe herself in love, and had been lied to.
At least Daniel wasn't misleading her about their
relationship.

But now she was his mistress, he thought,
staring down into her lovely green eyes. Though
she looked calm, she was also watchful, waiting
for what he'd do next.

And he didn't know what that was. Was he still
bothered by the fact that after all their intimacy,
she still hadn't told him what had happened with
Wells?

He pulled out of her and somehow managed
to sprawl at her side on the bench. She looked at

his cock, which was still erect as it rested on his stomach.

"Shouldn't we get dressed quickly?" she asked, starting to straighten.

He put a hand on her thigh. "No need. The coachman won't stop until I give the signal."

She glanced at him and spoke dryly. "Well trained?"

"As in, do I seduce women in my carriage on a regular basis? I simply gave him instructions before we left the Gardens."

She relaxed back against the seat. Their bare arms and thighs touched, and he kept waiting for her to awkwardly cover herself, but she didn't.

But again, a man's nudity was not new to her.

He had to stop thinking about that, so he looked at her breasts, resting high on her rib cage, pert and deliciously pink. He wanted to taste them again, and was about to when she spoke.

"Are you going to keep staring?"

"Are you?"

She blushed. "I am allowed to. But surely you must be used to the sight."

"Of you naked? Do you think I'm sneaking about your house watching you dress?"

"Other women naked," she corrected, reddening even more.

"In my limited experience—"

She huffed in disbelief.

"—every woman is different," he continued, ignoring her reaction, "from the color that graces the peaks of her breasts"—he trailed a finger up the side of her breast and touched the peak, which tightened for him, even as she trembled—"to the varied fullness"—he cupped one breast gently, holding and weighing it, before beginning a slow trail down her abdomen—"to the shape of a woman's nether lips." He threaded his fingers through her curls, watched her stiffen, and heard her indrawn breath as he traced her damp opening. "Shall I kiss you there?"

But he had gone too far. With a shocked gasp, she clamped her legs together. He didn't try to withdraw his hand, still cupping her, one finger sliding inside her.

He was trying to bring a reaction out of her, and wondered if he'd been attempting the same earlier. He'd brought her masked to Vauxhall Gardens, notorious for its mix of noblemen and commoners. She'd almost been unmasked by a woman who knew him—and would have known Grace. Scandal was something he was used to, but had he subconsciously wanted her to be a part of it? What reaction had he expected from others—from her? Caught together so blatantly, he would have been forced to marry her, or ruin her.

He would never hurt her, so did he want to marry her?

It was a new revelation for him, because he'd never found a woman who made him think of marriage as more than a convenience for the transfer of wealth and the continuation of the family into the next generation. Suddenly he thought about need and caring within a marriage, two emotions he had never wanted to feel, not when they could lead to so much grief. But there was joy, too.

And now Grace was naked in his carriage, mostly at ease. How would she react if she knew the path of his thoughts? She'd had her heart broken once. He didn't know if he could love her; wouldn't he know such an emotion the moment he felt it? Perhaps he couldn't feel it because he didn't know if she trusted him.

Yet she'd desired him so much she'd forgotten about the challenge, had given herself to him. Wasn't that a form of trust?

At last she eased her legs a bit, and he removed his hand. Deliberately holding her gaze, he brought to his mouth the finger that had just been inside her. When he licked it, her lips parted, and she stared at him, blinking in a dazed manner.

He gave her a wicked grin, and at last she groaned and looked away.

"So are you happy now?" she asked. "Is this everything you wanted?"

Happy? What was she leading him to? He had a moment of dismay as he remembered the warnings of his family, who thought she was trying to entrap him.

But how could there be any trust between them if he still worried about such a thing, after everything he knew about her? He had much to think about.

But he took her words as what they were, from a woman unsure of her sexuality, a woman who'd been used by another man and abandoned. If she was too embarrassed to voluntarily reveal her secrets, perhaps he could coax her.

"I'm happy," he began slowly. "Are you? Your first lover did not take care of you."

She stiffened, and predictably found her chemise beside her on the bench and pulled it on like a blanket, covering herself and what she thought of as her shame. "So it was obvious that I'm not a virgin. I did not lie to you; I'd always said I wasn't innocent."

"So you did. I just did not take the words so literally." He paused, giving her time. "Would you tell me what happened?"

She glanced at him in surprise. "Why do you want to know?"

"You said he hurt you. I don't want to do the same."

She smiled crookedly. "You're not. You explained up front your motives in pursuing me, and you've met your goals." She bit her lip and looked away again. "Baxter made me believe we'd fallen in love, even said the words to me as he promised to marry me."

"All to get you into his bed?"

With a shrug, she said, "I think so. Maybe he was even toying with the idea of marriage." She hesitated, and old sadness twisted her expression as she whispered, "But then I thought I might be carrying his child."

He took her hand and she let him, but he didn't think she even realized he was there. She had gone back into her own pain and fear.

"He was not overjoyed," he said matter-of-factly.

His tone seemed to ease her tension, for a faint smile touched her lips. "No. He accused me of trying to force his hand."

"He's a bastard," Daniel said in a low, angry voice.

She gave him a rueful smile. "He is. That's why I warned your cousin about him."

"Good of you." When she said nothing right away, he began, "What happened next?"

"He left me."

"When he thought you might be pregnant?" he asked, straightening up in outrage. Her voice was far too even, too calm, as if she'd spent a long time ridding herself of emotion.

She nodded. "He said he would not be trapped by a woman after his fortune. He would try to send money when the time came." Her laugh held no amusement.

"I should have taken him apart when I had the chance," Daniel said between gritted teeth.

Her hand touched his arm. "No, it's over. It was only a scare, not a true pregnancy. I had never felt so much gratitude and relief in my life when my . . . monthly came."

She glanced at him shyly, as if they weren't naked. It was endearing.

"But I knew I had come so close to losing my reputation, to losing . . . everything." She sighed. "But now you've proved to me that my lack of virginity will be apparent on my wedding night. I cannot lie to a future husband. Perhaps I should just be your mistress and be done with it."

In the face of her controlled emotions, he asked softly, "Is that what you want, a life beholden to a man's money?"

Her chin lifted; her eyes shot green sparks. "No."

"Then I haven't won yet."

"What?" she asked in confusion.

"The challenge was for me to make you my mistress, and you've said you won't be that. I'll just have to keep trying."

She studied him. "But the two weeks are over."

"Do you want the *challenge* to be over?" he asked, actually feeling nervous about her response. What would he do if he couldn't see her, try to seduce her, every day?

In a whisper, she answered, "No."

The relief he felt was almost overwhelming, giving him even more to think about. "Then let's get you home."

When she started to lift her chemise over her head, he took it from her and did it himself, When it was over her face, her arms upraised, he leaned over and kissed each nipple, feeling satisfied as she shivered.

Then she took his wrinkled shirt and pulled it over his head. When he tensed, wondering what she'd do, she surprised him by touching her tongue to his navel and giggling when he jerked in surprise. He didn't imagine she realized the effect of her hair brushing his groin.

When he could see her bright face again, he asked, "Can you ignore the corset?"

"Not and still fit into the gown. And am I just supposed to carry it inside?"

"I guess not."

He helped her pull the garment over her head and settle it into place over her chemise. Then he used his teeth to tighten the laces at her back. Instead of laughing, she gave a low moan, and his own passion began to rise again. The game was no longer about playing.

She helped him slide on his waistcoat. When she reached the bottom button, she leaned in and briefly kissed his mouth. She proved herself an expert in tying his cravat, and his reward for barely remaining still was another kiss, this time to his throat, and a dip of her tongue beneath his collar. He shuddered.

She had several petticoats, and she held her balance standing in the middle of the rocking carriage and stepped into them for him. As he tied each one, he nipped at her through her garments, first one thigh, then the other, then with his face pressed against the petticoats between her thighs. She cried out and held his head there for a moment, and he rewarded her by rubbing hard against her.

She pushed him back onto the seat, then lifted each of his stockinged feet to slide them into his drawers. She drew the garment up his legs, her body following as he parted his thighs. Her face just above his hard erection seemed like torture, and a lock of her hair slid over him, making him inhale harshly. Dipping her head, she let her hair brush back and forth over him, until he was gripping the leather bench to keep from launching himself at her. At last she pulled his drawers all the way up, though she didn't tighten the laces, which made him hopeful.

When she backed away, grinning with pleased satisfaction, he tried to remember how to move. He almost groaned as he reached for her gown, then held it up until she slid her arms in. As each inch of her face appeared, he pressed kisses over and over again, taking her damp mouth in a long invasion before following the gown even lower. As it settled into place halfway down her breasts, he thrust his tongue into the valley between, inhaling lavender and the unique scent of Grace. Her skin was moist and salty, and he could have continued there for much longer until she pushed him away with shaking hands.

"Your trousers," she whispered.

Once again he found himself easing backward on the seat, watching her from beneath half-closed eyes as she knelt before him and pulled the trousers up his legs. When he lifted his hips to allow her to pull them to his waist, she quickly placed a kiss on his erection through his clothing, and then pulled away as if she were embarrassed. But he would remember that innocent, curious kiss for a long time.

"Only my drawers are left," she said softly, not yet meeting his eyes.

All his desperation and desire welled up within him, and the thought of letting her go back to her empty bed seemed more than he could tolerate. He fumbled to open his trousers and drawers, then with swift hands drew her up and over until she straddled him.

"Drawers get in the way," he said against her mouth, and thrust up inside her.

She cried out even as her wet, hot walls accepted the length of him, sheltering him. He lifted her up and down himself until she understood what he wanted, then she rode him gracefully, wildly, feeling her way with her eyes closed. Her skirts poofed across his chest, but since he'd never buttoned the back of her gown, the bodice fell forward. It was easy to release her breasts from the low corset, and he played with them, teasing and plucking and rubbing them. She squirmed and ground herself into him, learning to feel her own pleasure as she drove him into a frenzy. It took all of his strength and control to hold back, to give her time. His breath rasped harshly in his chest, his jaw ached from gritting his teeth, his body was afire with the pleasure he held back, the summit of which he desperately wanted to reach.

At last she stiffened and flung her head back, arching her body as her climax swept over her. He gripped her hips in both hands and surged into her over and over, letting his release overwhelm and overcome him.

She collapsed gasping onto his chest. Weakly, she murmured, "I never imagined . . . *that*."

He chuckled as he swept the hair from her face and tucked some of it behind her ear. "Then there's a lot you never imagined, and I plan to show you."

She sat up again, and he sighed with bliss as that drove him deeper.

"But only if you win me as your mistress," she said with false primness. "One night does not do that."

Grace watched Daniel's harsh expression, his lowered brows, felt him move inside her. The tremors of her pleasure still rippled through her, and everything he did set off more waves of it. He filled her, stretched her. Now that they'd made love twice, she felt a little tender, but not enough to make her climb off him.

He sat up and wrapped his arms around her and kissed her. "Should we continue our ride through the city?" He nuzzled her cheek and moved inside her. "And our more private ride?"

With a sigh, she murmured, "I should return home."

"Then stop tempting me, woman, and let me dress."

She laughed as she slid off him, trying to hold all her skirts up. After they finished helping each other dress, Daniel rapped on the roof to get the coachman's attention. When the carriage stopped, he stepped out for a moment, then came back inside.

"I told him to take us into the alley behind your town house," Daniel said, "just in case your brother is home."

"A few weeks ago he would probably still have

been out, but now you never know." She felt troubled just thinking about Edward.

"He's changed, Grace," Daniel said quietly.

"I think so, but I've hurt him, Daniel."

"*We've* hurt him."

She gave him a searching glance, trying to read his expression, to understand what he meant. Did he merely feel guilty for his sake—or for hers, too?

They held hands until the carriage came to a stop, and she heard Daniel sigh when he reached for the door handle.

She put a hand on his back, wanting to say that she wished this night would never end. But would he think she meant only as his mistress? So she said nothing.

When he helped her down, and the coachman discreetly stepped away, she softly said, "Daniel, have you ever attempted to play my father's violin?"

He betrayed his surprise. Or maybe he was no longer trying to hide his emotions from her.

"No."

"I know we've decided to keep the winning of it still between us, but . . . perhaps because it wasn't really yours yet, you didn't try to play it. I think you should."

He gave her a wry smile and kissed her nose. "Let me see you into the house, Grace."

She put her arm through his. At the kitchen door, he waited outside until she'd lit a candle from the lamp. Smiling tenderly at him, she closed the door and locked it, watching through the windowpane as he faded into the black courtyard.

Only after she was in her room and wearing a dressing robe, Ruby already back to her own room, did Grace hear a knock.

Hoping it would be Daniel, she flung open the door.

Edward stood there, and he gave a sad smile when he saw her expression. "You even wish it was him."

She waved a hand at him, smiling. "Edward, you make too much of things."

He entered her room, and she noticed he was still dressed for the evening.

"What were you doing tonight?" she asked.

He stiffened. "I had a dinner party to go to."

"Who gave it?" she asked in curiosity.

"A Mr. Hutton. You don't know him."

"How do you know him?" She couldn't help her curiosity, for his manner seemed . . . different.

"He's a director of the Southern Railway."

"Ah, you know him through Daniel," she said happily. "And does he have any eligible daughters?"

Edward sank down into a chair before her bare hearth, and she recognized his evasions.

"Aha, so he does," she continued. "Do you . . . like one of them?"

He sighed and said gravely, "I do."

"Then you can thank Daniel."

"I know."

His agreement seemed most reluctant.

Edward cocked his head as he studied her. "Did you enjoy the Gardens?"

Now it was her turn to be evasive without appearing so. "I did. It was truly a fairyland."

"I know what's happening, Grace."

She stiffened, but didn't reply.

"You think you can reform him, like you've always tried to do to me."

"It worked for you, didn't it?" she challenged.

"I wanted it to, but does he? No gentleman tries to seduce young maidens. I would never dream of doing so with Miss Hutton."

"You're a good man, Edward," she said kindly. But maybe she needed a man not so good.

Yet did she deserve Daniel? A man was threatening her, and whatever his scheme, it could cost Daniel—and his family—respect. How would she feel then, when she could have solved the Cabot problem by cutting Daniel out of her life completely?

Should she have? Instead she'd surrendered to him, agreed to prolong their challenge because she could not imagine life without him. What was she hoping to accomplish? An offer of marriage? When she was withholding a truth from him? Was she trying to find a fairy-tale ending where there was none? Perhaps her dreams were just as false as the Gardens themselves.

Sex with Daniel had been the ultimate gamble.

Chapter 23

When Daniel awoke the next morning, he discovered that the previous night his house had been invaded—by his mother and her staff.

He stared at her in surprise as she waited for him in the breakfast parlor. With a smile, he came forward and kissed her cheek. "Mother, it has been almost twenty years since you were last in London. Did you come just to share toast with me?"

"Sit down, Daniel, before the food gets cold. You did sleep rather late," she added, eyeing him suspiciously.

"Yes, my lady," he said, pulling his chair to the table and nodding to the footman, who set a hot plate of eggs and ham before him.

"You were out very late," she said, buttering a piece of toast.

"As an adult, I am allowed to." He smiled.

"Were you with Miss Banbury?"

"I was." He eyed her with speculation. "You still disapprove?"

"I trust you to make a wise decision."

But she still disapproved—or a better word might be "worried," enough so that she had braved the risks of London after so many years.

"Her father has an antique violin, well over a hundred years old," Daniel began slowly. "It reminds me of the one Father used to have."

"Is it similar to the one that's on your library wall?"

He'd forgotten. "She let me borrow it."

"I see," she said shrewdly.

"Why don't you play anymore?" he suddenly asked.

"The violin?" Her gaze moved away evasively.

"The piano, your favorite instrument."

Then she pinned him with eyes very like his own. "Why don't you play? I always felt very guilty that you gave it up because of your father's tragedy."

"It was an accident, Mother. Most people know that."

It was the first time he'd alluded to the rumors surrounding her since childhood.

"It was," she said simply.

"Yet it must have hurt when people believed otherwise."

"It did, but that is the past, and now it's of no consequence. All I'd ever wanted was for you to be untouched by that scandal."

"And I was."

"But you created your own scandals. It must run in the family."

He smiled. "It's probably unnecessary now."

"But you started such a life to protect me."

Staring at her, he said softly, "I think so, although I'd forgotten that until someone made me realize it."

"Miss Banbury?"

He nodded.

"Perhaps there's another reason you keep your distance through scandal. Perhaps you're keeping marriageable young ladies away from you. Is that my fault, too? Did you think my heart was broken because of the way my marriage turned out?"

Before he could reassure her, she hurried on.

"Daniel, I would do everything again, regardless of the outcome, just to spend the few years I had with your father. Intimacy and love are worth the risk of any scandal."

She put her hand on his arm, and he covered her hand with his. "I'm glad you've come to visit," he said. "Now perhaps we can discuss why you should begin to compose again."

She blew out a breath of laughter. "We can't change everything about ourselves with just one conversation!"

But as they began to eat and talk normally, he couldn't help but wonder if she had come to protect him from being hurt by a reckless marriage. Though living in London, he'd spent his life outside its Society, just like his mother. Perhaps it was time they both came back inside.

It was a new day, and Grace told herself to be hopeful, that somehow she could make everything work out. But a black cloud hovered over her, and by the afternoon, she knew it was not just a rain cloud, but a thunderstorm. While she was working on needlework to calm her racing mind, Woodley announced Horace Jenkins.

She rose slowly to her feet, feeling the blood drain from her face even as her embroidery hoop slipped to the floor.

Mr. Jenkins stood just inside the door until the butler backed out. And then Mr. Jenkins deliberately closed the door.

"Please open that," she said, trying to be firm. "You know I cannot be alone with you."

"You're alone with Throckmorten."

"And if you know that, then you know that he's having you watched. He'll receive a report that you visited me here, and how will you explain that?"

"You'll explain it, Miss Banbury. You'll tell him that you welcomed my visit gladly. Your satisfaction will be obvious when we attend the soiree together this evening at Mrs. Bradley's."

"You wish me to accompany you?"

"I do. And if you refuse, *all* of your secrets will become known."

She swallowed, thinking frantically, but a solution did not occur to her. Whom could she tell without making this terrible situation worse? Not Daniel, not Edward.

"How long will you continue to threaten me, Mr. Jenkins?"

"You have forced me to use such methods to be

close to you, Miss Banbury," he said, his features softening as he took several steps toward her.

She kept the sofa between them.

He looked pained. "All I want to do is court you, to treat you as reverently as any lady that I admire."

"And do you blackmail all the ladies you admire?"

He winced. "I wish to spend time with you, Miss Banbury, and if this is the only way for you to get to know me, so be it. The others would never even give me a chance."

"If you think so highly of me, why should I believe you would hurt me so cruelly by telling Society what my mother did to me?"

"Because if I could not be with you, then it would prove how shortsighted a woman you are. And such a woman would deserve the scorn of others."

She was still gaping at him, struggling to see any logic in his argument, when he bowed to her.

"I will come in my carriage for you at seven, Miss Banbury. Please be waiting."

She stood still as a statue for several minutes after he left, but at last, she gathered her strength. If one good thing had come of Mr. Jenkins's visit, it was that he had reminded her of how inappropriate she was as a wife to Daniel. She would never be free of her past, of her mother's sins. She could not bring such tragedy down on Daniel or his family. To make him forget about her, she would have to make sure he found another wife.

* * *

At Mrs. Bradley's soiree, guests were having
conversations and light refreshments in one
drawing room, while dancing was going on in the
second drawing room. Mr. Jenkins had not left
Grace's side for an hour, during which Daniel had
also arrived. She'd felt his stare from across the
room the moment he'd seen her with Mr. Jenkins.
Although he'd betrayed no emotion, she could
read the anger too well in his eyes. She'd promised him she would be careful about Mr. Jenkins,
yet here she was, plastered to him.

Sadness clutched at her heart with real pain.
She loved Daniel. Hurting him like this went
against everything in her. She wanted to be safe
in his arms, but if she was honest with herself, she
knew their unconventional relationship would
never have led to a quiet, happy marriage.

But other guests had noticed that she and
Daniel didn't immediately come together. Many
gazes moved between them with speculation, and
Grace saw that Mr. Jenkins's pride was bolstered
with each whisper about them. This was what he
wanted. If he could not beat Daniel in a card game,
it was obvious he wanted everyone to know he'd
beaten him for a woman's attention.

So Daniel was forced for the moment to social-
ize with others, and Grace saw that a good deal
of them were young ladies. Daniel's frequent appearances at Society events of late had led to a rise
in his popularity. After all, the mamas could only
be forced to conclude that he was looking for a

wife. His faults could be overlooked. And if he was not with Grace, then he had yet to decide on one, making him fair game.

Only when Mr. Jenkins saw Daniel disappear into the dancing room with a young lady did he offer to retrieve Grace some refreshments. She knew she was disappointing him by her sad silence, and she really must stop, in order to keep him happy. Eventually she would have to figure out what to do with him, but for now, in front of London Society, she could only tolerate him and pretend to enjoy it. In the moment of solitude, where she was the focus of speculation, she took a deep breath and tried to ease the painful constriction in her chest whenever she thought about Daniel.

"Miss Banbury?"

Grace opened her eyes and looked up into the dark, dashing features of the duke of Madingley. She had known when he'd arrived, of course, by the flutter of excitement that had passed through the rooms. A duke's acceptance of an invitation was a rare gift to a hostess, and Mrs. Bradley had stumbled into the arms of her husband as if she would swoon. But in the end, the duke had made his courtesies to a fawning Mrs. Bradley, and then had searched out his cousin, as was both men's habit when they were at the same event.

But somehow Grace had lost track of the duke and had not seen his advance.

The duke smiled at her. "Don't tell me you're about to faint at my presence like our hostess. I will be forced to become a hermit if I keep having this effect on women."

She smiled back, enjoying his easy humor. "Of course not, Your Grace. I'm made of sterner stuff."

"So Daniel tells me."

She blushed as if she imagined he'd been told intimate details of her. Of course Daniel would never betray her like that. Instead, she was being forced to betray him.

She sighed.

"Miss Banbury, you are not enjoying yourself this evening," the duke said softly. "You and my cousin have not spoken."

"You should be happy about that, Your Grace," she said, beyond being polite. "Did you not wish to keep us apart?"

He blinked at her in surprise. Perhaps people did not regularly speak so forthrightly to a duke.

"I wished nothing of the sort, Miss Banbury. My only concern was that my cousin find happiness with someone who loved him for the right reasons. Don't we all wish such relationships for our families?"

She sighed. "Of course we do. Forgive my short temper."

"You seem to be the one staying apart from him, Miss Banbury."

She shrugged, hoping he'd believe that.

"Did you know that his mother arrived in town yesterday?"

Her eyes went wide as she met the knowing ones of the duke. "She did? But she never comes to town."

"I rather thought it was a good thing, myself."

"You don't think . . ." She trailed off, wondering if the family was rallying together to keep her and Daniel apart.

"That she's here because of you?" Madingley finished her thought.

"I would never be so presumptuous."

"I think she's here because at last she realizes that although Daniel is not a child, perhaps they still need one another."

"I hope he plays music for her," Grace said softly, wanting Daniel's mother to see that he was getting better. She straightened as she realized that Mr. Jenkins was standing across the room, holding two glasses, and looking as if he didn't know whether to interrupt a duke.

"Music?" the duke repeated questioningly.

"I think at last he's ready to return to it," Grace said. "Maybe you could encourage him."

"I will admit," the duke said, watching her with obvious bemusement, "that I have had several conversations about Daniel with young ladies in the last few years, but this is the most unusual. A woman always wants to know if he's interested in marriage, but—music?"

"It is not so strange in his family, Your Grace. And if you wish to talk about marriage where Daniel is concerned, I can give you several names of wonderful young ladies that might interest him."

If a duke would ever let go of his pride to gape, Madingley would be doing so, she knew. She'd just suggested other women for Daniel to marry.

And suddenly she wanted to cry. Her eyes burned with tears she could not possibly shed, so with a quick curtsy, she left the duke and returned to Mr. Jenkins, who watched her warily, but seemed to relax when she only gave him a smile as she took her lemonade.

She wished it were something stronger.

Daniel escorted the third young lady to her mother, bowed, and quickly took his leave. But he was too late to approach Grace, who'd left Chris and returned to Jenkins's side like a dutiful wife.

Daniel felt murderous, as he imagined what might have happened to make Grace behave like this. Obviously, he'd underestimated his opponent.

But mixed in with his anger was jealousy and bewilderment, and a pain that seemed like sadness, but was so much more. After the incredible passion they'd shared, why had she not come to him about Jenkins? The fact that she still didn't trust him was a blow that hurt worse than he'd thought possible.

"If you stare any harder at Grace, her dress will catch fire."

Daniel gave a start and glanced at Edward Banbury, who stood at his side looking coolly about the drawing room.

"I am not staring at her in so obvious a manner," Daniel said, his jaw clenched.

"Who is that she's with, making you crazy?"

"Horace Jenkins, the man I gambled against, along with your mother."

Now it was Banbury's turn to glare across the room. "The fellow you thought might be watching her?"

Daniel nodded. "And now she's with him. Did she make any explanations to you?"

"None."

"But surely you're happy she's not here with me," Daniel said with sarcasm.

"Strangely enough, that's not true." He sighed and looked down at the champagne in his glass. "So what are you going to do about this?" He motioned with his glass toward his sister.

"You're not going to insist it's your place to protect her?"

"You seem to want to take over for me in that department."

Daniel felt surprised that Banbury was relaxing his opinion. "Obviously, she doesn't want my protection, or she'd have told me what was going on."

"Then I think you need to insist."

Daniel hesitated. "And I have your permission?"

Banbury met his gaze with an impassive one. "For this. We'll take it on a case-by-case basis."

Daniel's amusement was short-lived. He nodded to Banbury and moved away. Jenkins was glued to Grace's side, so Daniel would have to wait until

Grace left him, so as not to arouse suspicions. And he didn't want to have a conversation with her in front of all the guests. He needed someone as a distraction.

He stole Chris away from a disappointed young lady and her mother, pulling his cousin out into the corridor.

"Am I rescuing you or annoying you?" Daniel asked.

"Luckily, the former," Chris said, smiling. "Is something wrong?"

"Talk with me here in the corridor. I'm waiting for Grace to come out here alone."

Chris arched a brow, and said mildly, "Then you're not escaping the attentions of so many women? Miss Banbury told me she could give you references on the suitability of several of them."

"*What?*" Daniel realized he'd spoken too loudly when two gentlemen on the way to the library gave him strange looks. "Tell me everything she said to you."

"She thought I should encourage you to return to music."

Daniel closed his eyes and groaned.

"And then she offered names of young ladies."

"That's all?"

"It seemed quite a lot to me. I rather believe she's fond of you, Daniel, and you seem to be so of her."

"Grace's offering to find me a bride is fondness?"

"Hoping that you'll find happiness seems to involve a sacrifice on her part," Chris said softly, "as if she's decided your happiness can't be with her. I'm rather impressed with her selflessness. I see I was wrong about her."

But Daniel ignored him as Grace herself left the far drawing room, her head bent, her pace quick. He left Chris without a word and followed her, taking her elbow before she could open the door to the ladies' retiring room. She trembled and looked up at him in true fear, and for a moment, he didn't know how to respond, but the relief and then wariness in her face brought him back to himself—and his anger.

He dragged her toward the back of the house, to the first empty room he could find. A small lamp was burning, and by the delicate sofa and ornate desk, he guessed it was Mrs. Bradley's morning room. Daniel closed the door, and when he saw a key in the lock, he turned it.

Grace gasped.

Instead of showing outrage, she flung herself at him. He fell back against the door in surprise, his arms full of warm, soft woman and yards of delicate fabric. She pulled his head down and kissed him, saying nothing, expressing her longing and passion with her moist mouth and soft moans.

And he was almost overcome.

But not quite. Some logical part of his brain rose amidst the hungry chorus of lust and protested her motives.

And then her hand was on his trouser buttons

as if she would disrobe him in Mrs. Bradley's morning room.

He grabbed her shoulders and held her away, feeling like it was his turn to swoon. "Grace, stop this at once!" he said in a soft yet firm voice. "You will not distract me."

"I cannot express how much I've missed you?" she asked, fingering the buttons of his waistcoat enticingly.

"And now you have. It's my turn to express my displeasure over your conduct."

"You don't want me kissing you?"

"I don't want you trying to distract me from my very justifiable anger. What are you doing here with Jenkins? And why did you not tell me that he'd contacted you?"

With a groan she pushed away from him, presenting her back, and prowled the room. "Daniel, this doesn't concern you any longer. You need to go find another woman to concentrate on." The last seemed torn rawly from her throat.

"You've spent all this time trying to change me, first by my redemption in the eyes of society, then by music. And now you want me gone?"

"I don't want to change you anymore. You are perfectly good the way you are."

He could have sworn she was holding back tears, but she was pacing, her head down. Some of his anger and hurt eased.

"Grace, tell me what is happening."

She froze in the middle of the morning room, and at last she turned too-bright eyes on him.

"He's blackmailing me. He's going to tell everyone about the bet if I don't allow him to court me."

Daniel inhaled sharply. If she loved him, wouldn't she have come to him for help? He thought he'd won her trust at last, but she couldn't trust him to keep her reputation safe. He realized that he was so hurt because he loved her. *I love her*, he thought again, in bewilderment and growing relief. This was love, to want Grace's happiness more than his own, to want to protect her regardless of whether it changed her opinion of him. This was love, he thought again, as the pain of her mistrust lanced even deeper into him. My God, if anyone deserved this punishment, it was he. But was he a fool to hope for something better?

"Grace—"

"No! You're going to try to be my gallant knight, and I won't have it! You've already done too much for me. I'm living in your house, on your money—"

"Your house. I've already put the deed back in your name."

With a moan, she turned away from him and covered her face. "And did you want to make me feel like even more of a mistress?"

He threw his arms wide. "I wanted you to feel secure enough to stand on your own, to make decisions that weren't out of desperation. We can take on Jenkins. Let me help."

He watched her head come up, her shoulders straighten, and when at last she faced him, her face was beautiful and too composed.

"No. Let me handle this, Daniel. I promise to come to you if I need help."

He didn't believe her, but he knew he could not convince her of anything in the state she was in. She walked past him toward the door, very careful not to allow even the hem of her skirt to touch him as she passed. She unlocked the door and opened it, even remembering to look both ways before she left and closed the door behind her.

Daniel swore under his breath, wishing he could smash something. He vowed to find a way to convince her that he was worthy of her trust.

Chapter 24

It was easy enough for Daniel to follow Jenkins's carriage through the London streets. From horseback, he watched Grace alight at the Banbury town house and hurry inside. Daniel waited tensely, wondering if Jenkins would be so bold as to follow her, but he didn't leave the carriage.

He followed Jenkins to his club, but knew that would be too public a place for a confrontation. So when the coachman opened the carriage door, Daniel appeared at his side, startling Jenkins, who froze in the doorway.

"Although we have not been properly introduced," Daniel began pleasantly, "I am certain you know that I am Throckmorten."

Jenkins nodded slowly.

"Then sit back down and have a private conversation with me."

Jenkins glanced at his coachman, who stared between the two men uneasily.

"There is no need for caution," Daniel said. "My good coachman, I will only be a few minutes, and you can remain right beside the door. If you hear any unusual sounds, by all means, fling the door wide and whistle for a police officer."

"As if he's supposed to call the law on a member of a ducal family?" Jenkins said with bluster.

Daniel smiled. *"We* give you permission," he said, stressing the royal "we."

He mounted the carriage steps, and Jenkins was forced to sit back.

Daniel took the bench opposite him, crossing an ankle over the other knee. "So you could not content yourself with only following Miss Banbury about town in a sulk because you did not win the card game."

Though Jenkins was obviously nervous, he lifted his chin arrogantly. "What did she tell you?"

"I forced her to tell me that you were blackmailing her although she wanted to protect your sordid secret."

"'Blackmail' is a harsh word, Mr. Throckmorten. I explained to her that since only I truly wished to marry her, I'm the man she should be with."

"And so that leaves her with no rights of her own?"

"She will see that I am doing my best to make her happy."

"Oh, she looked very happy at Mrs. Bradley's home," Daniel said sarcastically.

"She will be."

Daniel leaned forward, satisfied when Jenkins seemed to shrink back in his seat. "Let me tell you how things will be. If you breathe a word of Grace's troubles, you will incite sympathy for Grace, and I will make sure everyone knows that you're a blackmailer. You think you're on the fringe now, but I can put you out in the cold, as far as Society is concerned."

"I don't care," Jenkins blustered. "I spend little time in London."

Daniel grabbed him by the cravat and twisted, so that it tightened at his throat. The man made a strangled gulp.

"I will make you care when I'm through with you. Stay away from Miss Banbury. Leave her in peace."

Daniel flung Jenkins back in his seat, opened the door, and descended, straightening his coat sleeves. To the coachman, he said, "Thank you," then walked down the street to where he'd left his horse tethered.

He went back to the Banbury town house, almost surprised the cook in the kitchen, and had to wait in the courtyard for another half hour before the kitchen went dark. At last he let himself in the back door, went up to Grace's room, and knocked so softly, he didn't think she'd be able to hear. But she flung the door wide and faced him, still wearing her evening gown. She pulled him inside and shut the door.

"I said I'd come to you if I need help," she whispered with urgency.

"And I said I wanted to help. So I did. Jenkins will not bother you anymore."

Her mouth fell open before she could collect herself. "I asked you to let me handle this!"

"And I told you that I needed to help. I was a part of that game; it's up to me to handle the consequences."

"And I was the prize! I have a say, too. Did you threaten the man?"

"I did."

With a groan, she dropped her head back.

"You're angry with me?" he demanded, advancing on her.

She didn't back away, only put her hands on her hips and faced him down.

"Let me see if I have this straight," Daniel continued. "You're willing to trust a blackmailer not to betray you, rather than trust me to do what's necessary to help you. Did I ever have any of your trust?"

Her eyes widened. "Daniel, this isn't about trusting you! It's about learning to trust myself to solve my own problems."

"You've been trusting yourself all along, Grace. Don't lie to me—or yourself. Why can't you trust someone else? Has watching your mother's weaknesses, and then seeing them appear in your brother, made you so convinced that you're the only competent adult?"

"Competent?" She pointed a finger at his chest. "I am hardly competent. I have my own weakness, you know, and it's men!"

"Men?" he demanded.

"Very well—you! You muddle my mind; you

make me do things I swore I never would. And now you're trying to convince me that only you know best. Well I won't have it! I want you to leave."

Daniel stared at her, feeling his anger cool. She had a weakness for him? As if it were something bad?

Or as if it felt uncontrollable, like what she imagined a gambling fever felt like. He felt a little out of control where she was concerned himself. But she wouldn't want to hear that right now.

"I'll leave," he said neutrally. "But this discussion isn't over."

She said nothing, not even good night, when she closed the door behind him. He didn't imagine that Jenkins would try anything tonight, but Daniel stayed in the master suite just in case, not sleeping much, thinking about Grace.

Did that mean she loved him? Was he seeing their relationship the wrong way? Maybe it really was about trusting herself, and what she felt for him. It gave him much to think on.

After luncheon the next day, Jenkins returned. As Grace allowed Woodley to show him into the drawing room, she felt a little calmer, more in control. She could continue to allow his courtship for a while. She still hadn't come up with her own plan—and she blamed Daniel for that. Crying over him had kept her awake half the night, and she still hadn't recovered. She was feeling morose and confused, but she had to put that to the back of her mind.

Jenkins didn't even wait for her greeting as he closed the door and crossed the room to her. Her eyes narrowed as he took her hand and planted a wet kiss on the back.

"Mr. Jenkins!"

When she tried to pull away, he held tighter and turned her palm over as if he was going to kiss her again. And all she could think of was Daniel's dark head bent over her hand and the way she'd melted inside when he did so simple a thing as press his mouth there. She yanked harder and was free.

Jenkins's eyes narrowed. "You agreed to allow me to court you."

"Courting and forcing your attentions on me are two different things. You will act like a gentleman, or you will leave."

He glanced at the closed door, and it was as if she could read his thoughts on his face. He was wondering what he could get away with, feeling his power over her, and as with so many people, letting that power begin to corrupt him. He might have been a simple gentleman farmer, but now he was imagining that he could seduce her compliance.

Although part of her was affronted, another part knew that he was taller than she, and he might be able to overpower her. If she screamed, her servants would come running, and the situation could worsen. Servants talked to other servants. Secrets were difficult to keep in crowded London.

But she was getting ahead of herself, panicking at the calculating look in his eyes. What should she do?

And then Jenkins grasped her shoulders and pulled her to him clumsily.

"Let me kiss you," he said against her cheek, after she turned her head aside.

"No! Unhand me! A gentleman does not—"

"I'm certain Throckmorten is no gentleman, so you must be used to rough treatment."

Then he fondled her breast.

And in that moment, Grace's panic crystallized into a sense of melancholy calm. It was over. She would not hide the rest of her life over this. She could not give in and let him think he had power over her. And she would never consent to marrying a man like Jenkins. If Daniel could handle scandal, so could she.

She slapped Jenkins's face hard, and he gaped at her in surprise.

"How dare you risk angering me," he snarled in a low voice. "I can tell everyone—"

"Then do it," she said, putting space between them. "Prove yourself no gentleman, as you've already proved here. But I'm done with you."

For a second she thought she'd caught him off guard, but his expression hardened. "I am not bluffing."

"I'm not either, and I can bluff with the best of them. Do what you must with my secret, but remember how the telling of it will make you look."

"And how will it make your precious Throckmorten look?"

She gave a cold laugh. "Like a hero to other
men for winning a woman at a card game. You
can't harm a man with his kind of power. You can
only harm me—and yourself."

He drew himself up. "I'll return tomorrow and
we'll discuss this again."

"We won't. I've made up my mind. I don't wish
to see you again. Please leave."

He spun in place and marched out the door,
and only when he was gone did she sag back onto
the sofa. She'd fought back; why didn't she feel
more triumphant? She told herself that Jenkins
wouldn't dare take on Daniel or risk facing the
censure of Society. But she didn't know him well,
and perhaps he didn't care about those things.
Though she was shaking, she sensed it was a reaction to her escape. She was very glad she would
be seeing Beverly tonight because she desperately
needed a friend. Now all she could do was hope
that Jenkins had a conscience.

That night was one of the highlights of the
season—the Madingley Ball. The duke's aunt,
Lady Rosa Leland, was his hostess. They gra-
ciously opened their London town house—it
might as well have been a palace, Grace thought—
to everyone from the cream of the *ton* to country
gentry in town for the season.

She and Beverly sat in the Standish carriage,
waiting in a long line as people disembarked

beneath the columned portico of the mansion a block away.

"You're very quiet," Beverly said.

Grace glanced at her. The gas lamps outside framed Beverly's curious face against the rain-spattered window. "I'm sorry I'm not very good company tonight."

"Is it because of Mr. Throckmorten?"

Grace smiled sadly. "Indirectly."

"He seems to be at the center of much of what you do."

"Not anymore."

"Why not? I must admit, I thought for certain I would hear an engagement announcement from the two of you."

Grace's throat felt so tight that she almost couldn't get words out. "No, things have quite fallen apart. Edward found out about the challenge, and he and Daniel fought."

Beverly put a hand on hers. "Oh, Grace, I'm so sorry. But surely your brother calmed down. And isn't the challenge over now? It's been two weeks."

With a slight hesitation, Grace said, "We extended the deadline."

"Ah, surely that is proof that Mr. Throckmorten can't be apart from you."

"I don't know, Beverly."

"And you know, should anything go wrong, you could always move in with me until things improve for you and your brother."

Grace was again blinking back tears. She was

so tired of crying. "Your kindness moves me, but that won't be necessary. Daniel put the town house in my name."

"You own it?" she breathed.

Grace saw the way her happy expression turned hesitant.

"But . . . why?" Beverly asked.

Grace could not bear to tell her friend everything. "He wants me to feel secure, he wants me to trust him."

"But isn't that wonderful?" Beverly asked plaintively.

"I'm being blackmailed by another of the gamblers, and I don't want Daniel to be stained by my reputation. Perhaps even you should steer clear of me tonight, Beverly. I refused to give in to the blackmailer's demands, so everything might come out."

If Beverly were smart, she would take Grace's advice; instead, Grace found herself wrapped in a tight, warm hug.

"You poor dear. Do not believe I would ever abandon you in your hour of need. And neither will Daniel."

"And that's the problem, Beverly!" she cried. "I asked him to let me handle this, and he thinks I don't trust him, but I just don't want him separated from his family because of me! He's just beginning to accept himself again."

"You're wrong about him," Beverly said, "but no one can convince you of that but yourself. Promise me you will think everything through before you act."

"But I've already acted. I've stood up for myself. If I end up ostracized from Society, then so be it. But I won't drag Daniel down with me."

"Even if he wants to be there?"

Grace could barely breathe, so tight was her chest. The carriage jerked forward, and she managed, "It's our turn. Here comes the footman."

Beverly shook her head but said nothing as they both left the carriage.

Madingley House was ablaze with lights beneath the statues of warrior angels lining the roof. The full sound of the orchestra drifted out the front door as Grace and Beverly entered. They followed the line of slowly moving guests up the marble staircase that rose through the entrance hall. They passed impressive paintings the height and width of each wall as they circled up three floors to the ballroom, which took up an entire floor of the house. Huge carved columns supported a ceiling decorated in frescoes and paintings, and hung with massive crystal chandeliers.

Grace felt like the country miss she'd been raised as, so much did she gape at the luxurious surroundings. This was Daniel's way of life, a child and cousin of nobility. She felt small and inconsequential, so very out of her element. She would have turned around and fled, but that would only have made her a coward. She had to prove to Jenkins that she would not back down before his hollow—she hoped—threats.

Before coming to the front of the receiving

line, a footman announced their names to the ballroom, and Grace relaxed a tiny bit as barely anyone looked her way.

"See?" Beverly said into her ear.

All this proved was that Jenkins had not yet made the time to slander her. But there were hundreds of people moving about the ballroom, feathers fluttering and jewels glittering. The men in black evening clothes framed their ladies' colorful displays.

At last they were next in line to greet the Cabot family. The duke smiled at Grace warmly, and his lack of skepticism eased her. Somehow he had warmed to her. She sank into a curtsy before him, and then was introduced to his aunt, the hostess, and two female cousins and cousin-in-law. His sister, Lady Elizabeth, obviously remembered her, for after being introduced to Beverly, she grinned and took Grace's arm.

"Might I have Miss Banbury's attention for a moment?" Lady Elizabeth asked politely.

Beverly nodded. "I see friends I should greet, Grace. If you need me, I'll be near the arched entrance to the refreshment room."

Grace was grateful for the explanation because she couldn't imagine being able to find her friend again in such an immense crowd.

"And how are you?" Grace asked Lady Elizabeth.

"Excited! I'm finally old enough for my first Madingley Ball!"

Grace gave her an indulgent smile, for she well

remembered her first ball, though of course it had been nothing so extravagant as this. But there had been young men, and she'd finally been allowed to have their attention—and it was where she'd first been overcome by the persistent courtship of Baxter Wells.

"Have you seen Daniel yet?" Lady Elizabeth asked.

There were people on all sides of them, and Grace regretted that she did not have the height to search for him. "No, I only just arrived."

"Of course you did!" she said, laughing at herself. "Do you know that his mother is here as well? We are quite shocked and pleased that she's decided to leave her mourning at last—although she's still wearing gray, of course, but that is better than the black she's worn for twenty years. I've only ever seen her in that!"

Grace smiled, feeling exhausted by Lady Elizabeth's fast-paced monologue. "And I'm certain her reintroduction to Society is going well."

Lady Elizabeth lowered her voice. "We think so, and she has many friends to surround her, but there are always people who want to talk about that silly old scandal."

And at that moment, Grace saw Horace Jenkins. She tried to give him a polite smile, hoping he had understood that his power over her was finished.

Without breaking her gaze, he leaned toward the man he was standing with and spoke in an urgent manner. The man's eyebrows rose; he searched the crowd with his gaze—and found Grace.

She couldn't look away. The two men stared at her, Jenkins wearing a triumphant, tight smile, and the other man regarding her as if she were a piece of meat he wanted to snack on. Grace looked away, but the damage was done. The truth was going to make its way about the Madingley Ball, and her privacy would be no more. She felt unclean, as if she should thrust Lady Elizabeth from her before she could contaminate the girl.

But Lady Elizabeth was chatting about the young men she'd been introduced to, and it was a while before Grace could politely take her leave.

She wandered the ball alone, not bothering to look for Beverly right away. She ran into the occasional lady whose acquaintance she had already made, and was greeted civilly, politely, without a hint of lurid curiosity. Then Grace would move on again, swept up in the current of the ballroom, skirting the many couples dancing in the center of the room, passing the refreshment room.

And then she caught another man's eye, and instead of a polite bow, she received a shocked stare. He was speaking with an older lady, who gasped when she saw Grace, and began to speak even more forcefully to the man, using her hands to gesture wildly. And they continued to stare at her as if politeness would no longer apply to a woman whose own mother had sold her on a bet.

In the refreshment room was a long buffet table full of gleaming silver tureens and platters displaying tempting foods, but Grace couldn't eat. She was too busy holding her head high, nodding to people she passed, pretending nothing was wrong—pretending that she was above it.

She saw Daniel, and her heart beat wildly for a moment with just the pleasure of his looking at her. And then her feelings plummeted, knowing she could not allow it to continue. These past weeks, people had watched the two of them with interest, but now there was an undercurrent of ugly fascination. She wanted Daniel to stay away, but he came toward her with clear purpose. The crowd parted eagerly, watching, waiting. Surely a woman like her was only worth being his mistress.

He took her gloved hand and kissed it, and although she was warmed clear to her toes by the sweet gesture, it took everything in her not to pull away.

"Mr. Throckmorten," she began in a low voice.

"Miss Banbury, you look stunning as always."

His low, smooth voice made her shiver inside. How was she to spend her days without these wondrous feelings he inspired in her? She had to school her features, had to show the *ton* that she could be as remote as any of them.

But she knew she was foolishly smiling at Daniel, sealing her fate.

"We're quite the object of gossip tonight," he said quietly, holding up his arm to her.

She reluctantly placed her hand on his forearm. "I told you I could handle my . . . problem, and

I guess you feel that I haven't done a very good job."

"You stood up to a blackmailer," he said softly. "You have the courage of a lioness."

She blinked up at him in surprise, heat and tenderness spilling through her. "But . . . it didn't work. He has told people what my mother did to me. Can't you tell? You shouldn't even be seen with me."

"He's told everyone that I was a part of a base game where a woman's reputation was at stake. You are only the victim, while I was a knowing participant. It's been over an hour now since the rumors started. Do you know how the story has grown?"

Though he spoke with amusement, she felt her face drain of blood.

He patted her hand. "Don't worry. It will all come to right."

"How can you say that?" she whispered fiercely, her face frozen in a false smile. "What are they saying?"

"Grace—"

"Tell me!"

"The bet has grown from the right to court and marry you—which didn't bother many people, I might add—"

"Daniel!"

"Very well, the next version was that I won the right to your virginity."

She gasped. "Can the story become worse?"

"I can see you are not familiar with the deviltry

of the *ton*, my love, because now the rumor is that we have a baby together, which we just visited at Madingley Court."

It took her a moment to hear what he said, because the words "my love" were ringing in her ears and in her heart. *My love?* What was he saying? Was he trying to shore up her reputation? She felt ill thinking he'd feel like he had to save her—like she'd just trapped him into marriage by her foolish confrontation with Jenkins.

How could she ever know if he really loved her if he felt forced to marry her?

But maybe marriage wasn't even occurring to him. After all, she was just like her own mother—and his: giving her future children a scandal to live down.

Was she alone in this disaster?

Then her brother Edward approached them, and on his arm was a lovely young woman with striking red hair who betrayed a bit of nervousness as she stared all around her. Grace glanced about, and people were watching openly, as if they expected Edward to challenge Daniel.

"Grace, this is Miss Hutton," Edward said. "Miss Hutton, my sister, Miss Banbury."

Grace remembered to curtsy, and the other woman did the same. On a night like this, how could Edward introduce her to the woman who'd captured his attention? Didn't he know that this scandal might drive away Miss Hutton, leaving him all alone?

She felt Daniel's steady arm beneath her hand,

and she remembered to breathe. "It is so nice to meet you, Miss Hutton."

"A pleasure meeting you, Miss Banbury," she said in a sweet voice. "Your brother has told me so much about you, and said I'm supposed to ask you any questions I might have, but I'm not sure I could be so forward." She glanced at Edward with guilt. "And I think I probably speak too quickly."

But Edward smiled down at Miss Hutton with such fondness that Grace found some of her tension easing. She so wanted him to be happy. "Please, Miss Hutton, ask anything you'd like. And come to call on me, so we can become better acquainted. Have you met Mr. Throckmorten?"

"I have," she said, smiling up at Daniel. "He has been a guest of my parents. Good evening, Mr. Throckmorten."

While Daniel answered politely, Grace saw that the duke was approaching them, escorting Beverly.

And then Grace realized that all the people she cared about were rallying in support of her, showing the gossipmongers how little the scandal mattered. She could have cried.

But she couldn't imagine it would be enough to make her a valued guest in people's homes. Except maybe as an attraction, like at the zoo.

As Edward and the duke spoke with each other, Daniel said into her ear, "Grace, stay with Madingley. I have something I need to do, but we'll be together again soon—and no, I'm not going after Jenkins."

"I never thought so," she said solemnly. Looking up into his warm eyes, she murmured, "I trust you, Daniel."

He smiled and kissed her hand before he walked away.

Then it was Edward's turn to make his excuses for a moment, leaving Miss Hutton with them. Miss Hutton stared at the duke as if he were the Prince Consort himself, and Grace was amused at the duke's patient smile.

The orchestra finished playing a quadrille and did not begin another musical selection. Grace looked up at the duke in surprise, but surely he was not about to make a speech to the assembly since he was right beside her.

He smiled and extended his arm to Grace. "Will you come with me?"

"Of course, Your Grace," she said, wondering what he was about. There was no music to dance to. She glanced at Beverly and Miss Hutton, who both looked as confused as she felt.

The crowd parted for them, and people did not give her the shocked smirks they'd been giving her before, now that she was on the arm of the duke.

She still could not see through the crowd when she heard the first chords of a piano. Silence started before her, then spread all around as people whispered to others behind them. Grace didn't know what was going on, but the duke still seemed calm.

As they neared the corner of the room where the orchestra had been set up, the last of the guests backed away before them, and Grace saw who was playing the piano.

Lady Flora, Daniel's mother. Grace inhaled a shocked breath.

The light gray gown she wore softened the severity that Grace had first associated with her. Her face was full of concentration, and the next few lines of music were hesitant. But then confidence seemed to suffuse her, and she smiled faintly as she continued the piece. Grace thought she recognized one of Baldwin Throckmorten's compositions. Why had Lady Flora decided to renew her musical career in so public a place?

The first sweet strains of a violin made Grace's head turn swiftly. Daniel was walking toward his mother, the antique violin beneath his chin. He played from memory, and although his rendition was not flawless, since he had obviously not been practicing, the fact that mother and son performed together after all these years made her eyes start to water. At her side, the duke looked solemn, but proud, and she saw Lady Elizabeth blowing her nose into her handkerchief.

And then she began to wonder why Daniel and his mother were putting themselves on display for all the gossips in the crowd, resurrecting an old scandal about jealousy and betrayal and murder.

Did they want people to start talking again, or were they testing to see if at last the scandal had faded away?

And then Daniel met her eyes, and she caught her breath in sudden understanding. Tears began to run down her cheeks, and when she fumbled with her reticule, the duke handed her his monogrammed handkerchief, which she used unabashedly.

Daniel and his mother were doing this for her. They were distracting the crowd with memories of a worse scandal.

Daniel came closer, serenading her. The sweet notes of the violin were pure and touched her heart deeply. Did he love her? Could she risk telling him how she felt?

"He's quite good," said a dry voice in her ear.

She barely glanced at her brother, so focused was she on Daniel and the soothing effect he and his mother were having on the hundreds of assembled guests.

Then Grace looked more closely at her brother and saw a spot of blood in the corner of his mouth. "What did you do to yourself?" she demanded in a whisper.

"Showed Jenkins what happens when he hurts a Banbury."

She gaped at him. "You fought with him? Here?"

"Landed some really good blows," Edward said cockily, grinning down at Miss Hutton, who was full of admiration. "He only managed to hit me once. And the conservatory was quite empty, what with the show Throckmorten is putting on."

"You poor man!" Miss Hutton said, reaching up with her handkerchief to dab at his lip.

Grace blinked as she turned from Miss Hutton to Edward, who grinned back at her. He was going to be all right, in more ways than one. And so much of it was because of Daniel.

The last notes of the piece rang in the air, and the applause seemed more than just polite, easing Grace's fears. Daniel came toward their small group, and to her surprise, he handed Edward the violin.

"Thank you for allowing me to borrow this," he said.

Edward's expression was guarded, and Grace held her breath, but gradually he relaxed and smiled. "You're welcome. But whatever else you've borrowed, you have to keep."

Grace knew her face flamed red.

Daniel looked right at her, not bothering to hide the way his dark eyes smoldered at her. "I intend to."

She didn't know what to do with herself, how she should behave. She had no secrets left to weigh her down, and she felt like she was floating, waiting for an anchor to claim her.

Daniel took both her hands in his.

"Oh, you shouldn't do this," she said, feeling suddenly shy, knowing how many people were watching them. "You've done too much for me tonight. I feel like it's my fault that you and your mother tried to renew an old scandal."

"That wasn't a scandal. It was just my family, doing what we do best." He smiled tenderly at her. "Why don't you marry me and join two scandalous families? Maybe we could even be the normal couple. Unless you're too afraid to start a new scandal by marrying me?"

Beverly was waving her offer of a handkerchief, and Grace realized that tears were still streaming down her face, but she didn't care who saw.

"Oh, Daniel, if you love me," she said softly, "then I can bear anything."

He cupped her face in his hands. "Sweet Grace, I *have* fallen in love with you, with your generous heart and the way you care about everyone more than yourself. You would do anything to protect your family, and I would be proud to be one of them."

"But you've spent your life trying to protect your own family—perhaps not the same way I did," she added, grinning. "But you've made me see that I've been trying to please other people, as if I had to fix everything, as if I didn't deserve to be happy."

His eyes searched her face. "Will you be happy with me, Grace?"

"Oh yes," she whispered, and when he kissed her, she gladly leaned into him.

Someone cleared his throat, and they both looked up into the face of the duke of Madingley.

"Is this correct behavior for a ball?" he asked, his expression impassive, even though his dark eyes twinkled.

"It is for a Madingley Ball," Lady Elizabeth piped up. "It's everything I ever dreamed of!"

Grace and Daniel laughed, accepting the well wishes of the family and friends gathered around them. When they had a moment to breathe, she turned to him and said, "You know, life with me won't be easy. You forget that I have a mother, too."

"How could I forget your mother after such a memorable introduction? Don't worry, I have the perfect little property picked out for her. I'll even give her a little spending money."

"Do you trust her with a home of yours?" Grace asked in disbelief.

"I have to reward her—she's the reason I have you." He kissed her lightly on the mouth. "But we can't possibly have her living with us—she'd teach the children how to gamble."

Grace laughed. With Daniel's arm around her shoulders, she felt sheltered from the world—and loved.